GO SEEK

Michelle Teahan is a qualified Medical Scientist but her passion has always been writing stories. She loves creating strong female characters, putting them in the worst types of situations and seeing how they react. She lives in County Cork, Ireland, with her husband, two young daughters and a giant ginger cat. *Go Seek* is Michelle's debut novel.

GO SEEK

Michelle Teahan

HEADLINE

First published in 2023 by Headline Publishing Group

1

Cataloguing in Publication Data is available from the British Library

ISBN 978 1 0354 0557 2

Typeset in ITC Giovanni by CC Book Production

Printed and bound in Great Britain by Clays Ltd, Elcograf S.p.A.

Headline's policy is to use papers that are natural, renewable and recyclable
products and made from wood grown in well-managed forests and other
controlled sources. The logging and manufacturing processes are expected
to conform to the environmental regulations of the country of origin.

HEADLINE PUBLISHING GROUP
An Hachette UK Company
Carmelite House
50 Victoria Embankment
London EC4Y 0DZ

www.headline.co.uk
www.hachette.co.uk

For Christina and Johanna,
who I would do anything for

Hindsight ‣ [noun] understanding of a situation or event only after it has happened or developed: *with hindsight, I should never have gone.*

Oxford Dictionary of English

PROLOGUE

What have I done?

This was bad. This was very, very bad, she thought as she paced up and down the brightly tiled hallway.

Picking up the receiver of the mustard-yellow phone attached to the wall, she dialled the same number she'd already tried three times.

You have reached the mobile phone number of 0-8—

She slammed it back onto the mount, cursing loudly as it inevitably fell down, and took more care to replace it despite the shake in her hand. Running her hands through her hair, she returned to her pacing.

Her daughter had sworn blind that if she bought her a mobile phone for her sixteenth birthday, she would be contactable at all times, but in the three months since then her daughter had answered her a grand total of once.

She grabbed the receiver again, punching in the same numbers with a force that risked knocking the entire unit off the wall. A sweat had broken out all over her body.

Please, please, please, she thought, *I really need this to be the second time you answer my call.* It started ringing and she held her breath. *Please* – she squeezed her eyes shut – *please.*

You have reached the mobile phone number of 0-8-7—

'Damn it!' she shouted, forcing the phone back onto its mount. It fell down again. This time she didn't bother replacing it. Instead, she returned to the path she was wearing through her hallway.

She'd never felt a fear like this before. *How could I have been so stupid? Right outside* his *hotel.*

Despite the sweat, a cold sensation had crept through her veins, and she needed to do something, anything, to stop it.

She knew what that something was, where she had to go, who she had to turn to. It wasn't what she wanted to do, but she had been left with no other choice. Not if she wanted to ensure her and her daughter's safety. It was the lesser of two evils. Taking a deep breath, she stopped her pacing, a sense of calm taking over. She'd be fine, there was time. She and her daughter would be safe. Everything was going to be fine.

She made her way to the kitchen and started pulling open every drawer in turn until she found a blank piece of paper. Then she repeated the process, looking for a pen, before leaning over the kitchen counter to scribble a note.

She signed off, then filled the kettle. She would need a cup of tea to settle her nerves before doing what needed to be done, but as her finger paused over the switch, the doorbell sounded. She looked down the hall towards the front door.

Maybe everything wouldn't be fine.

1

Now

Kent, England

The toilet flushed for the second time in less than two minutes.

'Abbie, out of the bathroom now, please. There's no way you have to wee again.'

I sighed. There was a strong chance the toilet would flush again in the next couple of seconds. Potty training had been relatively straightforward with my two-and-a-half-year-old until she'd developed an obsession with repeatedly going to the toilet – all so she could press the flush.

I looked down at my nursing baby, happily suckling, her hand wrapped around my hair, then towards the bedroom door that led out into the hallway. At the other end of the narrow landing was the bathroom where my toddler was no doubt gearing up to send more water rushing into the toilet bowl. I glanced at the digital clock sitting on my bedside locker. It was 8:35 a.m. My husband, Christopher, was probably finishing up a leisurely hotel breakfast on his business trip in Milan right about now.

Pushing my head back against the grey crushed-velvet headboard of my super-king bed, I took a deep breath and looked at the ceiling. How in the name of Christ was I going to get out of here and to the GP's surgery, which was a good twenty minutes away, for our nine o'clock appointment?

Taking another deep breath, I pushed down the overwhelming feeling of being trapped; physically on this bed beneath a feeding baby, and in this house with a toddler who had a tiny bladder, but also figuratively in this life by the titles of mother and wife.

Looking back down at the baby in my arms, whose eyelids were dipping lower and lower, those feelings drifted from me like receding waves on a shoreline. Destined to return but gone for now. Smiling down at thirteen-month-old Sarah, I knew I was exactly where I needed to be, where I *should* be. Contentment filled every inch of space inside me that had just been vacated by the feeling of confinement. How could I not be content with my wonderful family and—?

The toilet flushed again.

'Abbie! Get out of that bathroom. NOW!'

My face was flushing red and beads of sweat were sliding down my spine when I finally reached the surgery and scrambled into the nurse's office.

'I'm sorry we're late, it was so busy out there with the school traffic and I had to park halfway down Elmwood Avenue, and—'

Nurse Rose held up a hand to stop me while simultaneously tapping away on her phone, without even looking up.

'Come in and sit down, Mrs King,' she said, finally, returning to her computer screen.

I hadn't even crossed the threshold of her office and I already felt like a naughty nine-year-old being told off by her teacher instead of a thirty-two-year-old mother of two.

Nurse Rose pushed the vaccination consent forms across the desk towards me as I took Sarah out of her buggy and warned Abbie to behave. I reached out and signed them awkwardly while trying to keep a wriggling Sarah, who desperately wanted to join her sister, in my arms. I could feel more beads of sweat rolling down my back. I should have taken off my coat before I took Sarah out of the buggy, but if I sat her on the floor with Abbie there would be no getting her back. Not willingly, at least.

'Sorry for cancelling last month,' I said, in an effort to fill the awkward silence that followed. 'It's just she was miserable with a head cold so I didn't want to put her through a vaccination.'

'It is a twelve-month vaccine, not a thirteen-month one,' Nurse Rose said, rummaging in her drawers for supplies.

I didn't know what to say to that so I turned in my seat to see what Abbie was up to.

'Oh God, I'm sorry,' I gasped when I realised that the reason for Abbie's silence was that she'd been methodically emptying a wide metal cabinet of its files.

Nurse Rose looked over and sighed. 'Could you ready the child, please?' she asked, with a pointed look at Sarah.

'Oh, yes. Sorry. Of course.'

The nurse tutted as she watched me struggle to remove Sarah's tights. 'Loose-fitting trousers are what we recommend for vaccination days,' she stated firmly, tapping her manicured fingernail on the syringe she held, needle pointed towards me accusingly.

I had in fact dressed Sarah in loose-fitting trousers, but she'd leaked through her nappy on the drive over, and a pair of tights, which almost definitely needed a wash, was all I could find in her changing bag. I didn't say any of that, of course. Instead, I gave the nurse a small, tight smile and apologised once again.

By the time Sarah was vaccinated and settled in her buggy, and I'd wrestled Abbie away from her filing cabinet destruction, I felt like the worst parent to have ever entered Nurse Rose's office.

Back at the Ford Kuga, which I had abandoned earlier on a quiet street around the corner from the GP's surgery, I had already replayed the entire appointment with Nurse Rose in my head. I hated myself and my parental inadequacies even more the second time.

A familiar sadness settled on me when I thought of my own mother and how wonderful she had been. She wouldn't have been late to my vaccination appointment, and she certainly wouldn't have had me wearing clothes in need of a wash.

Forcing Nurse Rose and my mother from my mind, I pushed my foot down on the buggy's brake paddle, still gripping Abbie's small hand. I looked at the car and weighed up my options. I could put Abbie in first, but her seat was on the side of the car out on the road, which would mean leaving Sarah alone in her buggy on the footpath. Or I could put Sarah in first and keep Abbie by my legs, but Abbie had a tendency to run off if something interesting enough caught her attention. What had I done earlier? Jesus, when had simple things become so complicated? Looking around the car at the empty road, I decided to put Sarah in her seat before she fell asleep in the buggy. Right from birth, it hadn't mattered if Sarah had been asleep thirty seconds or thirty minutes, if you moved her, she woke, and there was no going back.

'Abbie, stand right next to Mummy while I put your sister in her seat, okay? Arm around my leg and hold on tight. Don't move from my side.'

I unhooked the straps from which Sarah had somehow mostly escaped and placed her in the car seat. The consequence of trading her morning nap for a brutal stabbing with a sharp needle came with a vengeance as Sarah started to scream and straighten her body. I thought of the pushy sales assistant who had tried to convince me and Christopher to fork out the extra money for a car seat that turned sideways. We had walked away laughing, thinking she had mistaken us for inexperienced, first-time parents. Well, I certainly wasn't laughing now as I edged one foot into the car to try to wrestle a screaming baby into her seat. How did something so small suddenly have so much strength the second you tried to manoeuvre them?

After singing her a medley of distracting nursery rhymes, completely off-key, I sighed with relief as Sarah finally relaxed into her seat. At the same moment, the pressure of Abbie's small arm left my leg.

'Hold on, Abbie! Be a good girl now, don't make Mummy cross,' I called as I pulled the straps over Sarah's shoulders.

The pressure didn't return.

'Abbie?' Panic caused me to fumble with the seat buckles as I tried to stretch sideways to see outside the car.

'Abbie!'

The clips finally snapped into place. I pulled the straps to check Sarah was secure and jumped out, my eyes searching the area around the car.

'ABBIE!'

I couldn't see her.

'Abbie, where are you?' I screamed, walking into the road. I started turning in circles, but it was as if the world was rotating in the opposite direction and I couldn't process what I was seeing. How was she not there? Why couldn't I see her?

I should be able to see her.

'Abbie, where—?' I stopped dead.

The familiar pattern of white daisies on purple boots was sticking out from beneath a parked car on the opposite side of the road. I couldn't breathe. She had crossed the road. Why would she do that? What if a car had come? Had one come? Did it hit her? A barrage of questions swarmed around my brain as I ran towards those small boots. I threw myself down, feeling as if my heart was clamped in an ever-tightening vice. I placed a hand on a boot, and instantly the sound of the most beautiful, high-pitched giggle filled my ears. The boots pulled away and crawled out from beneath the car.

'Abbie, Abbie, Abbie.'

I couldn't stop saying her name, reassuring myself that she was okay. That she was there in front of me. That she was safe. It had only been seconds, but it had seemed like an eternity. In that time, the bottom of my world had fallen out, and I had felt paralysed by fear. Folding Abbie into my arms, I held her against my chest. She was mumbling some-thing, but I wasn't listening. I just wanted to feel her against me. Everything that had gone through my mind, the things I'd thought – but none of that mattered now. Now, she was safe in my arms.

It took a few seconds for my breathing to settle and the panic to evaporate sufficiently for me to speak. I held Abbie away from me, my hands clamped on her arms, terrified that she might disappear again. Annoyance pushed its way through my relief.

'Why did you do that to me, Abbie? Why did you run off like that?'

My voice verged on hysterical, but reining in all that emotion was proving difficult. Abbie looked as if she was about to cry so I held her face between my hands and rubbed her cheeks with my thumbs.

'Don't worry, love. I'm not angry.' I was relieved my voice sounded more natural. 'I just want to know why you ran off like that?'

'Sorry, Mummy,' she dropped her eyes to the ground. 'I was only playing hide-and-seek.'

The adrenaline coursing through my body finally abated. Hide-and-seek. That made sense. It had become the game of choice in our house. Christopher and Abbie could play for hours, with Christopher selecting his hiding places so that he had an unobstructed view of the TV. I would have to talk to Christopher when he got home. We'd need to stress the rules of the game to Abbie; when it was and wasn't appropriate to play. He'd think I was overreacting, but if he hadn't taught her the damn game, she wouldn't have run off just now and scared me half to death. What good could possibly come from teaching a child so young how to hide from her parents? Just thinking about what might have happened made me sick to my stomach.

'You can't play hide-and-seek without telling someone,

sweetheart. It's dangerous to play on your own when no one's looking for you.'

'Wasn't playing on my own, Mummy.'

'I wasn't playing, Abbie. I was busy with Sarah. You knew that.'

Abbie's bottom lip pushed out in response to the reprimand.

'No, Mummy, not you.'

'Oh, is that right?' A smile spread across my face, ready for her to name and blame yet another imaginary friend. 'Who were you playing with, then, missy?'

'The man.'

I stopped smiling.

'What man?'

'The man with the black, shiny coat.'

I couldn't move. I couldn't breathe. My heart was pounding in my ears, and Abbie's face dimmed and darkened in front of me.

She leaned in close. 'Your turn now.'

'What?' I asked, my mouth dry, everything inside of me turning cold.

Abbie smiled, a beautiful innocent smile, a complete contradiction to the words she spoke.

'Go seek, Mummy.'

2

Every muscle in my body responded to Abbie's words. I jumped up and ran back to the car, dragging Abbie behind me. She stumbled as I pulled her up onto the footpath, urging her towards the car door, still wide open. I threw myself around the door and stopped. I let go of Abbie's hand.

She was gone. Sarah was gone.

The space that my younger daughter had occupied, only moments earlier, was empty. No, not empty. There was a white, blank business card tucked into the headrest. The headrest where my daughter's head should be nestled.

I stumbled back from the car, turning in circles, a desperate repeat of moments earlier. I looked up and down the street, trying to take everything in, but terror flooded my body, dampening my senses. This time, I knew I wouldn't find her.

The silver Hyundai parked behind us was still there, as was the green Mitsubishi in the driveway up the road, the red Ford Focus behind that, and the silver Toyota across the road, where I had found Abbie hiding. Nothing was different. Everything was the same as it had been when we'd returned from the clinic. I turned again. No, something was different. The dark blue Peugeot 508 that had been parked across the driveway of the last house in the row was gone. Had they simply left their house to go to the shop? Or had someone been waiting here for me? But there was nothing. There was no one around. No sign that something terrible had just happened – except for the empty car seat and that hateful fucking white card.

I screamed, the sound coming straight from my gut, as I fell to my knees. Abbie was crying as she rubbed my back, trying to soothe me as I had done to her so many times before. Still on my knees, I turned to Abbie and my screams became tears as I looked at her beautiful face. She had big blue eyes, just like her father, and small rosebud lips, a brush of colour against her perfect pale skin. There was a smattering of freckles across the bridge of her nose, and a mess of red curls falling across her forehead, the only physical attribute I had given her. An older version of the baby who, moments earlier, had been safe and sound in the car.

Safe. I thought she'd been safe.

I'd made the ultimate mistake. I'd dropped my guard and the most unthinkable thing had happened. *I* had let it happen. All of those surreal worst-case scenarios that kept me awake at night while I listened to Christopher's heavy, restful breathing beside me, carefree and oblivious to the imaginary scenes in my head, and now the most terrifying one of all had just happened. The nightmare that plagued me the most had become a reality, and none of the worrying, none of those sleepless nights, had prepared me for it.

My head throbbed, but I couldn't stop the tears. Abbie wrapped her arms around me. 'It's okay, Mummy. I don't like seeking, too.'

I cried harder, so hard that I couldn't breathe. I wanted the world to stop, to give me time to process what had happened, to let me figure out what I should do, what I *needed* to do to get my baby back. But that didn't happen. The earth continued to spin, and time continued to tick relentlessly, unconcerned by my desperation.

I had no idea how much time had passed with me kneeling on the footpath, tears flowing down my face. Abbie had stopped rubbing my back and was sitting beside me, knees pulled up to her chest, hugging them tight. Seeing my toddler sat so still when she normally never stopped moving dragged me back from the dark place my mind had retreated to. I forced a deep breath into my lungs and stood, scooping Abbie up and kissing her frightened, tear-stained face. I squeezed her little body against mine, soothing her as best I could while trying to ease the physical pain that ripped through me the second I saw those loose, limp car seat straps and that vulgar white card, so out of place.

Closing the door, with Abbie secured in her car seat, I took one last pointless look around the quiet, unchanged street.

As I did, I saw how it must all have played out. The man in the black coat is crouched down behind my car, beckoning Abbie with a smile and his finger to his lips. Abbie doesn't hesitate. Why would she? There is no one in her world who doesn't care for her, who'd want to hurt her. She doesn't yet see danger.

She's walking towards him, her little fist balled up, covering her mouth to keep from giggling, red curls bouncing as she creeps away from me. He's explaining the game to her in a hushed voice, pointing to the hiding place. His hand is on her back as he guides her there, watching as she crawls beneath the car before walking off, back to his vantage point, where he watches the game he's set up play out. And there I go, unwittingly playing the role of the panicked and distraught mother, the role I had been scripted.

I'm crossing the road, running towards those small boots, completely unaware of the other faceless person creeping towards the open car door and the unguarded baby within. And while I'm on the other side of the road, reassuring myself that my child is safe, my baby is being pulled from her car seat and taken out of sight.

Of course it was Sarah. It was always going to be her. The one who couldn't speak, who couldn't scream out for her mummy, kick out, wriggle away, run off or cry for help. Sarah made the most sense. She was easy to travel with, to take where they needed to go. Where *I* now needed to go.

Home.

I blinked, and the street was empty once again.

I walked around the back of the car, returning to Sarah's car seat, and pulled the white card from the headrest, shoving it into my pocket before climbing into the driver's seat and starting the engine. But I couldn't get my body to cooperate and start driving. I couldn't leave. It was as if I was deserting Sarah, even though I knew she was long gone.

'Get it together,' I muttered to myself, gripping the steering wheel until my knuckles blanched. I took a breath, in for a count of four, held it for a count of four and released it to the count of four. Box breathing; a calming technique I had learned years ago when life had suddenly become a lot more complicated than I was equipped to manage. 'You can fall to pieces later, when your baby's life doesn't depend on you. You've fucked up already, you can't afford to do it again, Maeve.'

It worked, something inside me slammed shut. The raw, unbearable pain that had been threatening to destroy me became trapped behind an efficient, albeit temporary, barrier. I adjusted the rear-view mirror away from the empty car seat and focused it on Abbie.

'Okay, time to get going.' I was telling myself as much as her.

'But, Mummy, we need to find Sarah.'

I forced a reassuring smile to my face.

'Don't you worry, sweetheart. Mummy will find Sarah. I promise.'

*   *   *

On the drive home, I obeyed every stop sign and speed limit, took care at every junction and signalled at every turn. I needed to act quickly, but that also meant efficiently. Getting stopped for speeding, or having an accident, was not an option. There was no time to waste, so I drove as cautiously as I could bear to, despite every single one of my nerve endings screaming at me to push down on the accelerator as we traded the busier town streets for quieter country roads.

As we drove through the large, gated entrance of Redmond Row, my body was vibrating with all the adrenaline I was trying to suppress. My right foot ached from keeping it steady as we passed the red-brick homes, each with varying amounts of trees and greenery surrounding them to provide even more privacy in an already gated community.

The second I pulled into the driveway of our large, four-bed house, I cut the engine and retrieved Abbie from her seat, keeping my eyes focused on the task at hand, refusing to glance towards the identical car seat on the other side, which was now empty.

Abbie ran off to the living room as soon as I opened the front door, no doubt to return to the mound of books and the game of 'library' she'd been playing that morning before we'd left.

Before all three of us had left.

Standing in the hall, I looked into the kitchen at the highchair, which was tucked in awkwardly at the dining table. Only two mornings ago, we had all been sat there eating pancakes, laughing at the flour that had found its way into Christopher's neatly cut, dirty-blond hair. I had looked around the table at my family – Sarah rubbing chocolate spread into her face, Abbie joining in and filling in the gaps Sarah had missed, while Christopher mock-grimaced – and wondered how I deserved a life with such a loving husband and two beautiful daughters. Thinking back on the memory, I felt as if I was about to lose it all over again. How had everything changed so quickly? If only I'd known then that there'd been a timer counting down above our heads.

A wave of nausea hit me, but I pushed it down. It was almost eleven, according to the clock in the kitchen. I didn't have the luxury of more time to panic.

That morning, time had seemed important. Rushing out the door so Nurse Rose wouldn't be waiting too long for us. But it hadn't been – not at all. What I wouldn't give to rewind the clock and be sat in bed, feeding Sarah while listening to the toilet flush. And now that time truly was important, it would continue to pass at precisely the same pace. It didn't care that my daughter was gone, that she had been taken from me. It didn't care that I was without her or that, for every second that ticked by, it felt like my heart was breaking into tiny, useless pieces. Time didn't care that the hours about to pass would be the most difficult and important hours I would ever endure. Time would pass both slowly and quickly, all at once.

I knew exactly what I had to do with that time, and where I had to go.

I was going back to Ireland, back home to the place I swore I'd never return to – where I'd lost so much – to find the people I ran from.

The people who now had my child.

3

Abbie insisted on packing her own bag when I told her she was going for a sleepover at her grandparents'. And of course, the only bag she wanted was her *Frozen* one, which we hadn't seen in weeks. Struggling to keep calm and act normal, I showed her an array of other options, none of which were acceptable. I even offered her my Louis Vuitton travel bag, which I rarely used myself in case anything happened to it, but I may as well have been showing her a black bin bag.

A pink backpack with white clouds almost satisfied her, until she realised pink was no longer her favourite colour. I started pulling out drawers and digging through toy boxes, searching for the bag and hoping I'd find it quickly or that Abbie would let it go. Panic bubbled up inside me, but I refused to lose my cool. Abbie had been through enough, and I'd already failed one child.

I finally found the *Frozen* bag, flattened at the bottom of a toy box, only for her to frown at it and say that maybe the pink one would be better.

'We'll pack this one now we've found it, Abbie,' I said, keeping my tone as light as I could, between clenched teeth.

'Okay, Mummy.' She shrugged, trying to put the clothes I'd laid out for her into the bag.

To stop myself screaming at Abbie to go faster, I went to my room and threw a few things into the Louis Vuitton bag, since the thought of wasting even more time by rummaging around for another made me feel sick.

'You excited for your sleepover at Nannie and Grandad's?' I asked Abbie as we made our way out the front door.

She demonstrated her enthusiasm for the impromptu sleepover by jumping up and down and turning the words 'nannie' and 'grandad' into a tuneless sing-song as she skipped her way to the car, the trauma of the morning's events seemingly forgotten.

Thank Christ for that, I thought as I followed behind her.

I'd already phoned Christopher's parents, Beverly and Ian, from the hands-free set in the car on our way home. A necessary and efficient use of travel time. They were delighted at the opportunity to have some quality time with Abbie, as I knew they would be. Since I'd moved to England to be with Christopher, and especially since the girls had arrived, Christopher's parents had done their utmost to find the balance between being involved yet unobtrusive in our family dynamic. But they were always eager, desperate even, to take the girls for some unsupervised quality time without me or Christopher there, forcing them to adhere to our rules.

There were times I thought Beverly might actually cry if I didn't allow her to give Abbie the chocolate she had bought especially for her. It wasn't like I was a health freak when it came to the girls – and it wouldn't be so bad if it was ever an appropriate amount of chocolate, but the bars she had waiting for Abbie were almost the size of her head. She had no understanding of how drastic the drop from a sugar rush of that magnitude could be. Christopher often marvelled at the fact that he had never even tasted chocolate until he was fourteen and bought it himself from money he'd saved cutting his neighbour's lawn.

I was anxious at the idea of leaving Abbie, but I had no other choice and, sugar overdoses aside, I knew she would be safe with her grandparents until Christopher returned tomorrow.

Their house was a little less than an hour away, en route to Gatwick airport – something I never thought I would be so grateful for – and it was under constant surveillance by a private security team. Christopher's mother had been a high court judge and had spent her career putting a lot of nasty people behind bars – people who were always threatening to seek retribution for their punishment, or people who had someone on the outside willing to look for justice for them. It made sense for them, as well as us, to take extra precautions. So when we first began looking for a home to buy, they had insisted we implement our own security measures. And while I didn't like the idea of having cameras everywhere, with strangers watching our every move, Christopher had suggested a gated community. He said it would be worth the expense to ensure the safety of his family. He earned enough money as HR director of an accounting firm with bases all over Europe, and if I was being really honest I was relieved about the extra security it gave us. Of course, they assumed that my relief came from concerns over Bev's ties to the criminal world. In reality, I was glad the gated community we settled on was on the opposite side of Kent from his parents. As good as Beverly and Ian were at giving us our space, I didn't think that would be the case if we were within walking distance.

I phoned Christopher on the way to his parents and told him the same thing I had told them. That my mother's friend Marnie had suddenly taken ill, and I thought I should go see her – just in case. She had lived on the same street as us and had taken care of me directly after my mother's death when I was just sixteen. Christopher agreed, just like I knew he would. He was a softie at the best of times, but throw in the possibility of an old family friend passing away and he would likely have returned home early if I had hesitated about going. The truth was, I hadn't spoken to Marnie in years. I felt bad, as if I was wishing ill health on her, and I didn't like lying to Christopher, taking advantage of his empathy, but it had to be done. It was the only way to ensure he didn't question me too much. Then came the even harder part. The part that pushed my guts up into my chest cavity and threatened to spill my morning muesli all over the steering wheel.

'I'll take Sarah with me, Chris. It wouldn't be fair to leave her when she still looks for the occasional breastfeed.' It was one of the most difficult things I had ever done. I struggled to keep the devastation from my voice as I spoke aloud the sentence I had practised, over and over, in my mind before making the call. It was one of the worst lies I could ever tell my husband.

As I spoke the words, they wounded me like a knife to the gut. In another world, some parallel universe, where my daughter was still with me and Marnie really *was* ill, what I said would be true. I would have taken Sarah with me. She did still want to be nursed. Not often, and more for comfort than sustenance, but she would look for me. She would want to crawl onto my lap and wrap her tiny hands in my hair while she nursed. She would want to, but she couldn't. Because she wasn't with me. She was with someone else. Someone who wouldn't know what she wanted. Someone who wouldn't care even if they did.

The image of Sarah looking for me, sitting on a floor I couldn't even picture, arms outstretched, crying and calling 'Mama, Mama' through her tears, and me not being there, made me feel as if all the oxygen had been syphoned from my lungs. Christopher often joked that she hadn't learned to walk yet because she had no need for it, with me ready to sweep her up into my arms whenever she asked. Every time, I pointed out that I'd done the same with Abbie and she was now racing around the house. For the millionth time since Sarah disappeared, I wondered how I was going to keep it together.

Christopher encouraged me to take my time, but to keep him updated. He would pick up Abbie from his parents' house as soon as he got home tomorrow evening, if I was still in Ireland. He didn't question me, but why would he?

For one brief, desperate moment I wanted to scream and cry and tell him everything. Beg him to make it better, to help me find our girl. But that foolish part of me, the part that didn't want to do this alone, didn't want to be wholly responsible for my daughter and everything that happened to her, was weak. I couldn't afford to be weak.

Get it together, Maeve. You need to stay focused. For Sarah. You're no use to anyone if you break down now.

Easier said than done, but I had no other option. Emotions were dangerous. This was too important. There was too much at risk. And so, I took another deep breath and flicked that imaginary switch inside me, turning my emotions off, as I continued talking to Christopher. I kept the rest of the conversation light. Even managed to laugh at some joke he made about needing to detox Abbie after her stay with his parents. I just hoped it didn't sound as forced as it felt.

'Goodbye, Chris. Abbie will see you tomorrow and,' I gulped down another quick breath, 'Sarah and I will see you as soon as we can.'

I hope, I added in a whisper when the call disconnected.

4

I kept my goodbye with Abbie short, much shorter than I would have liked, but it seemed like time, the ever-constant bastard, had sped up out of spite. I ushered her up the drive and in through their front door before either Ian or Beverly could come outside to meet us at the car.

By way of a greeting, I explained that I had booked a last-minute flight to Cork, leaving in the next hour, so I really needed to hurry.

'We'll walk you out and say a quick hello and goodbye to little Sarah before you leave,' Beverly said as she stroked Abbie's face, delighting in the affectionate hug she was receiving. Affection, no doubt, motivated by the promise of chocolate the moment I was out of sight.

I bent down, giving Abbie a quick smile and a wink, before kissing her forehead. 'No, Bev, there's no time. Sorry. I need to get going – and Sarah's asleep, anyway.'

Beverly's face fell as I stepped backwards out the door to make sure she wasn't following.

'I'm sure I'll pay for this nap when she's like a live wire on the plane,' I added, with a smile, hoping it'd ease the rejection of not letting her escort me to the car.

It worked. Beverly smiled and gave a small laugh. 'Not at all, she's a great baby.'

'You really are blessed with her,' Ian added.

'That I am,' I said, turning before they could see the tears beginning to gather in my eyes.

'Be a good girl for Nannie and Grandad,' I called to Abbie as I hurried back down the drive, trying my best not to run. 'And remember how much I love you, missy.'

'Love you, Mummy,' her little voice replied as I reached the car.

On the drive over, I had explained to Abbie that the game of hide-and-seek with Sarah was a secret. Just between us. I hoped that would keep her from talking about it. But chances were, if she did, they'd assume she was regaling them with one of her adventurous, fantastical and, most importantly, fictional tales.

Airport check-in went smoothly, a fact that cut through me when I realised it was because I had no children with me. As the plane took off and forced itself up into the sky I sat back in my seat, pressed my head into the cracked-leather headrest and took another deep breath. The struggle to remain calm was constant but I needed to use the travel time to strategise. For that, I had to think logically and methodically and, under no circumstances, lose my composure and break down. Something which would happen in seconds, if I let it. I warned myself to hold it together – for Sarah's sake.

A baby cried as the plane continued its ascent, the changing altitude all too much for those tiny ears. I thought back to our first holiday as a family of four. Sarah was barely two months old and slept the entire flight, while Abbie randomly placed stickers in a sticker book, Christopher pointlessly trying to convince her to stick them in their designated spots. I shook my head, pulling myself out of the memory before it all became too much. I checked my watch, just gone two. Almost five hours without Sarah. It felt like an eternity.

The seat belt light dimmed out and the urge to race to the toilet, lock myself inside and cry, was overwhelming. I wanted to cry. I wanted to cry because I was devastated, because I was terrified, because I was angry, but, above all else, because I was so very lonely. I missed Sarah as I would a body part – an arm or a leg. I'd never left her with anyone besides Christopher since she was born. Even then, never for more than an hour. But she wasn't with her dad now. She was with—

I stopped myself. I wanted to fall apart and spend the next hour pushing out all the sorrow bubbling around inside me, releasing my emotions, but it wasn't an option. If I did, I'd be as good as burying my daughter.

Instead, I sat back, closed my eyes and thought about what needed to happen next, ticking through every place I had to go and everyone I needed to see, filling in the gaps of the plan which had been formulating in my mind the moment I discovered Sarah was missing. No, I corrected myself; taken. The moment I discovered Sarah had been *taken*.

Since becoming a mother, I had doubted myself and my decisions every step of the way. Always worried I was doing the wrong thing, the wrong way, at the wrong time, making all the wrong choices. But sitting on that plane, bound for my hometown of Cork, I knew exactly what I needed to do. More than that, I knew for certain I was capable of doing it. A first for me as a mother.

I couldn't stop myself, I leaned out of my aisle seat to get a better look at the crying baby. The father was holding him up on his broad shoulder, gently bouncing him up and down. He wasn't more than a few weeks old, wrapped in a blue woollen blanket. His cries became quieter and quieter, and just like that, he was asleep. Was Sarah sleeping? Whose shoulder was she resting on?

I sat back in my seat again. I'd have her back soon, I told myself. I'd get her back, or I'd burn the world down trying.

After another forty minutes in the air, the pilot announced we were beginning our descent. It still amazed me how close my new home was to Ireland. Over four and a half years earlier, when I left, it was as if I'd escaped from another world, leaving behind an entirely different planet. That small, unobtrusive island coming into view beneath me hid more depravity than its unassuming inhabitants could ever imagine. They had no idea what malignancies grew across their green isle. Perhaps it was easier that way. Easier to go about their lives, happy and carefree, oblivious to their country's sins. Ignorance is bliss. I reminded myself of that, time and time again, over the months and years, whenever the urge to share my deepest, darkest secrets bubbled beneath the surface.

By the time the plane touched down in Cork, every detail of the plan was clear in my mind. My daughter was in Ireland, I knew that, and I also knew what had to be done to get her back. The only thing left to do was to pray for everything to play out in my favour. It was a shame I had no faith in God, but for the first time in a long while, I was beginning to have faith in myself. Regardless of faith, however, luck had an important part to play. I couldn't afford for the universe to conspire against me. There was no margin for error. I would have to remind myself of that every time my chest felt as if it might cave in under the weight of missing my daughter.

And so, as I stepped off the plane, I left the grieving, devastated mother behind. The moment my feet met Irish soil, I became the woman I'd left behind all those years ago. Before I ever met Christopher. Before ever becoming a mother. If old scores were to be settled, I'd make damn sure they were, and permanently. I would be retribution personified.

As I left the airport and made my way to pick up my rental car, there were two things I was certain of. First, I was going to get my child back. And second, nothing like this would happen to my family ever again. *That* I would make sure of.

5

County Cork, Ireland

I drove out of the airport car park, relishing the power and torque of the 5 series BMW I'd selected, but careful to keep an eye on the speedometer once I hit the main road. I'd chosen it for its engine power and fast acceleration, but the last thing I needed was to get stopped for speeding.

However, once I turned off the main road and navigated the meandering country lanes, my right foot increased the pressure on the pedal. There was a sense of urgency building inside me the closer I got. Muscle memory kicked in as I headed south, manoeuvring along the narrow, winding roads. I'd forgotten how much I loved to drive fast. The quick, smooth gear changes helped me careen around the bends with the least amount of under-steer. It had been a long time since I'd thrown a car into corners. Children had been a very effective way of altering my driving habits.

The speed and absolute concentration it required was a

welcome relief from all the thoughts buzzing around inside my head, threatening to penetrate the internal barricades I'd erected earlier. I focused entirely on the movements of the car and how to keep it on a straight course between the roadside ditches as I sped along.

Twenty minutes later, I pulled up outside the secluded lodge house, sitting on the edge of a fifteen-acre patch of woodland. It was as though no time had passed at all; the excitement I had felt at leaving my life in Ireland behind me, and starting anew with Christopher, was still fresh in my mind. For a moment, I sat in the car, taking in the red wooden door and the small, white sash windows I'd once thought were so pretty. Now all I felt was dread. The idea of stepping back into that life had felt unimaginable and unthinkable – until now.

The Dunpool Woods were situated about ten minutes west of the busy fishing town of Kinsale. The lodge house, built with dark grey stone mined from the quarry a couple of miles down the road, was called the 'Stone Lodge' and had once been the servants' quarters to the Dunpool Manor House, which had stood proudly in the centre of the woods. Another lodge house known as the 'Gate Lodge', which once served the same purpose, sat on the opposite side of the woods. While the manor house was now no more than a crumbling ruin, providing hikers through the woods with an extra place to explore, both lodge houses had been restored and sold. The Stone Lodge was mine, and I paid the retired couple who lived in the Gate Lodge a generous monthly fee to maintain it and keep it ready for occupancy at short notice. I'd always hoped that payment would turn out to be money wasted, but here I was. And a part of me always knew I would be.

The afternoon was already starting to darken, a sure sign that winter was closing in. Looking around, I couldn't help but marvel at all the beautiful oranges and browns autumn had brought to the woods. Such beauty in the death and decay of their foliage, but soon it would be November and every tree would be stripped bare.

I remembered how I used to sit on the black wrought-iron chair outside the back door, drinking coffee and breathing in the pure, clean air, with a view of nothing but tall oak trees, thinking how small and insignificant I was compared to them. They had been there, standing tall and strong, long before I ever existed, and they would still be there long after I was gone. That thought had always brought me a strange sort of comfort.

I pulled a familiar set of keys from my bag, the ones I'd taken from beneath the false bottom of my wardrobe. I sorted through them until I found the dull bronze key I knew would fit the rusting keyhole of the red door.

Keys in hand, I slid my arm through the handle of my bag so that it rested in the crook of my elbow, and made to leave the car. I stopped.

Could I really do this? Was I deluding myself into thinking

I was even remotely capable of doing what it would take to get my child back? All that earlier confidence evaporated, like a song I'd once known but couldn't quite remember the tune of.

Every day since becoming a mother, I had felt as if I was letting my children down. That I wasn't enough for them, that I didn't deserve them. They were so wonderful and perfect, and the guilt ate at me every day because they deserved so much better than me. I whispered in their ears as they slept, apologies that they had been given me as a mother.

But I could do this, couldn't I? This was the kind of thing I was actually good at, wasn't it?

I screamed and slammed my palms into the steering wheel, but all that I achieved was a cheerful beep from the car horn, the sudden flight of a murder of crows from some nearby trees, and the need to pick my keys up off the floor.

No, now is not the time.

I pushed open the car door and headed to the lodge.

It was like stepping back in time. Everything was as I'd left it, a little over four and a half years ago; the coffee mugs were hanging motionless and silent on their wooden pegs under the kitchen cabinets, and a red chequered tea towel was threaded through the handle of the oven. Had I even left at all? I ran my hand along the kitchen counter. It was spotless. Opening the cupboard at the end of the kitchen, I reached in and flicked on the switch for the central heating.

I peered in and saw that the timer was set for an hour every morning and evening. At least the Gate Lodge couple were earning their fee.

I sat at the small, square kitchen table and took a moment to absorb the fact that nothing had changed in my absence, and reacclimatised myself with the once so familiar surroundings. I had loved this lodge once. When I first came here, I felt as if I'd won the lottery. I'd been twenty-two and, thanks to a hefty inheritance left to me by my late aunt, able to afford a home that was all mine and free of any terrible memories. I really thought I'd lucked out. I was a naive fool.

I pushed myself back from the table before I got lost in the memory, and hit the switch on the kettle. Engrained memory had me reaching for the same lilac mug I'd used so many times before. Moments later, leaning against the kitchen counter, sipping hot black tea, the bicycle helmet hanging by the front door caught my eye. I smiled and ran my tongue along the scar spanning the entire length of the inside of my bottom lip. The one I had earned the last time I wore that helmet. It was also the first time I had met Christopher. I laughed to myself, picturing his face, pale with horror, as he ran over to help me up off the ground.

That had been another day when I'd needed to use speed to keep my mind occupied. Except that time, it was atop a mountain bike, taking an off-road path I didn't know, downhill through the woods near the lodge. I'd been concentrating fiercely on every slight movement of the handlebars, to keep

36

myself upright. Anything to keep my mind off my life. One thing I hadn't expected was that anyone else would be out in those woods, on a cold February evening as the light was fading, but Christopher was. You couldn't convince him to run in less than perfect conditions now, but back then, apparently anything went.

I'd thought he was an idiot. I'm sure he had some choice opinions on me, too, that day – seeing as he was the one running on a designated track, while I was the one careening down through a thick wood across his path. Okay, maybe I was the idiot.

One sharp tug on the handlebars to avoid ramming straight into him was all it took to send me flying over the front of the bicycle and into the rocky verge. And so, at the ripe old age of twenty-eight, I had my very first fall off a pedal bike – a rite of passage I could have happily done without.

I landed face first. Good for keeping all my limbs intact, but less than optimum for my face. Marks peppered my face but it was my bottom lip that had taken the brunt of the fall. It was almost entirely split in two.

Christopher didn't hesitate when he saw me lying there, despite the colour draining from his face. He scooped me up, helped me walk to the small car park on the outskirts of the woods where he'd parked, and took me straight to the emergency department at Mercy University Hospital. We barely spoke during the thirty-minute drive. I couldn't, thanks to my lip hanging open. I was holding it together with a towel

Christopher had pulled from a gym bag on his back seat. I
expected him to leave once we got there, but he walked me in
and sat right beside me on those interconnected, hard plastic
chairs that shifted and squeaked every time anyone on the
row moved. For a little over three hours we sat in silence as
I clutched a blood-saturated towel to my face, with bits of
leaves and dirt trapped in the red curls that had sprung out
wildly when I'd released them from the helmet and were now
falling down my back. It was actually entertaining to see the
looks people were giving him every so often, no doubt wondering if he was the cause of my battered face. Technically, he
was, but not in the way they were thinking. He shifted in his
seat every time someone tutted or shook their head at him.

He could have left. Stood up and walked out of the
waiting room from hell, but he didn't – he stayed. Every
so often, when he wasn't looking, I took the time to study
him. His neat, cropped hair was a bright blond thanks to
the summer sun, and in the fluorescent lighting I could see
his deep tan. I was drawn to his pale blue eyes. Having dark
brown eyes myself, I'd always envied the opposite. He was
about my age, I guessed, maybe a bit older as some lines had
settled into the skin on the outer corner of his eyes. He wasn't
my type, though he was handsome, there was no denying
that. I observed him out of a combination of curiosity and
boredom more than anything else.

After a quick patch-up and twenty-odd stitches, which
took a fraction of the wait time, he drove me back to the

lodge, apologising for the hundredth time as he walked me to the door. I shook my head and waved his apology away, too afraid to speak in case I burst my stitches. No way was I going back to the hospital waiting room.

And that was it. He said one last 'sorry' and went on his way. At least, I'd thought that was it, until the next afternoon when he appeared back at my door with a bouquet of yellow tulips and a cheeky smile I couldn't help but return, despite the strain it put on my stitches.

Christopher always refers to that disastrous meeting as our first date. Over a bottle of wine with friends he'll top up their glasses, regaling them with the same details they've heard a hundred times before. But he loves to tell it, and so together we recite the story like a well-rehearsed scene from a play.

Things between us moved fast after that, probably faster than was technically healthy since I had just come out of a very serious relationship and was in the middle of trying to decide which European city to run away to, but it felt right. And, most importantly, *I* felt right when I was with him. Something I hadn't been able to say before. Two weeks later, Christopher's work trip was over and he was getting ready to return to the UK.

'I'll come with you,' I had blurted out as I passed him a freshly folded shirt to add to his suitcase.

For a moment, I thought I'd said the wrong thing, ruined the wonderful couple of weeks we'd had and completely misread what was between us.

But after almost a full minute of him staring at me in silence, he dropped to one knee and grinned up at me. 'Will you marry me?'

Those four little words changed my entire life.

I shook myself out of the past, rinsed my mug and left it to dry upside down on the draining board. I'd been selfish to leave with Christopher, to marry him when he proposed, and I'd been even more selfish to have his children. Christopher was in danger, the second his life became intertwined with mine, and the girls were a target the moment they came into existence – all because of me. I did this; I put them all in this position. And the worst thing was, they had absolutely no idea what kind of monster I really was. Christopher's daughter was in danger and he didn't even know. The pain burned in my chest; I knew that if my husband and children knew who I really was, and the things I had done, they would hate me.

I made my way into the hallway, which was essentially a small, square space with four doors off it – one on each wall. Reaching for the brass handle of the door on the left, I pushed down. Locked. Just how I'd left it. I took the set of keys from my pocket again, separated the toothy, golden key from the others and slid it into the lock.

Nothing had moved in there either, but unlike the kitchen, everything was covered in a layer of dust, and the smell of stale air had me breathing through my mouth. A single bed was pushed against the opposite wall, a small window above it. I crossed the room and pulled the heavy curtains closed before turning towards the only other piece of furniture in the room: a white wardrobe. Beautiful and ornate, yet grotesquely oversized in the room, it took up almost an entire wall. It didn't fit in the room. Not just physically, but it stood in awkward contrast to the basic, timber-framed bed, the brown bedclothes neatly made up, and the plain brown curtains, only notable for their weight and ability to quench the light in the room. The wardrobe looked almost absurd. I smiled, knowing that when I opened it, it would be empty. Well, almost.

6

I tugged at the wardrobe's silver handles, pulling open the heavy doors, and stared at the empty space. I reached up to the back panel and felt around in the top right-hand corner for a thin gap, so small I could just about squeeze my finger-nail along the crevice. I carefully peeled the panel towards me, ignoring the pain shooting through my nail bed. As I did so, the thin sheet of wood started to loosen halfway down, enough that I could grab it at its edges. With one swift yank, the entire back wall of the wardrobe popped out. Balancing the board against the opposite wall, I turned back to the now-hollow wardrobe and stepped inside.

It may have looked free-standing, but the wardrobe was in fact built in, extending back through the thick stone wall that sat behind it.

Inside, I raised my hand above my head and felt around for the small switch nestled in the corner, which lit up the space in an artificial white glow. At the back of the wardrobe – the true back – there were six deep shelves that extended from floor to ceiling, each holding an array of items. Squatting down, I removed a small step stool from the bottom shelf and climbed up onto it, scanning along the selection of wigs perched up high. I grinned, thinking of the times I'd worn each one. My hand itched to reach for the black wig styled in a short pixie cut. The last time I'd worn it, even those closest to me hadn't recognised me. This time, things were different, though. Very different. I needed those same people to know *exactly* who I was, the second they caught sight of me. I needed to make an impact. To appear like a ghost on the streets of Cork City, to haunt those who still haunted me.

I freed my red curls from the tight ponytail I had pulled them into earlier that day, shaking them out and letting them hang loose around my shoulders.

At fourteen, there were few things worse than standing out, so I'd spent my early teenage years straightening my curls and begging my mother to let me dye them with a permanent hair colour, instead of those cheap ones that washed out whenever you got caught in the rain. But she always refused, taking it as a personal insult that I didn't like my hair, as it was identical to hers. Motherhood had thinned my mop of hair somewhat, but there had been plenty to spare, and it was about the same length – give or take an inch – as it had been when I'd last been here. When I'd first moved to England, I had cut it short, and kept it that way for some time, but since having children I'd grown it back out. And once Sarah was born, I made sure to keep it long, as she liked

43

running her fingers through it every night as she fell asleep. My heart gave a leap. What was she going to do tonight?

The space inside the wardrobe was suddenly too tight. There wasn't enough oxygen. I stepped out, gulping down air, desperately trying to fill my lungs and make myself breathe. Before both my body and mind succumbed to undiluted panic, I pushed it all back down, slowed my breathing and allowed my body to relax. I was a mother but also a woman who shouldn't be crossed, and it wouldn't be long before I was reminding people of that.

Returning to the wardrobe, I grabbed some bits and pieces from the next shelf down. Make-up: strong, dark shades. And jewellery: big, flashy pieces. Stuff Mrs Maeve King, Mummy Maeve, the Maeve I was now, would never wear. Not in a million years. I rummaged around until I found what had once been my favourite lipstick – Ruby Woo by Mac, still in the box, the only shade of red that didn't clash with my hair. I ripped open the packaging and tucked the lipstick into the back pocket of my jeans for later.

Beneath the accessories was a row of deep wicker baskets, each containing an entire outfit. Tops, trousers, under-wear, right down to shoes. I rummaged through one before replacing it and choosing another. Inside were a pair of black, skinny jeans, an oversized grey woollen jumper and lace-up black boots. *Perfect.* I added the make-up to the basket and threw it onto the bed, before leaning back into the wardrobe to retrieve a shoe box, tucked away behind the baskets.

I opened it and began flicking through an assortment of driver's licences, the same photograph featured on each of them – a woman with auburn curls, dark eyes, and a handful of freckles scattered across pale skin.

Maeve Murphy, Maeve Davis, Maeve Keane, Mae Daily, Mae Keeffe. Some variation of my forename was on every licence because, whatever the situation, it was always safer to keep the same first name. It was much easier to explain away a discrepancy in surnames: 'That's my married name,' or, 'That's my maiden name,' or, 'My father was a murderer and I wanted to distance myself from the family.' The excuses were endless, and all easily relayed if needed. Justifying a different first name was a much trickier feat. There are few things that can as effectively accelerate your heart rate as being in the presence of people who think your name is Jane when someone who knows you as Rachel walks in. That's when things can become very dangerous, very fast.

I replaced the lid and carefully returned the box to the shelf without removing anything. I already had a driver's licence tucked inside my wallet, which I had taken from beneath the false bottom of the wardrobe back home in Kent. It had a picture of me next to the name Mae Murphy, with a random address listed from some village in Westmeath. It was Mae Murphy who had rented the BMW parked outside.

Then I turned my attention to the most important shelf of all. Unlike home, where the most dangerous things were kept on the highest shelves, out of reach of small inquisitive hands, here they were low down and within easy reach. Displayed across the width of the bottom shelf was a collection of handguns, each one a different make and model. They were the only possessions I'd found difficult to leave behind.

I ran my hand over each of them as if they were old photographs, which they were, in a way. The feel of each one beneath my fingertips sparked distinct memories, and my past came rushing forward. I paused at the Beretta M9. A limited-edition 9mm semi-automatic matte black finish with wood grip panels and a subdued gold emblem and screws. The Italians did a lot of things well – food and cars, to name but two – but, by God, they made one beautiful gun. In my hand, it felt like an extension of my arm, not some cumbersome weapon. With this gun, I had seen my fair share of action. I ran my thumb back and forth over the scuff on the handle and remembered the day it had happened. I'd thought I was going to die, that day.

A gunfight had become a fist fight, and in the nerve-shredding venue of an active train track. The grappling had knocked us into the path of an oncoming train, and while the gun had got off lightly, I had been less fortunate. It could have been a lot worse. Though it could've been a lot better, too, if I'd managed to clear the track in time. I'd been jumping from the line, with my arm outstretched, gun pointed behind me, anticipating the bullet I expected would follow me. It turns out, the force of a speeding train is enough to send you spiralling, even if it only makes contact with your hand.

Almost every bone in my right hand and arm had shattered on impact, but it also left me with five cracked ribs and a body so bruised that it was a long time before my pale skin returned to its normal colour. The healing process was painfully slow, and the only comfort I had was that the person most eager to take advantage of my weakened state had enjoyed a much more intimate meeting with the same train.

Shuddering at the memory, I returned the M9 to its designated place on the shelf. It hadn't been used since. Too much had gone wrong that day and, while the logical part of my brain knew it wasn't the gun's fault, the superstitious part of me, however small, worried it would bring me the same bad luck.

I picked up the Glock instead. It was uglier than the Beretta but efficient, so would do the job. I loaded it with ammunition and slid the full clip back into the gun before shoving it into the back of my waistband.

I was feeling calmer. Just handling the guns made me feel more confident in my abilities, more certain that I was capable of getting my daughter back. I'd do whatever needed to be done.

Back in the kitchen, I devoured the sandwich and yogurt I'd grabbed at the petrol station on the way from the airport. Not the most filling dinner but it would do. I finished and returned to the spare room to gather my selections. I brought them to what was once my bedroom. The double bed was dressed and neat. Both bedside cabinets were bare, except for a small silver lamp on the left side. The side I always slept, closest to the door. The only other piece of furniture in the room was a large dresser. Empty, except for any items that may have been left behind when I hurriedly emptied the contents into suitcases.

I dressed as quickly as I could, but it required some strategic jiggling to get my looser tummy inside the skinny jeans that had belonged to my former self. With the button fastened, albeit under more pressure than it was designed for, I dragged the jumper over my head and across my waist and went to stand in front of the full-length mirror hanging on an otherwise bare wall. Staring back at me was a reflection frighteningly similar to the one it had shown years earlier.

After brushing out the hairspray that I'd applied liberally that morning to my hair, allowing its natural volume and wildness to take over, I applied the heavy make-up and finished it off with the lipstick.

The look worked, I could admit that, but it wasn't me. I despised that woman staring back at me in the mirror. I thought I'd seen the last of her, that I had banished her, but here she was.

I stepped forward. However much I hated her, I needed her. I needed her more than I'd ever needed anyone. Our hands reached towards each other, fingertips touching as we spoke.

'Welcome back, Maeve Deane.'

7

Returning to the BMW, I sat with the ignition off for a few minutes, box breathing. From the second I'd seen my reflection in the mirror, my heart rate had increased, and I needed it to settle before I drove off. Deep breath in: one-two-three-four. Hold: one-two-three-four. Out: one-two-three-four. Pause: one-two-three-four. After a couple of rounds my heart rate settled and my concentration sharpened. Exactly what I needed, since I was city bound and heading to a bar I'd hoped never to enter again to find a man who'd once promised me payback for a broken nose and bruised testicles.

After a twenty-minute drive, I parked in a multi-storey car park in the heart of Cork City. Walking out into the cool evening air, I tightened the worn leather coat around myself, the one that had hung limp and abandoned on a hook by the front door of the lodge for years.

The city was buzzing and as I made my way along the main street, lively conversations, laughter and jazz music spilled from the mouths of every bar and restaurant I passed.

It was jazz weekend in Cork City – a weekend-long music festival, drawing jazz lovers to the city from all over the world since the late seventies. It's always one of the busiest weekends of the year and was something I had always loved. Now, I wanted nothing more than to shove the slow-moving revellers, who were meandering from place to place, sampling the sounds of different bars and clubs, out of my way and into oncoming traffic.

After a number of evasive manoeuvres, most of which involved precisely timed body swerves, I reached a quiet street on the south side of the city and turned down an obscure laneway that appeared to lead to nowhere. As my boots crunched on the worn concrete footpath, its surface unlikely to ever see repair, I absent-mindedly touched the gun in my waistband.

I stopped outside a large boarded-up window that sat beside an old wooden door. Above the window was a faded sign: 'Horgan's Bar and Eatery'. On the outside, it looked as if the place hadn't been opened to the public in decades, but unless things had changed drastically since I'd left, I would bet my life on there being a hive of activity behind that ageing door. I would almost guarantee that behind the sealed-off window there were small groups of men and women, sitting in dim lighting, huddled over their drinks, and scheming in low voices.

I banged on the door. Nothing. My breath caught in my throat.

What if I was wrong? What if this place was no longer used as a hang-out? I had been out of the scene for years. So if things had changed, how would I find the people I needed to track down my daughter?

I knocked again. Nothing.

I held my wrist, to stop it shaking, and pounded on the door with the side of my fist. It opened a fraction. Relief washed over me.

'Yeah?' asked a male voice, younger than I'd expected.

'Was looking for a drink.'

'Back the way you came and around the corner,' the voice said, pushing the door closed.

I pressed my shoulder against it, gaining just enough space to wedge my boot in the gap and stop it from closing on my face.

'What the fuck!'

I pushed my weight against the door, putting the gate-keeper under as much pressure as I could.

'I'm sorry,' I corrected myself. 'I phrased that incorrectly. Was looking for a drink *here.*'

There was no way I wasn't getting through that door.

I let the pressure off the door for a second before quickly slamming my entire weight into it. The sudden jolt threw the owner of the voice off balance, and he stumbled back, allowing me to swing the door open wide. Close to a dozen sets of eyes turned towards me as I crossed one leg over the other, planting my toe into the ground, while leaning against the door frame with my arms folded. Maeve Deane: the perfect picture of dangerous nonchalance. I hoped.

'So, who missed me enough to buy me a drink, then?' I asked, feeling a sly half-smile settle on my face with surprising ease.

The owner of the previously disembodied voice at the door was staring at me with his mouth hanging open on his childlike face.

The sound of chairs moving and scraping across the floor filled the room as most of its patrons stood and made their way towards me, shouting greetings mixed with a variety of obscenities. I smiled at the sing-song Cork accents and the speed at which they spoke, knowing that just hearing them would bring out my own accent and make it stronger. It was like finally hearing the correct way to say a word that you have been pronouncing just a little bit wrong.

'Well, holy shit, look who isn't dead!' a man in his late fifties called as he threw his arms around me. He was unshaven and wearing a dirty, dark green woollen hat, despite the heat of the room.

I almost winced at the bad language, having spent the better part of the last two years trying to avoid it at all costs – determined to prevent it coming out of tiny mouths, with their ever-listening ears.

'Ah, Mike, I couldn't have gone off and died without having you propose to me one more time, now, could I?' I returned the hug, patting him on the back.

52

Another man was standing behind Mike, head down, hands shoved deep into his pockets.

He greeted me with a nod. 'Maeve,' he said, without making eye contact.

'Alan,' I replied, with my own nod. I was the last person he wanted to see.

I remembered the time Alan and I had been standing outside an old farmhouse in East Cork. A house being rented by a man who worked as a debt collector for our boss. A man who, it appeared, was misplacing a large proportion of that collected debt.

In the ten minutes we stood there, waiting to confront the man when he arrived home, Alan put his hands in and out of his pockets close to fifty times. That's when I saw the beads of sweat that had formed across his brow. Until then, I'd had my suspicions about Alan, who played courier between our boss and the debt collector, but standing there watching him squirm, I knew. One prod and the truth spilled from him. How he'd needed the money for hospice care for his sister, who'd been diagnosed with cancer and at twenty-seven was lying drugged in a hospital bed waiting to die. He was going to stop when she was gone; he swore it. When the debt collector arrived, I informed him his services were no longer required and doled out his punishment as per instructions. I told the boss that the debt collector had confessed to everything, and I told Alan that he owed me one.

'Anything,' he'd said.

An easy promise to make back then, when he didn't have much, but I'd kept an eye on him over the years. His name popped up in articles here and there when I scanned through the Irish newspapers online. Now, he had plenty. He was a well-known businessman who had invested his ill-gotten money at the right time. He appeared to own apartment buildings in Cork, Galway and Dublin cities, as well as holiday homes scattered along each of their coasts, though it seemed that was his only legal business. He'd done well for himself.

'I never thought I'd be seeing those beautiful cheekbones again,' said a short, curvy woman in her early forties with a severe bob that was an unnatural shade of black.

'Lena.' I wrapped a hand around her head and kissed her cheek. 'I can't believe you're still hanging out in this shithole.'

'All for the whiskey,' Lena smiled.

'Well, if it isn't Ms Deane, as I live and breathe.'

The voice alone was enough to send my adrenaline production into overdrive. I was relieved that he was here, but now I knew I was probably gearing up for a fight. I shoved my hands into my jacket pockets, willing them not to betray my nerves. My stomach tightened and everyone around me stopped their salutations in their tracks and parted in front of me. And there he was, the reason I'd come to this dingy little bar, sitting alone at a table, in a heavy wooden chair facing away from me, towards the bar. One hand was hanging lazily over the small wooden arm, and he was smoking a cigarette with the other, his legs stretched out in front of him, feet crossed.

Davey O'Leary, one of the most infamous criminals on this entire island and the man who either had my daughter or knew who did.

I took a deep breath.

'Davey . . .' I hoped my voice sounded bored, though I could feel the strain in it.

'We'll let you two catch up,' Lena mumbled, patting me on the elbow.

As quickly as they had assembled around me, everyone dispersed back to their seats, eyes glued to their drinks, affording us the privacy Davey would expect.

Here goes.

I walked to the other side of his table. As I did, he reached a foot over and pushed out a chair. Same old Davey, controlling every detail, even where I would sit. I resisted the urge to pull out the chair next to the one he had chosen for me, but the last thing I wanted was to piss him off before getting the information I needed. I had to find out what he knew, and how he was involved in all of this, because there wasn't a doubt in my mind that he was – somehow.

Softly, softly.

Every cell in my body was screaming at me to catch him by the throat, knock the chair out from under him and push my gun into his forehead to make him talk, but I had to be careful. Davey had a loyal following. He was a master manipulator, able to use love, affection and fear with almost enviable skill to get exactly what he wanted from people. I had once seen him break a man's leg and convince him that it hurt him more to do it. The fool practically thanked Davey before we'd left. That's what made him so dangerous, and here I was, about to sit down and have a drink with him.

I took my assigned seat, and Davey gestured to the bartender for two more drinks. He said nothing, just sucked on his cigarette and looked me up and down. I sat back, crossing my legs, with my hands still stuffed inside my pockets. I would let him do this his way – for now. I stayed silent and studied him, almost as intently as he was studying me. I stared at his tanned skin, his firm jaw creating a face far too beautiful for the dangerous soul it housed. The only imperfection in his features was the way his nose dramatically kinked out to the left side of his face. His looks were just another weapon in his arsenal. Whether it was dealing drugs to young college girls for an extortionate mark-up, or talking his way into some place he shouldn't be, to do something he shouldn't be doing, his looks always helped convince people to trust him.

I'd always been wary of Davey. He was a man used to getting what he wanted – or simply taking it. I'd always been nervous around him, and he'd played on that, but if he had anything to do with my baby being taken, then I'd make him wish for the simplicity of a bullet to the head.

'You're looking good,' he said, taking another drag of his cigarette.

'You, too.'

I took a glass, half filled with whiskey, from the same boy who had been working the door. He didn't look much more than eighteen. One of Davey's latest recruits, no doubt, someone he'd taken under his wing and manipulated into doing his dirty work. Someone whose life had made working for a man like Davey his only option. I felt a pang of guilt for leaving Davey here to take advantage of people like that. I'd convinced myself, at first, that he really was looking out for the young people he took in, giving them simple, straightforward drug runs to keep them from worse fates. He was their saviour. If only I'd known then what I know now, maybe I would never have allowed myself to be drawn so deep into this dark, miserable world with these damaged, dangerous people.

Reaching for my whiskey, I was relieved by my steady hand, and lazily removed the other from my pocket.

'Wasn't expecting to see you again,' he said, finally looking me in the eyes.

'No?' I asked. 'Are you sure about that?'

A small smile lifted the corners of his mouth. He uncrossed his feet, sat up and leaned forward. I tensed. Every muscle in my body prepared for an attack, ready to move when and if I needed to, but he just reached for his whiskey before returning to his slouched position. He drank deeply from the glass, licking his lips as he finished.

'Well, a man can always hope, can't he?'

The gentle approach at gleaning information was already

starting to grate on me. I wanted answers. I wanted out of this all too familiar hellhole, and I wanted my baby back in my arms so I could go home to my family.

'Cut the shit, Davey.'

His smile vanished and his eyes narrowed. He looked much more like the Davey I remembered, but I'd been intimidated by him enough to last a lifetime. There would be no backing down now. I was here for a fight that I had no intention of losing. I reached into my jacket pocket, pulled out the blank white business card that had travelled here with me from England, and laid it in front of Davey.

'You know why I'm here.'

He smiled down at the card. 'Yeah, I suppose I do.'

8

My heart was pounding in my chest. Everything I had suspected was true. My stomach turned at the confirmation that my daughter really was with these people. I had known it from the moment she was taken, but that smile on Davey's face as he spoke made the gravity of the entire situation hit me hard. I watched as he leaned forward again, stubbing out his cigarette in the large glass ashtray, which was already half full of wrinkled orange filters. I urged the rising panic to stop and allow me to think straight.

I slid the white card away from him and put it back in my pocket, for no other reason than to force myself to concentrate on something else for a moment. The noise in my head quietened enough for me to realise that whatever admission Davey had just made didn't mean that Sarah was with him, it just meant that he knew about her, which could still mean it wasn't him who had orchestrated all this.

Davey pulled another cigarette from the pack and placed it between his teeth.

'Davey—'

'Shut your fucking mouth.' Davey slammed his fist down on the table, his fresh cigarette falling to the ground.

I jumped, as did the rest of the bar, though no one dared look over. My heart rate quickened, but aside from the involuntary reaction, I refused to show any fear. And besides, I wasn't afraid of him. Not for myself. In that moment, the only thing that truly scared me was not getting my baby back. Davey taking my daughter and leaving that white calling card was the best-case scenario. Davey I could handle.

My eyes flicked to the clock behind the bar. A quarter past seven, almost bedtime. Right now, I should be convincing Abbie to keep still as I brushed her teeth; she always fanned her mouth, claiming it was 'bunning'. Sarah should be in her cot, calling for me, impatiently waiting for her bedtime story. But I wasn't at home. Instead, I was here in this dive of a bar and Sarah . . . well, I had no idea where she was or whose arms she was in. Would they know to put her to sleep by eight? How would she fall asleep? Would they rock her? My chest ached so much, it felt as though my ribcage would burst open and my heart fall out, right there on the ground in front of Davey. He wouldn't give a shit, even if it did.

My breasts tingled in anticipation of milk production for bedtime, still blissfully unaware that I didn't, and wouldn't, have my baby in my arms tonight. That for the first time in her short life, her mummy wouldn't be putting her to bed. That tonight, she would have to fall asleep without me, and there was absolutely nothing I could do about it. I closed my eyes.

Don't you dare cry. Don't you even think of showing weakness in front of him. If you do, he'll think he's won and won't be satisfied until he's destroyed you.

I had to keep it together and get this done. Sarah didn't need her mummy right now, she needed the woman I once was, the woman who could hold her own going toe-to-toe with some of the most notorious criminals in the country. It wasn't my breastmilk that would save Sarah, it was the revival of the ruthless, conniving, underhanded woman I'd once been. That was who she needed, and that's who I'd be.

I leaned back in my chair, uncrossed and recrossed my legs as I summoned the most arrogant, insolent smirk I could muster. I knew it would piss him off, but the second he told me to shut up I switched tactics and decided to make him as mad as hell instead. It was the mental state in which I'd seen him make the most mistakes over the years. Anger could make him sloppy and, as dangerous as that could be, it was a necessary gamble, with time pressing down on me.

He relaxed back into his nonchalant pose, trying to regain his composure, but I could tell by the twitch of his jaw he wanted nothing more than to get up from his chair, knock me to the hard wooden floor and kick me in the stomach until I coughed up blood – a move he had a particular fondness for.

'How about *you* shut the fuck up for a change, Davey?'

The words, combined with the calm, almost sweet voice I used to deliver them, did the trick. Davey didn't move but I could see fire in his eyes as hate morphed his features into something far less handsome.

'I wouldn't talk to me like that if I were you, darling,' he said, quietly. 'You, of all people, should know what I'm capable of if someone pushes me far enough.'

It was true, I'd seem him react to what he classified as 'disrespectful behaviour', time and time again. But I'd also seen him piss himself, while snot streamed into his mouth, as he was put back in his place one time when he'd stepped too far across the line.

'I'm well aware of the temper tantrums you're capable of throwing, don't you worry.' I leaned forward, forcing myself as close to him as the small round table between us would allow, and kept my voice low. 'Now tell me who has my child, Davey, or I swear to Christ I'll make you wish I never walked through that door.'

He gave a small laugh but, despite all his bravado, he knew I was entirely capable of following through on my threats. And, if our past encounters gave him even a momentary pause, he should be a lot more cautious now that my child was involved.

'You're not a fool, Maeve, you know exactly what that card means.'

'No, Davey, that's exactly it, I'm not a fool, and I know there are others who would use that card to trick me into starting shit with the wrong person.' I was starting to lose my temper. 'Now, tell me who the fuck has my child.'

'Careful now, you wouldn't want to end the game prematurely.'

I smirked again, desperately trying to keep my own temper under control. 'Something *you'd* know all about, I'm sure.'

He gave another quiet laugh, before he spoke again. 'Ah, there's the smart-mouthed Maeve Deane I know and hate. I'm sure your mother would be so very proud of you if she wasn't rotting in the ground,' he sneered.

That was as much of the conversation as I could take.

'I wouldn't bring up mothers if I were you, Davey,' I said, through my teeth.

He grinned. 'Good old Maeve, still with the same buttons, ripe for pressing.'

I sat forward. 'My mother was taken from me, Davey but yours,' I gave a small laugh, 'she ran fucking screaming from you.'

Davey reached across the table so fast I didn't even have time to take a breath before he wrapped his big, meaty hand around my throat.

'Don't you fucking dare speak to me like that.' He could barely get the words out through his clenched teeth.

Well, that worked, he'd lost his cool. But maybe it had been too effective, I thought, as I struggled to take in air.

Say something, I willed him, *let some detail slip – anything.*

His hand remained tight on my throat, cutting off my air

supply with frustrating ease. A stark reminder of the physical advantages most men are born with, immediately putting them in a position of power over women. I tried to contain my panic and refused to struggle for the oxygen my lungs desperately wanted. His hand tightened. The look on his face now told me that the hot-headed prick was going to kill me. I've seen that look many times before, but only once have I been on the receiving end.

Years ago, when I had been living in Cork City, Davey had called by the house under the guise of relaying details of an upcoming job. When I'd opened the front door wider, to hear what he had to say, he forced his way in and pushed me up against the wall, hands roaming everywhere and slipping easily beneath my thin pyjamas. And for one terrifying moment, I froze.

With Davey, it was always about power, and I would bet my life that the attack that night was more about getting one over on those around him than anything sexual.

The shock had worn off quickly, followed by a nose-breaking head-butt to a once perfectly straight nose, and a knee to the testicles that I hoped would prevent him from ever procreating.

He made me a promise that night. 'You'll pay for that, you bitch. The worst thing you can imagine will be nothing compared to what I'll do to you.' Then he left, nose bleeding into one hand and cradling his balls with the other.

And that's exactly why I was here. To see if Davey had finally followed through on his promise.

I thought he had. But now, as his hand squeezed tighter around my neck, I wondered if he would go to all the trouble of abducting my daughter just to kill me like this, in his bar, without regaling me with the details of everything he'd done.

But if it wasn't him, I needed answers. Firstly, to one very important question: who was he working for? Davey was high enough up the ranks that there were only three potential answers to that question, all of whom made my blood run cold, but I would have to deal with that later. Right now, I needed to get this bastard's hands off my neck.

In a different scenario, one where my windpipe wasn't being crushed, the effect I was having on him would almost be flattering. It wasn't every day a woman could turn a cool, calculating dog like Davey into an impulsive, kill-despite-the-consequences type of mutt. What an achievement. Yet, all good things must come to an end, and as a black haze encroached on my vision, I reached into my jacket's inside pocket and removed my switchblade. Davey didn't notice. His eyes stayed fixed on mine, determined to watch the light dim from them.

I thought of that night when he had attacked me and how he might be involved in my child's abduction. The anger bubbling in my gut kept me conscious long enough to flick out the blade of my knife and drive it up into his wrist.

Davey roared, his chair clattering to the ground as he

scrambled back with my knife still embedded in him. I was on my feet the second his fingers left my throat, gulping down air.

A handful of Davey's men, who had been scattered throughout the bar, came towards us, while everyone else rose quietly and, with practised precision, slipped out of the bar. They were smart enough to avoid bearing witness to the proceedings that were about to unfold.

A blonde woman, skirting somewhere around mid-to-late-thirties, had run from behind the bar, screaming and frantically trying to see Davey's hand.

'Davey, Jesus Christ, Davey, get it out of your wrist!'

Davey, however, only had eyes for me. The way he was looking at me, his breathing ragged as he grasped the handle of the knife, made his earlier expression resemble a look of adoration. I couldn't help the smile that spread across my face.

'You'll regret that,' he said, yanking the knife from his bloody wrist and sending it skittering across the floor.

'I highly doubt it,' I said, still smiling. 'The look on your face right now is one of the best things I've ever seen.'

My reluctance to aggravate him was truly out the window, but I still needed to know who was calling the shots. And now that it seemed like it wasn't him, there were much more interesting ways to find out.

Davey was practically vibrating. Only four other men remained after the impromptu bar evacuation. Including

Davey, that made five. I didn't count the blonde, who was now clutching a blue-and-white chequered tea towel, desperate to staunch the steady flow of blood pulsing from Davey's wound.

I turned in a circle, taking in the faces of the surrounding men. The two I recognised looked suitably nervous, but those I didn't – the ones with less creased faces – smiled with confidence, hands twitching eagerly.

Davey took a step towards me, adrenaline and rage sustaining him despite the injury.

'Tut, tut, Davey, aren't you about to piss off someone important with all this impulsive carry-on?'

'She'll get over it,' he growled.

And there it was. Everything I needed to know. Davey stilled, eyes widening as he realised his mistake. Our eyes locked and, for a moment, neither of us moved.

One tiny word, a simple pronoun, had upped the stakes of the impending fight.

There was only one 'she' on my list. Only one woman with the ability, the audacity and the ranking to pull this off. The same woman who, we both knew, would have no qualms about making Davey suffer for his little slip-up. He may have *wanted* to kill me before, but now he *needed* to. The only way I was getting out of here alive was if he couldn't stop me. The proverbial fight to the death.

Davey lunged, but before he could reach me I stepped towards him, grabbed his injured wrist with both hands, turned my back into his body, and used his momentum to propel him over my hip. I steered him, by his seized arm, towards the man standing directly behind me. The other three didn't wait for Davey's nod after seeing him crash into their colleague. They started to close in on me.

I paused when I realised that the youngster who was both doorman and server was among them. He took my hesitation as fear and charged at me, but inexperience, or perhaps reluctance, led him to attempt capture rather than attack. Rounding me, he grabbed me from behind, pulling my arms to my sides, and announced, 'I've got her, I've got her.'

Despite his youth he was strong, and I was, technically, 'got', but he should have known better after seeing me send a man twice his size barrelling across the floor moments earlier. Silly boy.

His grip was tight around my waist as he swung me from side to side in assumed triumph. He had a few inches on my five-foot-six frame, but in order to keep his hold on me I was practically on my tiptoes, which meant his head, and more importantly his face, was positioned directly behind my own. Tilting my head down, I buried my chin as deep into my chest as I could, until I felt an uncomfortable pull down the back of my neck, as if it was an elastic band I was pulling taut. I released it, snapping my head backwards, with as much speed and force as it was capable of, straight into his young, triumphant face. A sickening crunch, accompanied by a surprisingly high-pitched scream, and I was free. His hands dropped and flew to his face in an attempt to contain the fast flow of blood now coming from his freshly broken nose.

'Sit this out,' I warned him, before turning back to the other two, who were now approaching in a much more cautious manner, both with their fists raised in an old-school defensive boxing stance.

Davey and the guy who'd unwillingly broken his fall were back on their feet but seemed happy to let the two boxers have their shot while they tended to Davey's wrist, wrapping it with a cloth that was quickly becoming saturated in his blood. He'd need to head to the hospital after all of this, I mused to myself, as I stepped towards the two on their bouncing feet with their bobbing fists guarding their jaws. They were fooling themselves if they thought I would only aim for their faces. They'd have been safer standing there cupping their testicles like soccer players awaiting a free kick.

The bigger of the two stepped up first. He was older than me, about mid-forties, and his head was so bald that, even in the dimly lit bar, there was a glare off it.

A sudden sense of urgency rushed through me as I watched one of the many obstacles standing between me and my daughter come towards me. No, I had no more patience left for any of this. I strode towards him and, while maintaining eye contact, sent a roundhouse kick straight into the side of his kneecap. His leg buckled, but he was strong and solid, and only faltered for a moment.

He swung a heavy right hook at my temple, which I

swerved, bending low at the waist. He might have been strong, but it was to the detriment of his speed. It takes a lot more energy to swing and miss than it does to swing and hit.

It had taken me a long time to accept that this was the key to fighting men. Most men are stronger than most women. A fact I had tried desperately to rectify by spending hours lifting weights, followed by even more hours sparring in boxing rings. It helped, but not enough – not enough by a long way. Nine times out of ten, the men I came up against were still stronger, which not only pissed me off but also put me in danger. It took time, but eventually I realised that if I was going to survive in the life I'd chosen, I'd need to learn how to get the upper hand in a fight with a man, and so I'd switched tactics. I spent more time studying aikido, Brazilian ju-jitsu and basically any martial art I could find that focused on using an opponent's weight, strength and movements against them. It had helped – a lot.

Another grunt, another swing, another easy dodge. By the way his left arm muscles were bunching, I could tell he was going to swing from his left again. So, instead of avoiding the strike, I took a step to the right, turning side-ways as his arm straightened, and grabbed his exposed wrist with both hands. I pulled him towards me, simultaneously kicking his left foot out from under him and propelling him straight into the ground. The combination of surprise and my remaining grip on his left arm caused him to land on his face – hard. I stepped over him, placing one foot on either side of his body and, still gripping his left arm, yanked it up behind him until he roared out in pain. I would have kept going until his shoulder popped from his socket, if it hadn't been for the very distinctive pressure against the back of my head.

'Enough of this shit now, M.'

'Bollocks.' I released the man's limp arm and raised my hands above my head. 'Now, now, Davey,' I said, turning slowly to face him, 'you know I don't like it when you shorten my name down to a single letter. Makes me feel cheap.'

'It's more than you deserve.'

Judging by the spittle flying from his drying lips and how steadily his right hand held the gun pointed at my head, I knew I was in a dire situation. Riling him up and inflaming his temper may have been the fastest way of getting information, but now a surge of anger could lead him to squeeze that tiny, lethal trigger – and then it was game over.

What would happen to Sarah then? What would happen if I didn't come for her? Panic surged through me, so I pushed it down with all my might. I needed to get him talking, to make him realise that *she* would be a lot less forgiving if he ended the sick game she'd put so much effort into setting up, by adding my brain matter to the other questionable stains on the bar floor.

'Davey—' I began.

The blonde woman from earlier burst through from the back room with a phone to her ear, and cut me off.

'Davey?'

He didn't so much as blink at the sound of her voice.

'DAVEY!'

'What?'

'It's for you,' she said, matter-of-factly, stretching her arm out towards him with the phone in her hand, lit up and displaying a Dublin phone number.

Davey looked at her, narrowing his eyes suspiciously.

I smiled. It looked like blondie had just told on Davey for not playing nicely with others.

His eyes returned to mine. A look of uncertainty flashed across his face. He still wanted to kill me, there was no doubt about that, but I could see him beginning to process the repercussions of pulling the trigger.

Time paused for almost an entire minute. Davey staring at me, gun poised and ready, me staring back at him, waiting to see if this phone call would save my life, while the blonde woman stood holding the phone out towards him.

The frenetic rate of my heartbeat eased a fraction when he took the phone awkwardly with his injured hand, covering it in blood as he tucked it between his shoulder and his ear before dropping it to his side again.

He wouldn't have accepted the call if he wasn't going to do what he was told from the other end.

But, as confident as I was about that, I wasn't out of here yet. Davey was still a temperamental bastard with a gun trained on my head. No, I couldn't rely on whatever the voice at the other end of the line said to get me out of this; I could only rely on myself.

I was itching to grab the gun from the back of my waistband, but timing is everything, and it wasn't the time yet.

'What?' he snapped, knowing what he'd be told, and already angry in response to it.

The bar fell into an uncomfortable silence, once again, as Davey listened, giving nothing away.

'Fine,' was all he said, before firing the phone into the chest of the blonde who'd waited by his side.

She may have contacted whoever was on the phone, but judging by her reaction to the hole in his wrist it seemed they were in some kind of relationship. Lucky woman, considering there was probably a bruise blooming across her breast from the force of that throw.

'Ah, not allowed off the lead today, then?' I taunted him, despite the loaded gun still pointed at my head.

'Don't be so sure,' he sneered, taking a step towards me. 'Maybe I got the go-ahead to take care of an irritating problem sooner than expected!'

'I don't think so, Davey.' I matched his step, closing the gap between me and his gun. 'I suspect you were told to stand down, let the game play out, and be a good boy.' I reached the gun in his outstretched hand. 'Except there's one thing they don't know, isn't there?' I pressed my head against the muzzle of his gun. 'That you've let a piece of the puzzle slip and, in true Davey fashion, it was premature.'

I moved fast, ducking under the gun before grabbing his arm and forcing it upwards, while serving him a quick, hard knee to the testicles at the same time.

The bullet I knew he'd squeeze off lodged itself above the door frame on the wall behind me, sending the remaining occupants of the back room scrambling to get outside.

Davey folded over and fell to the ground. There's something deeply satisfying about the fact that, despite all their physical attributes, men carry their most fragile parts dangling in front of them at perfect kneeing height. A small, karmic attempt at levelling the playing field, I guess.

I stamped down on his good wrist, still clutching the gun. There was a satisfying crack, and the gun came away in my hand.

I trained the gun on him and his head dropped to the floor. He was beaten.

I was halfway through a sigh of relief when a faint but familiar click behind me caused the breath to catch in my chest.

With my left hand, I pulled the gun from my waistband, and with Davey's gun still pointed at him, aimed my own behind me before I'd fully turned towards the sound.

My heart sank at the sight of the young, multi-functional floater staring back at me with a gun aimed at my chest. *Anyone else*, I thought, *anyone else*.

'Drop it.' His voice was calm, his gun held steady with both hands.

'Not going to happen, I'm afraid.' And I truly was afraid, afraid of what I might be forced to do to get out of here.

'What are you going to do, then, M?' Davey sneered. 'Kill a child?'

'I don't know, Davey, he looks over eighteen to me.'

Standing there, in the middle of a dingy bar, both arms outstretched with a gun in each hand, trained on two different heads, I couldn't stop my mind from returning home. I was back in my living room with two small hands grasped in mine as we danced in circles singing 'Ring a Ring o' Roses', while two smaller hands clapped with delight.

A noise from the bar brought me back. The blonde woman stood frozen, hands at her mouth, trying to hold in another scream. She looked terrified. I followed her fearful look to the boy with the gun trained on me.

'You don't have to do this, you know. You don't owe him anything.'

'You're right about that, lady, but I'm hardly going to stand back and let you kill my dad, now am I?'

'Dad?' I almost choked on the word, as I thought back to that knee to his testicles years earlier and how it had clearly been much too late. Turning back to look at Davey, I asked, 'Since when have you been "Dad"?'

Davey shrugged. 'We all have to step up and take responsibility for our actions eventually,' he said, with a smile. 'Not that you'd know anything about fathers coming back into your life.'

'Fuck you, Davey.'

My conception had been the result of my mother's drunken one-night stand with a man who suddenly found work he couldn't refuse in England when she told him she was pregnant. That had been my mother's one and only indiscretion in her life. She'd been twenty, mourning the loss of her mother from breast cancer the month before, while still reeling from her father's death from a heart attack a year earlier. She had always told me it was the single greatest thing she'd ever done, because it gave her me.

'No. Don't!' Davey shouted over my shoulder.

I turned towards his confused-looking son, and Davey seized the opportunity. He threw himself at my legs, knocking me to the ground and sending the gun I'd taken from him spinning across the floor. How had I fallen for that?

'Do it! Do it now, son!' Davey roared.

The boy hesitated. I did not. Before he could obey his father, like a good son, I rolled onto my back, squeezed the trigger of my remaining gun and sent a solitary bullet flying between me and Davey's offspring. A scream from the blonde woman filled the air, not unlike the one that had escaped from my lips earlier that morning.

My bullet struck its target, and as the boy fell to the floor I was on my feet and running for the door. I paused at Davey's son, lying still, eyes wide.

'You'll be fine, kid,' I said, patting him gently on the face as he blinked up at me.

The bullet had barely grazed his upper arm. Jumping over him, I scooped up my bloody knife, retracting the blade, before returning it to my pocket. Then I ran out the door I had been unwillingly let through earlier, and straight into Davey's brother – my ex-fiancé.

9

Then

The first time Jamie noticed Maeve, in a crowded Cork City bar, was not actually the first time he had seen her. He didn't recognise her as one of the teenagers he had once employed when he was nineteen to sell drugs on the streets of the city. He didn't realise that she was the girl with the straight, dyed black hair who'd lived across the street from him, the girl whose mother had been murdered during a break-in. No, he didn't recognise her at all. Instead, he sat at his table in the crowded bar and watched her as she ordered a drink. He couldn't tell what it was, but it wasn't an obnoxious, artificial colour so it had to be something decent. She threw it back in one swift movement, before turning and leaning against the bar. As she took in what was going on around her, Jamie drank her in. Her long, curly, dark red hair was the first thing that caught his attention, but her body came in at a very close second. The term 'hourglass' had never applied to a woman's body so well. She was dressed casually, her simple top and jeans making her stand out among the masses of sequins, leopard print and short dresses.

There was no denying she was a beautiful woman. Heads turned, both male and female, not-so-subtly checking her out, but that wasn't enough to get him out of his chair. Jamie never put much effort in when it came to women. He didn't need to. He was handsome, which attracted some women, but he also knew it, which attracted most women. Jamie knew that nothing got the ladies more interested than a man with confidence, and he was the very definition of confident. That's why he was so successful – not just with women, but in life. He knew that most people would consider him a criminal, but he thought the term 'entrepreneur' was more fitting. Jamie was a businessman of the highest order, but yes, thanks to the illegality of his business adventures, he supposed he could also be classified as a criminal.

He watched as she scanned the crowd. Was she waiting for someone? Why was she alone?

The woman who had sashayed over to him at the start of the night, with her skirt up around her ass and a double vodka and Red Bull in each hand, was now nuzzling into his neck, and it was beginning to irritate him.

'Why don't you go get some more drinks?' he said, shrugging her off.

It was a dismissal, not a question, and she'd been around the scene long enough to know she should heed it.

He continued to watch as the woman at the bar ordered another drink. This time, he could see the bartender fill the glass from the large whiskey bottle mounted on the wall behind him – Jameson. Well, whoever she was, she had taste, and judging by how much whiskey filled her glass, it was a double, which meant she could handle her drink. That, or she would be falling around the place in the not too distant future.

She was still facing the bar when a man came up behind her, hands roaming. Jamie sat back. *Well, that's that*, he thought, surprised by his level of disappointment. She looked over her shoulder at the man attached to her. Jamie was about to look away when the man reached around her opposite shoulder and dropped something into her whiskey.

Jamie leaned forward, gripping the railing of the bar's upper level from where he was observing her. He looked up and down the bar, but it seemed that no one else had seen what had happened. Jamie called out, but the cacophony of voices swallowed up his voice, and his words were lost in the soundtrack of tinny pop music. He could go down there, but by the time he made his way through the crowd on the stairs and across to the bar, the prick who'd spiked her drink could have steered her out the side entrance.

He was about to signal the security guard to get on the walkie-talkie to the bouncers downstairs when she turned to face the man. For a second, it seemed as if she knew him. There was a smile on her face that made Jamie shift in his seat. Her lips were moving. Whatever she was saying, the man took it as an invitation and pressed himself against her. As soon as he did, she buried her knee in his genitals. She stayed pressed against him, whispering something in his ear, not allowing him to fold over on himself, as is both customary and compulsory when a man's testicles are under attack. Jamie smiled. She wasn't finished yet. Pushing him back, she swung her right fist at his face, and down he went.

Jamie had seen his share of fights: bar, street, fair, not-so-fair. But he'd never seen anyone cause so much damage with so much grace and fluidity. Her movements reminded him more of a dancer than a fighter. She turned back to her drink. Jamie was about to shout out uselessly into the wall of sound again when, without hesitation, she dumped the contents of her glass over the pathetic bastard writhing around on the ground. It was the smile on her face as she did it that had Jamie heading for the stairs. She was definitely worth getting out of his chair for.

10

Now

Jamie looked at me as if I was a ghost and held tight to my arms to stop me from disappearing. I pressed my hands against his chest to steady myself.

For one brief second, time paused. I stood there, staring into his dark eyes as they searched for something in mine.

'Maeve,' he whispered, as if he was discovering something precious.

His hands ran up my arms to my neck, where they paused with a gentleness and warmth so unlike the hands that had been on me earlier, his thumbs resting just below my jaw-line, every movement so familiar. We had stood in that same embrace hundreds of times before – in bars, nightclubs, restau-rants, streets, warehouses, hotels – but this was the first time we'd stood like this since I'd left him, nearly five years ago.

Jamie, my ex-fiancé, Davey's younger brother and possibly the man who had abducted my child.

'I need to get out of here,' I said, snapping out of whatever time warp we'd stepped into.

He didn't even hesitate. 'This way,' he said, grabbing my hand before I could protest.

He led me back down the street and around the corner to where he was parked.

'Get in,' he ordered, opening the passenger door of a black Jaguar that was almost identical to the one he had driven before I'd left him – except this one was brand new.

He shut the door behind me before striding round the car and climbing in the driver's side. He took off at speed, easily navigating his way through the city streets before pulling onto the main road that leads out of the city.

Had I done the right thing getting into his car? I couldn't, or perhaps didn't want to, believe that Jamie could take my child, but deep down, I knew he had every reason to want to make me suffer. After what I'd done to him.

I looked over at him, his eyes fixed on the road ahead. He was handsome, even more handsome than his older brother. In fact, he was a far better man than Davey in every way. Yes, he was still a ruthless criminal, but nothing like the prick I'd left bleeding back at the bar. I'd always thought Jamie and Davey were the perfect example to put any nature-over-nurture debate to rest.

Their mother had left them both when they were nine and ten. Although, in her defence, that's not technically correct. She left their father, a man who thought that it was his God-given right to do to their mother as he pleased. Ger beat her regularly and after a particularly bad incident, when she realised it was only a matter of time before he went too far and killed her, she tried to run.

Unfortunately for her, the night she chose to leave, Ger had decided to leave the pub early for the first time in years and he found her leaving the house, laden with backpacks, a small boy holding each hand. He caught her by the throat, pushed her up against the front door and gave her just what she wanted. He told her to get the fuck out of his house, but there was no way she was taking his sons with her.

This is where the brothers' versions of events differ. Jamie says she hesitated and held tight to their small hands, even while their father tightened his grip on her neck. Then he remembers her falling out the door as his father kicked her hard in the back of her thigh, promising that if he ever saw her again, he'd kill her and the boys. Davey, however, remembers no such hesitation. He claims that his mother simply dropped his hand and walked out the door before it slammed shut, trapping him on the other side with his father.

Either way, they never saw their mother again and endured the worst five years of their young lives, until their father died. He'd been travelling the wrong way down a dual carriageway in an attempt to evade the Gardaí after robbing a post office, when he came head-to-head with an articulated lorry. He died on impact.

Jamie remembers his mother as a caring, loving woman

who did the best she could with the horrible hand she was dealt; a woman forced to leave her children if she had any hope of surviving, rationalising that their father had never laid a hand on either of the boys. Davey remembers a mother who had spent her days passed out from painkillers and sleeping tablets, a mother who had abandoned him, leaving him with an evil bastard who subsequently redirected his violent tendencies towards the sons she left behind.

It didn't matter, though. Davey could have been brought up by a loving father and a present mother, and he'd still be the same today. Davey was always going to be exactly who he was.

'You want to tell me what's going on?' Jamie asked, flicking on the cruise control.

'Are you saying you don't know?' Although I believed Jamie was, at his core, a good person, I still had to ask the question. After all, on paper he was your average run-of-the-mill 'bad guy', and sometimes a very bad guy.

'Trust me, if I'd known you were here, I—' He stopped himself, his voice catching with emotion.

I snuck a glance at him and could see he was trying to compose himself before continuing. It was the last thing I needed, to come face-to-face with the man I walked out on, leaving nothing more than a short note, scribbled on a torn piece of paper. I never allowed myself to think about him, or the hurt I caused when I left, and now was certainly not the time to start. There was nothing more important than getting Sarah back. Nothing.

'Is it bad?' he asked, finally.

'Yes.'

'Well, then, you'd better get talking, and fast. There's a roundabout ahead, so it's time to tell me where you need to go.'

'Dublin, maybe? I'm not sure. I need to find Rita.'

Jamie glanced over at me, confusion creasing his brow.

'Rita has kidnapped my daughter,' I explained, answering his silent question. Admitting it out loud made me feel even worse.

Rita Regan, the 'she' Davey had referred to, had once been the general manager of Hotel de Vie, now known as The Harmada – the same hotel where my mother had worked as a receptionist. It sat on the quay in Cork City, a short walk from my mother's home. Rita also happened to be married to Ireland's most notorious crime lord, Martin Mulvihill. The same Martin Mulvihill who owned The Harmada. The same Martin Mulvihill who, for decades, had managed to evade every single investigation into him and his criminal activities. The same Martin Mulvihill who was my former boss – and the last person I wanted to contemplate having any contact with my daughter.

People often referred to Rita as Martin's lapdog: small and always willing to do his bidding. Of course, no one dared call her that to her face. She may be small, but Rita had a big bite and a dark side that made her the perfect fit for Martin.

'Rita? I just don't get it. Why would Rita do something like that? And after all this time?'

Jamie's response didn't surprise me. Rita had fostered Jamie and Davey when their father died, and while Davey had used Rita's address as no more than a way to keep social services at bay until he came of age, Jamie and Rita had become close and formed a pseudo mother–son relationship. Regardless, both boys did exactly as she told them.

Rita would say it was out of the goodness of her heart that she took them in but, after getting to know her, I suspect it had a lot more to do with keeping some of her best underage drug runners out of foster homes where she couldn't reach them. Everything Rita did was calculated and benefited her, in one way or another, but she was formidable at dressing it up to look as if she was doing her best for other people. I could tell that from our very first meeting, but I also knew never to voice that opinion to Jamie. I was aware that she didn't like me, but that hadn't bothered me much, since I didn't like her either.

'That's exactly what I keep asking myself.' I took a breath. 'But there was a blank white business card left in Sarah's place, and Davey said "she", so . . .' My voice trailed off.

'I just don't get it,' Jamie repeated, quietly.

'I don't either,' I said, putting my head in my hands. 'I thought they had allowed me to leave without retribution – I was vetted!'

That was part of the deal when joining the upper ranks of

a criminal gang – vetted when you join, vetted if you leave. If there are any doubts about your loyalty on either occasion, then you pay, usually with your life. It's not a risk any sane person would take.

'You were.' Jamie paused, taking a breath. 'When you left, everyone decided that it was safe to allow you to go. You were clean.' He glanced at me, for the first time since I'd run straight into him. 'I'd have warned you if they'd thought any different.'

I turned to him, but his eyes had returned to the road ahead.

'You don't think she'll do anything to—?'

I didn't have to finish the question. He knew what I was going to ask.

'No, no way. Rita would never hurt a child. Your daughter's safe.'

I couldn't tell if he was trying to convince me, or himself. The tightness in my chest didn't ease. Rita may have been like a mother to Jamie but she was anything but maternal.

'But if Martin's involved . . .' he added, the sentence hanging in the air between us.

'He's in Barcelona, though,' he continued, turning to look at me again. 'He was called over there to manage an emergency with a coke deal, and flew out late last night, so that's good news at least.'

I was still looking at him when he returned his gaze to the road in front of him.

'You know,' he grimaced, 'that he's not in the country right now.'

My heart rate accelerated. Everything was pointing to Martin orchestrating this – Rita's involvement, his white calling card – and if that was true, I was suddenly on the wrong side of the most dangerous man in the country.

I had been so sure that card had been left by Davey, that he'd managed to track me down and thought the perfect way of paying me back for that twist in his nose and that ache in his testicles was to take my child and leave Martin's calling card, causing me to come back to Ireland and start shit with the one person I did not want to start shit with. I'd come back here, thinking I was too clever for that. Thinking I'd make Davey pay and show him that trying to mess with me was an incredibly stupid idea. But it was starting to look as if I was the stupid one.

'No,' I said, rubbing my hand across my chest and trying to ease the pain. 'If this was Martin, I'd be dead already, wouldn't I?'

Jamie gave a small shrug. We both knew, if that was true, it left some important questions hanging in the air. If Rita was doing this alone, then why? Did the fact that Martin was out of the country at the time this was all happening mean Rita could be doing this behind Martin's back? Why would she do that? Why would she risk everything, risk Martin's wrath, just to get at me? Even the fact that Davey was involved in some way didn't help me. He was just as likely to follow

Rita's orders as Martin's, and was one of the few people who wouldn't report back to Martin if Rita told him not to. The more I thought about it, the less sense it made.

'Where's Rita?' I asked.

'I honestly don't know,' he said. 'I haven't been in contact with her for a couple of days.'

I looked at him. Was he telling me the truth?

'Can you find out?'

He didn't answer.

We sat in silence for a few kilometres before he pulled into a lay-by and took out his mobile phone. Jamie tried Rita's number but it went straight to voicemail. He made a few more calls, and while he gleaned no concrete intel as to where Rita was, all signs pointed to Dublin.

A few more probing phone calls and Jamie figured out that Rita had last been seen conducting business at The Pirate Rooms nightclub. Another business owned by Martin, which also functioned as a base for his illegal activities. Without being too obvious about it, Jamie had tried to ascertain if there was anyone with her, but it seemed that she had been alone. I didn't know what that meant. I didn't know if it was a good sign or a bad sign that no one seemed to know anything about the baby who should be with Rita.

That, combined with the Dublin number I'd seen on Davey's phone, led us to the Cork–Dublin motorway. I told Jamie he could drop me at Kent train station, but he insisted that he had business to attend to up in Dublin, anyway. I knew he was lying, and while I didn't relish the thought of an awkward two-and-a-half-hour car journey along a monotonous motorway with my ex-fiancé, I was glad of the opportunity to shave some precious time off the journey and avoid any more delays, in case Davey decided to have me followed.

We sat in silence for a long time, so long that when Jamie eventually spoke, I jumped in my seat.

'So, you have a daughter?'

I squeezed my eyes shut and took a deep breath as quietly as I could. This was exactly the conversation I didn't want to have.

'Two,' I answered, turning to face my reflection in the dark passenger window.

'Did you marry him?'

I knew the 'him' he was talking about. The same 'him' I met shortly after leaving Jamie. The same 'him' I fled the country with. My husband, Christopher.

'I did,' I said, to my reflection.

'Do you love him?' he asked.

'I do,' I answered, with a nod.

Jamie went quiet and I stared into the eyes of my reflection. Even after the years apart, the two children, a marriage, fleeing the country, it still felt strange to talk to Jamie like this, about how I loved another man.

I broke the awkward silence that followed by telling Jamie everything that had happened this evening with Davey, which evoked a mixed response from him. He only really seemed concerned when I mentioned Davey's son – who, it now occurred to me as I was talking, was his nephew.

'Don't worry, he's fine. I barely skimmed his arm, I promise.'

'Good, that's good.' Relief flooded his face.

For a moment I could see Jamie as he stood over me years earlier, watching as I repeatedly punched the face beneath me, over and over, long after he'd stopped moving, but I wouldn't have killed that boy tonight. Would I?

It's always a gamble to shoot with any intention other than to kill, especially when someone has a gun trained on you. Shooting to injure always carries risk; there's the danger that by leaving the person alive, they'll still get a bullet off. I didn't want to think about it too closely, because even though I'd known I was taking a chance, I had felt confident I'd get out of there by causing minimal damage. But what if I hadn't? What would I have been willing to do, to get out of there alive? The answer was simple: anything. I'd have done anything I needed to do, to get out of there and find my baby. I could have done it. I could have shot his nephew dead. No doubt his father had expected me to, the second his child hesitated, but I hadn't, and that's all that mattered.

Despite every heinous, horrible thing I had done over the years, I had never squeezed off a kill shot. I may have witnessed it many times – even contributed to some, in an indirect way – and those stains will remain on my soul forever, but I had never killed anyone in cold blood. I'd never even seriously considered it. Until now. Now that my child was the prize at the end of all this, nothing was off limits if it meant getting to her. I let that thought settle on me and took a deep breath as another piece of my soul darkened.

'How did that happen, anyway?' I asked, to distract myself from my thoughts.

'How did what happen?'

'Davey? Being a dad?' I elaborated.

'You saying you don't know how that happens?' Jamie laughed.

I joined him, briefly. 'No, I mean, how does he suddenly have a, what is he, eighteen, nineteen-year-old son? Who, as far as we knew, didn't exist four or five years ago.' It was strange talking about 'we' as me and Jamie, but there was something comforting in it, too. It made me feel less alone, back here in this life again.

'Yeah, that surprised everyone,' he said, hitting the indicator as he accelerated into the fast lane to overtake a line of slow-moving cars. 'He's nineteen. Insisted on finding Davey when he turned eighteen and figured his mother couldn't stop him. She followed him here from Northern Ireland.' Jamie was shaking his head. 'This wasn't the life she wanted for him, so she spent his entire childhood trying to keep him away from it, but here he is now, working with his dad.'

I couldn't blame her for trying to keep Davey out of her son's life. Her instincts had been spot on. Even at seventeen,

Davey had been trouble and caught up in a life no mother would ever want her child anywhere near.

Jamie assured me it was unlikely Davey would follow me. He figured Davey would sit back, let it all play out, and, when the dust had settled, hope that as little as possible had landed on him. I didn't point out that, if that was the case, I probably didn't need his help – but need and want are two entirely different things.

I looked sideways at Jamie and took another deep breath. Rita Regan had my daughter. The thought kept pounding through my head. I didn't know how it made me feel, knowing that it was Rita who had my child. As much as I'd like to believe Jamie, that she wouldn't hurt a child, the thought was immediately tarnished by the fact that she'd orchestrated Sarah's abduction. There was nothing friendly or innocent about that. It made no sense that she would do this off her own back, without Martin's say-so, but Davey had said 'she' and he'd been pissed when he realised he'd let it slip. If Rita was going to go behind Martin's back, Davey was the perfect person to have on her side. He was probably more loyal to her than he was to Martin. But why? I couldn't understand Rita's potential motives for doing this to me after all this time – and Jamie seemed to be just as much in the dark.

Or maybe I was overthinking it all. Maybe the most obvious and most terrifying answer was the right one. Maybe Martin was finally punishing me for leaving his employment.

Jamie looked down at my hands, my thumb cracking each finger in turn, before turning his attention to a small screen to the right of his dashboard and pressing a couple of buttons.

'There's a manned Garda speed-check up ahead,' he said.

I didn't reply, just kept pressing down on my fingers.

'About seven or eight kilometres.'

I nodded.

'So, what do you say?' he asked, swinging the Jag into a lay-by.

'What do I say about what?' I snapped, startled by the sudden pit stop.

'Maeve, you need to relax, to focus. You need—'

'What I *need*,' I interrupted, turning to face him, 'is to get to Dublin. What I *need* is to get my daughter back. What I *need* is to get away from this hellhole of a country and back to my family.' With every word, my voice level increased so that by the end I was shouting.

Silence filled the car. For a few moments we just sat there looking at each other. I felt bad for snapping at him, but I didn't apologise. Everything I'd said was true.

Jamie reached over and took both my hands in his, gripping my thumbs.

'I get it, Maeve. But to do all that, you need to focus – and right now you're anything but focused.'

I raised my eyebrows at him and looked down at our entwined hands. He released them immediately.

'Play the game. You know it will help,' he said, folding his arms across his chest as he sat back in his seat.

He was right, it would help. I knew it would, but that still didn't make it the right thing to do.

'I can't afford any delays.'

He smiled, sensing my impending submission to his plan. 'We both know this will probably speed up your arrival in Dublin.'

'Fine,' I said, rolling my eyes as I struggled to keep the smile from my face.

'Excellent,' he announced, opening his door. 'You have a look through the sat nav in case you need a refresher, and I'll sort the plates.' He jumped out, closing the door behind him and heading to the boot.

Alone in the car, I allowed myself a small smile. Jamie certainly knew me well. This would help focus me, but he didn't know me well enough if he thought I'd need to remind myself of the roads around here.

'Let's go,' I said to no one, before getting out of the car and making my way around to the driver's side. Climbing in, I adjusted the rear-view mirror and settled my grip on the supple leather steering wheel.

The game was simple; pass the Garda and his speed camera as fast as possible and then don't get caught. After that, it was all about the driving. Getting off the motorway and taking to the narrow, winding country roads where I would lose them. Then it would be as simple as pulling over, clipping off the fake licence plates Jamie had attached, and getting back onto the motorway to complete our journey.

Jamie leaned across from the passenger seat for a better look at the monitor displaying the Garda checks up ahead.

'Two kilometres,' he said, sitting back into his seat and getting comfortable.

I pressed the sport button before easing my foot down on the accelerator. The deep rumble from the engine filled my chest cavity and pushed up through me, forcing my lips into a smile. A soft laugh from the passenger seat had me turning my head towards Jamie.

'Where's my soundtrack?' I asked.

'At your command,' he answered, pressing a few buttons on the display panel before Metallica's 'The Four Horsemen' blasted through the speakers.

My foot sank further and my head bobbed to the music.

'We ride!' Jamie shouted, throwing his hands in the air.

We were both laughing as we passed the blue-and-white blur of the Garda car.

'What do you think you hit?' Jamie asked.

'At least two-forty.'

'Well, then, you'd better ease off,' he laughed. 'Or they'll think there's no point coming after you.'

'Careful what you ask for,' I said, pushing down hard on the brake pedal and sending us both pressing forward into our seat belts.

Jamie was laughing as he righted himself in his seat. 'You never did like to do things by halves.'

I turned to look at him, as we were now travelling at a much more respectable speed of 140 kilometres.

'All or nothing,' he said, grinning.

'All or nothing,' I echoed, grinning back.

The flashing blue lights behind us snapped my attention back to the road.

'Oops,' I said, looking at the speedometer, which had dropped below a hundred. 'Overcorrection.'

'We ride again,' Jamie announced as I plunged the accelerator pedal to the floor, forcing us back into the tan leather bucket seats.

I turned off at the next slip road, indicating as I did.

Jamie laughed as he turned up the music.

It had worked. The thrill of the high speeds, the sharp turns down narrow roads, the satisfaction of knowing a squad car was still patrolling the surrounding area looking for me, all of it had settled me, calmed me down and allowed me to focus.

Back on the motorway, and back in the passenger seat, we fell into silence once again.

I could see him out of the corner of my eye, looking in my direction every so often, as if he wanted to ask me something. Of course he had questions, I'd left without so much as a backward glance, but this wasn't the time, and he knew that. For me, I don't think there ever would be a time for that conversation. Since the day I left him, I'd never allowed myself to think of him, the life we'd once had, or the life we could have had together. I couldn't, because I was always afraid that if I did, if I really thought about it, I'd be back in his arms before I could fully consider the consequences. But I knew I owed him that conversation, maybe someday.

For the last half-hour of the journey I closed my eyes and leaned back against the headrest, easing the pressure on my neck. I needed to get some rest before we reached Dublin, and even if I didn't sleep, I still figured feigning sleep was a good way to avoid any more awkward small talk or conversations about the past.

I drifted off for some part of the drive, but it was a fitful sleep, with dreams of Sarah crying out for me in the arms of a stranger whose face I couldn't see.

11

Then

Jamie couldn't believe he'd fallen in love, and not just the keep-her-around, get-married-and-have-a-child-or-two kind of love but the all-consuming, couldn't-imagine-her-not-being-in-his-life kind of love. He'd never felt anything like it before. To be honest, he'd never felt anything even remotely like affection towards any woman, aside from Rita Regan, after his mother had been forced from his life. But then, he met Maeve Deane.

It took three nights in a row out drinking together before he finally realised he had met Maeve before.

'Maeve Deane,' he said suddenly as he arrived back to their table, drinks in hand.

'Oh, the penny finally dropped, did it?' Maeve laughed, accepting her drink as Jamie sat down and pulled his chair closer to her.

He remembered when he'd been nineteen and she was

just some sixteen-year-old who had done some work for him selling drugs to college students, but being truthful he'd never taken much notice of her, barely even realised when she'd upped and left for England after her mother died.

She had been a child back then, but this Maeve sitting next to him, sipping her Jameson as if she was relishing every burning mouthful, was all woman. She had changed a lot in six years.

'I still can't believe you're that small, awkward-looking girl that used to try to get my attention by wandering up and down the street,' he smirked, leaning closer to her so she could hear him over the deep bass of the music.

'Yeah, yeah, you wish,' she smiled back. 'You were just more concerned with how much money I made you.'

'That's true.' He downed the end of his drink. 'I do enjoy making money with minimal effort.'

'Oh, I'd say you're a minimal-effort kind of guy across the board,' she smiled.

He closed the remaining space between them. It had been three nights of talking, laughing, dancing and drinking, without so much as a peck on the cheek, and it was driving him crazy. But the look in her eyes as she flirted with him was more than he could take.

He grabbed the back of her neck and brought her face to his. She smiled as he drew her near and he felt something in his chest, something he had never felt before. Fear at how strong his feelings were caused him to stop, but she put her hand against his face and rubbed her thumb along his jaw-bone. This was unknown territory for him. It was almost as if he had no choice as he closed the gap between them and kissed her gently on her full, soft lips. That was their first kiss, but it definitely wasn't their last, and after three long days before getting to that point, they were both more than happy to continue back at his house.

'All or nothing,' she had said, smiling against his lips as she pushed him through his bedroom door.

'All or nothing?' He laughed. 'I like it.' And that was it.

They were together every moment they could be. He couldn't get enough of her, and she was just as eager. Everywhere they went, they ended up in some public toilet, storeroom, or quiet side street, with him buried inside her. She was his drug of choice, and he had no intention of cutting back.

A few weeks into their relationship, Maeve woke him by running her tongue along his neck. A very efficient method to get him up, in every sense of the word.

'I've been thinking,' she began as she slid a leg over him, taking him inside her with a satisfied groan.

'And?' he asked, delighted with her choice of wake-up methods.

As she began moving slowly on top of him, he really couldn't care less about what she'd been thinking. He slid his hands around her, grasping her ass, relishing its rhythmic movements.

'That maybe getting back into dealing would be a good

idea, after all.' Her breathing was getting heavier as her hips moved faster. 'With you,' she added, almost breathless.

'Really?' he gasped, both from her movements and what she had just said.

'Really,' she moaned.

He had mentioned the idea of them teaming up and Maeve trying her hand at something a bit more lucrative, but she had brushed it aside almost immediately and he hadn't brought it up again. The closer they had become, the more afraid he was that she would no longer approve of his choice of career. He'd seen plenty of people develop a conscience and readjust their morals as they got older, and perhaps Maeve was one of them.

Excited by the prospect of a joint endeavour, he pushed himself up, tightened his grasp on her ass and flipped her over, taking top position.

'I'd love that,' he said, pulling out of her.

She was about to protest but he swallowed whatever she was about to say, kissing her deeply before moving to her neck and then trailing kisses lower and lower.

'Let me show you just how much.'

A moan as she arched her back was the only response she could give.

'Oh, I don't know, I think I need to see the platinum ones again.'

Maeve, wearing a shoulder-length brown wig with a thick,

heavy fringe, pushed the plush blue tray of gold rings back towards the sales assistant, who was called Natalie, according to the shiny silver name badge pinned to her chest. This was the fifth time Maeve had requested to see something else, and Jamie could see the fixed smile on Natalie's face becoming more and more strained.

'You know what, why don't I just leave out both trays for the time being, so you can compare?'

Bingo! No jeweller wanted to leave too much out on the counter at any one time, and they sure as shit didn't ever plan on leaving you alone with anything, but Maeve was an artist when it came to manipulating people and situations like this. Jamie just came along for the ride and, keeping his back to the security camera trained on the counter, followed her lead every step of the way. He knew Maeve's next move was to get Natalie to want to be anywhere other than near them.

'Christ, I don't know. Matthew, can't you give any input?' Maeve turned to him, the perfect picture of a pissed-off girl-friend. 'Did you have this much trouble picking a ring for that slag you proposed to last year?'

Natalie cleared her throat and took a step away from the counter but didn't leave.

'Or do you only pick out the rings for the girls who drop to their knees every time you ask?'

Natalie's throat-clearing turned into a full-on coughing fit.

'I'm sorry, if you'll just excuse me a minute, I need to get a glass of water.' She turned from the counter and hurried to the back room.

Maeve smiled at Jamie as he looked at her with absolute adoration. He couldn't be prouder of her if he tried. Quickly and efficiently, they had the most expensive rings from the pads bagged in seconds.

Jamie grinned at her as they made their way out the door, hand in hand. He ensured his face remained out of the camera's sightline, while Maeve blew a kiss towards it. Turning down a side street, Maeve pulled off her wig and shoved it into her bag before shaking out her hair. Resting her head on Jamie's shoulder, she watched as he slipped the biggest diamond from their booty onto her ring finger.

'All or nothing?' he asked.

She gasped, looking up at him.

'All or nothing,' she answered.

He smiled back at her, before stopping and kissing her.

People smiled as they walked around them on the footpath, seeing a perfect happy couple, in love and newly engaged.

12

Now

It was coming up to ten at night by the time Jamie pulled up to a row of terraced red-brick houses. He shut off the engine, jolting me from my sleep, my eyes going straight to the digital clock on the dashboard. Sarah should be asleep by now, but then again, she should also be at home in her cot, safe.

It was so late and I hadn't checked in with Christopher or his parents. No doubt there were missed calls and messages waiting to fill up the screen of my phone the second I turned it on, but I couldn't look, not yet. Those simple things just seemed so difficult right now. As soon as I was away from Jamie, and had a chance to think, I'd get on to them – I would have to make up some reason for the delay. I sighed. I missed Abbie and Christopher, of course, but it was different knowing I could return to them at anytime. Not being able to get to Sarah, and not knowing when I might see her and hold her again, was killing me. The fact that someone had done this to me, had taken my baby, stirred an anger in me I hadn't known I was still capable of.

I took a deep breath to calm myself. This wasn't the time for uncontrollable rage. Every move I made needed to be the exact opposite: completely and utterly controlled.

Jamie and I sat in silence as I watched three full minutes tick by on the clock before he finally spoke.

'The key's in the glove box,' he said, still staring straight ahead into the darkened street, which was poorly lit by the street lamps lining it, most of which had been strategically smashed to keep the area in darkness.

I knew exactly where we were. It was Jamie's house – the same house he and I had always stayed in when we were working in Dublin. It was a rough area where people knew to keep themselves to themselves, which had made it a perfect base for us.

'Help yourself to anything inside you might need.'

I retrieved the key from the glove box. 'Thank you,' I said, not looking at him.

'I missed you.'

I started at the sudden confession and turned towards him, to find him staring at me.

'I'm sorry.'

'No. Don't be sorry. It was the right thing for you to do.' He reached out and took my hand.

I didn't pull away. I couldn't.

'And that made it all okay,' he continued, smiling at me.

Despite everything, I smiled back. 'I'm still sorry, though.'

He squeezed my hand before letting it go. 'Now, go get your daughter – and make sure you watch your back.'

'I will, don't worry.' Before I could change my mind, I leaned over and, holding one side of his face, I kissed his cheek. 'Goodbye,' I whispered, before pulling back and quickly jumping out of the car, closing the door behind me.

It was almost five years too late, but I'd done it. I'd finally said goodbye to my ex-fiancé.

Jamie had driven off before I'd made my way to the front door. He'd answered a call as I was getting out of the car; he was needed back in Cork. A part of me had wanted him to stay, and while I suspected that if I asked him, he would have, we both knew he couldn't be involved in this. We were on different sides of this particular game.

I hated this place. Not just this street, but this entire city. I hated that I had to come here to find Sarah. I hated that my daughter was so close to this shithole. There was a part of me – the irrational side of me that belonged to the old Maeve whose gun choice was crucial – that thought this city was cursed. I had a lot of enemies in Dublin, more than in the rest of the country combined. Everything that had ever gone wrong in my criminal career had gone wrong in this city. The time I was shot; the time I had my eye socket broken so badly that there was a serious concern that my eyeball might sink back into my head; the time I dislocated and relocated my shoulder, all within sixty seconds. All that was here, in 'the big smoke'.

I let myself into the small house for the first time in years. I couldn't even remember the last time I'd been here. The terraced house was one of a line of three small single-storey houses at the end of a row of larger two-storey houses. It was even smaller than the Stone Lodge. When I walked in, I was immediately in the kitchen-cum-living room. Directly off the living room was an average-sized bedroom. I locked the door behind me and slid the deadbolt into place. No one should know about this house, and more importantly, no one should know I was here, only Jamie. I hoped I was doing the right thing in trusting him, but it was such a relief to have some place I could hide and plan my next step.

I made my way to the bedroom, which contained nothing more than a small double bed, dressed neatly in dark blue bedclothes, and a bedside locker on the side of the bed closest to the door. Glancing around the room, I moved to the other side of the bed, where you'd expect to find another bedside table, and squatted down to examine the dark brown carpet. Carefully, I peeled it back from the skirting board to reveal a blank concrete floor. There was no room for a wardrobe in this room, so Jamie had dug down into the floor to create storage space for some of his more important items. I pushed down on the grey flooring, which gave way under the pressure, allowing me to grab hold of what was actually a panel of thick grey foam, and pulled it away from the floor.

The black safe we'd installed there so many years ago looked up at me. It only occurred to me then that Jamie might have changed the combination lock at some point over the last few years. I turned the dial right, then left, then right again, inputting the numbers we'd agreed on so long ago. Nine-three-nine – the ninth of March 2009, our third date. The lock clicked. I smiled; he hadn't changed it.

There was no selection of outfits hidden here, only necessities. Cash, handguns and ammunition. I pulled a thick wad of cash from the safe and tucked it into my jacket's inside pocket. I stopped when my finger brushed against my mobile. I'd turned it off when I got on the plane and hadn't turned it back on. I'd tried to; I'd pulled it from my pocket as the plane was taxiing to a halt and everyone else rushed to get their lives back online, but I couldn't do it. I couldn't turn it on and see Abbie's and Sarah's faces smiling back at me from the screen saver, or read my messages from Christopher asking me about the flight and how I'd managed with Sarah. I couldn't have feet in both worlds right now. I needed to be a woman so very different to the one whose life was contained and displayed within that phone. But pulling it out of my pocket now, I had an overwhelming urge to remind myself of who I really was. Abbie and Sarah's faces lit up as the phone came to life and I smiled back as tears filled my eyes. I sat down, my back against the bed, the safe momentarily forgotten, and stared at the precious faces as notifications from Christopher popped up.

How was your flight? Ryan Air as glamorous as always?

You all settled there? Sarah behaving? How's Marnie?

Just letting you know I've cut my trip short and I'm waiting for a flight home now. I'll have Abbie home and all before bedtime so don't be worrying about her going into a diabetic coma or anything from all the chocolate.

I know you're probably catching up now. Just give a text when you can so I know you made it over safely. Me and Abbie are home watching Toy Story AGAIN. Don't worry, I'll put her to bed soon.

The last message had been sent two hours ago. I was so incredibly relieved that he was home and with Abbie. I quickly typed out a reply, guilt crippling me for not making contact sooner. Of course he'd worry. Usually, when I went anywhere, I messaged asking about the girls every fifteen to twenty minutes.

—So sorry, phone died and just had a chance to charge it. Hope you weren't worried. How come you cut the trip short? Not that I'm complaining. It'll save us having to detox Abbie. Lol! Marnie's in good spirits, but she definitely looks a lot older than the last time I saw her. I guess that's just the joy of time. Sarah's being a sweetheart. Hope you two are asleep now. Love you both, talk tomorrow. Xx

111

I let out a breath as the message sent. What a mess. I hated lying to Christopher. I had already told him so many lies about my past, and to assuage my guilt I had promised myself that I would never lie to him about anything else, ever. Yet here I was, lying again.

Not to mention the pang of guilt I felt every time I mentioned Marnie. I pictured myself sitting on her grey crushed-velvet couch that she had spent a fortune on when I was about nine. It was easily the most expensive thing in her house and it stood out dramatically, but she would never get rid of it. I remembered sitting there sipping tea – with too much milk added, no matter how quickly I shouted 'when'. Then I let myself remember our last conversation, years earlier. What was a little more pain on top of what I already felt?

Marnie had been leaving work through the side entrance of Debenhams, off St Patrick's Street, when Jamie and I were discussing some business with a dealer who we had happened across, after some difficulties trying to pin him down.

'Maeve? Maeve Deane!' Marnie had called, rushing towards me.

'Marnie!' I'd tried to put as much distance between Jamie and me before she got to me, but it hadn't been enough.

She knew Jamie, she knew who he worked for, and she knew what me being with him meant.

'Oh,' she'd said, stopping just short of me, outstretched hands dropping to her sides.

'Marnie, you don't need to worry,' I'd said, grabbing her

upper arm and turning her so that she was facing away from Jamie and the conversation with the dealer, which was becoming more and more heated.

'Maeve,' she'd dropped her voice, but she was clearly furious, 'what are you doing with him?'

'It's okay.' I had laughed, desperate to put her at ease, to smooth out the creases that were lining her face with horror. 'Honestly, it's not what you think. You don't need to worry about me.'

'Your mother would roll over in her grave if she saw you hanging around with the likes of him, Maeve. What have you got yourself involved in?'

That's when I had known. Known that Marnie would keep going. Keep pushing me to get away from Jamie. Keep involving herself with people she shouldn't, trying to protect me.

I had had no choice.

I'd folded my arms across my chest and laughed again, but there was no humour in it. 'Still the pathetic woman you always were, Marnie, I see.'

She had taken a step back from me, as if I'd hit her.

'I mean, that's why your husband left, ran off with that young one. And why your own son moved to the other side of the world just to get away from you.'

Marnie's wide eyes had looked into mine as if she didn't know who I was. My chest had ached as I saw tears fill her eyes, but I kept going.

'I mean, let's be honest, the one good thing to come from my mother's death was that she doesn't have to listen to all your pathetic bitching and moaning anymore.' I'd smirked, my arms still crossed, fingers leaving purple marks on my skin – marks I would see later in the shower as I cried beneath scalding water.

That was the last time I'd spoken to Marnie. I promised myself that I'd never form another friendship and run the risk of having to treat someone like that again.

I put my phone back in my pocket now, and felt the handle of my switchblade. I pulled it out and set it on the ground next to me so I would remember to wash Davey's blood off it before I left. Returning my attention to the open safe, I pulled my gun from my jacket and placed it inside, before removing a different one. In the unlikely event that there were legal repercussions from the bullet I had sent through the arm of Davey's son, I didn't want to have that gun anywhere near me. Be prepared for anything – advice that was as important for criminals as it was for mothers – even though the likelihood of Davey going to the Gardaí was about the same as the moon falling from the sky and crushing me as I walked out the door.

I took the new gun apart, to check everything was correct, before reassembling it and loading it to full capacity with the bullets sitting at the bottom of the safe. There were even a few of my fake driver's licences scattered along the bottom. Jamie hadn't thrown them out. Did he know I would be back and need them sometime? I scooped out Maeve Molroy and tucked her into my wallet. No doubt I'd be needing her, since my previous alias, Mae Murphy, had rented and subsequently abandoned a BMW back in a Cork City car park. I dropped her into the safe. There was nothing dodgier than carrying around multiple IDs.

The time was ticking on towards eleven. Late in the world of a mother, but just beginning in the world of a woman about to wreak havoc in a Dublin nightclub. I went to the small bathroom to freshen up and, after a rummage around in the drawers, found an old eyeliner and mascara. Probably not recommended, and completely unhygienic, but needs must. I layered them both heavily on my eyes, replenishing the make-up I'd applied earlier. It hadn't fared too well after a gunfight and an impromptu journey to Dublin. Dark, overly made-up eyes had been a trademark look of mine, back in the day, and once again I was heading into the lion's den where I needed to be as recognisable as I could be, despite motherhood having aged my face.

'Time to hit the club,' I said to the handgun, before tucking it into my waistband and heading for the door.

13

I made my way into the city centre, stopping in a small super-market to buy a pack of cigarettes. I hadn't smoked since the day I met Christopher. Christopher didn't even know I'd once been a smoker. Maeve King would never smoke, it's a dis-gusting, unhealthy and expensive habit. But here in Dublin I was Maeve Deane, and the combination of stress and the desire to revive my former persona to intimidate people had me slipping into my old ways with unnerving ease.

'A box of matches, too, please,' I requested of the young shop assistant as I eyed the collection box for St Anthony; the patron saint for finding lost things. I rolled my eyes, wondering how much I'd have to offer to entice him to help me now. Nonetheless, I took my change and slotted two euros into the small wooden box with the smug-looking saint painted on the front – just in case.

I started unwrapping the pack as I walked towards the door, placing a cigarette between my teeth and pulling out a match, ready to strike the second I stepped out of the shop.

As I took the first drag of a near-perfect concoction of chemicals and sweet, sweet nicotine, a group of teenage boys rose from their stake-out spot on the windowsill along the shopfront and blocked the footpath in front of me.

'Here, give us a smoke, will ya?' one of the boys, who couldn't have been more than thirteen, called to me, his white hood hanging low over his eyes, forcing him to tilt his head back to make eye contact. They began closing ranks, in an attempt to intimidate me enough to hand over my cigarettes and avoid any hassle. I smiled as I took another deep drag of cigarette smoke, which slid down my windpipe with surprising ease, and pushed my way through them.

'Nice try, boys, but I've no intention of sharing. Find someone else to scare with ye're cool hoodies.'

The surprise alone was enough to get me past them, and I smiled as I continued on my way down the street, leaving them gaping behind me, no doubt waiting for the opportunity to intimidate some other poor smoker.

If only they were the worst type of thugs I'd have to deal with tonight.

The city was busy. It was always busy. Walking down a side street off O'Connell Street, I couldn't help but notice that so many storefronts had converted to e-cigarette shops. Bookshops, boutiques, cafes, it seemed like no business was safe from the spreading chain of vape shops.

Turning the corner at the end of the street, I stopped.

Some things hadn't changed at all while I'd been away – things that really should have.

I turned back the way I'd come and retraced my steps until I reached the Tesco Express I had passed moments before. Passing through the sliding doors, I pulled out my phone and checked the time again. I could afford these few minutes.

Making my way back down the street, I felt the handles of the plastic bags in my hands already stretching under the strain of the weight in them. With two full bags in each hand, I could only hope that they'd hold out until I made my way around the corner.

They did, but barely. Reaching the doorway of a closed clothing store, I placed the bags on the ground beside a small blue tent with a tear along a seam that ran almost its entire height. Stopping for a moment I stared at the faded chalk squares of a hopscotch game on the dirty dark footpath. Another child playing a game in a place she shouldn't even be, I thought, before turning back to the tent.

A small head with light blonde hair, pulled back in a neat, low ponytail, peeked out at me from the tear in the tent. The same girl I had seen on my first attempt to walk down this street. She'd been standing outside the tent then. I'd guessed she wasn't more than five, maybe six, but up close I wondered if she wasn't a couple of years older. It was her eyes, her pale grey eyes that looked at me with suspicions and fears a child her age should never have.

'Hi there,' I smiled, crouching down. 'Nothing to worry

about, just dropping off some food for you and . . .' I tried to see through the tear into the tent, but her head retreated.

Sighing, I stood up and continued on down the street, until the sound of a zip made me turn back around. The little girl stepped out and made straight for the plastic bags, rummaging through them without a second look at me. I walked back towards her but didn't speak again, afraid of scaring her off. I wanted her to eat so that she could sleep with a full stomach.

I tried to stop myself from looking inside the tent. I was afraid of who I might see, or perhaps not see. There was nothing more I could do to help, so I should just leave. Looking down the street, there were tents or sleeping bags or flattened cardboard boxes filling almost every available shop doorway as far as I could see. Shaking my head, I crouched back down; I needed to know if this young girl was going to be okay. I needed to know because I didn't know if *my* child was okay.

Inside the tent was a woman sleeping on her side, curled up into the foetal position. There were no blankets, pillows or bedding of any kind. They may be inside a tent, but they were as good as sleeping on the hard ground. Her eyes opened, and she looked directly at me. I almost fell backwards as she sat bolt upright, calling for the little girl.

'Katie? Katie?'

'It's okay,' I explained quickly. 'She's right here, I just brought you some food. She's right here.'

I beckoned the girl back to the opening of the tent. She dived inside, landing on the woman, arms laden down with a variety of buns and bread rolls.

'We have food, Mammy,' she said, in between bites.

'Thank you,' the woman said to me, arms now around her child as she evaluated me. She was suspicious.

Looking from her to the girl, I thought about all the dangers waiting for them each night when the streets darkened. I wanted to rip their tent even more, to stand up and scream at the occupants of every doorway to get up, that this wasn't fair, none of it was fair, that they needed to do something, go somewhere. But there was nothing to do, and nowhere to go.

'Have you been living like this long?' I asked, nodding to the tent.

'Three months,' the woman answered, her arm tightening around her daughter.

I said nothing else, just stayed crouched there, looking at the woman and her daughter.

'Are you from one of the churches?' the woman asked.

My silence made her nervous. I could see her trying to wriggle herself and her child further back in the tent, already pushed against the shop door.

'I'm sorry,' I said, shaking my head, 'I was trying to think of something.'

She looked at me, eyebrows knitted together.

'Oh no, I'm not from any church,' I answered. 'One second,' I said, standing and returning to the plastic bags

120

I'd brought. From one, I pulled out a colouring book and some markers I'd picked up. I lowered myself onto my knees, breathing through my mouth so as not to be overwhelmed by the smell of urine. I ripped a blue marker from the packaging and folded open the colouring book to write on the cover.

A rustling noise came from the tent. The little blonde head peeking out to see what I was up to, no doubt being held by her mother to stop her coming out. I smiled at her before returning to the colouring book and writing out everything I needed to.

Back at the tent opening, I reached inside and handed the woman the colouring book. She took it slowly, cautiously. After reading what I'd written, she looked up at me, shaking her head.

'Do you have any addictions?' I asked.

'No,' she answered.

'And you can work,' I probed further, 'while she's in school?' I looked at her daughter.

'Yes, but without an address or clothes or . . .' She trailed off, shaking her head.

I could tell she'd been through all this, time and time again. She was like any mother, desperate to do right by her child, to protect her, and yet she'd still ended up here.

'Well, that is an address,' I pointed to the colouring book cover. 'I want you to go there. Now. Don't wait until morning, don't keep your child out here another night. You will tell them you need to speak to Alan. He's in Cork at the moment, but insist they get him on the phone. Tell him he's to set you up in one of his rental apartments and to give you a job cleaning his holiday homes along the coast. A flexible job that will allow you to take care of your daughter but that also pays well above minimum wage.'

Her eyes were wide as she listened to me, and I wasn't sure she was taking everything in.

'Don't worry, it's all written there, anyway. Read that out to him. Word for word.' I reached into my jacket pocket and pulled out the thick wad of fifties I had taken from the safe in Jamie's house. Pulling one out for myself, I tossed the rest to the woman, now looking to her daughter, who simply shrugged as she shoved an entire chocolate mini-muffin into her mouth.

'I don't understand,' the woman gasped, looking at the money.

'That's fine,' I said, standing up and dusting the grime from my knees. 'You don't need to. Mind yourselves.'

I started back down the street, knowing they'd be okay, because under that address and list of instructions I had included a note written with the blue marker:

Time to pay your debt, Alan. Bet you didn't think you'd get off this easy.
Maeve Deane.

I made my way to Market Street, home to The Pirate Rooms. Of all the bars and nightclubs littering the city, The Pirate

Rooms hadn't changed its name since opening; it had never come under new ownership. It had never closed down, not even in the darkest moments of the recession, but then again, why would it? That was when criminal activity skyrocketed. I'd never been so busy or so flush with cash. My substantial savings accounts consisted mostly of money earned during that time. Perhaps I should feel guilty for having that money, but I didn't. I felt enough guilt and shame for the past, but the money was mine, regardless of how I came by it. I'd earned it doing my job, which made it mine to do with as I pleased. Besides, spending it on my family and my girls negated the lifestyle attached to it, as far as I was concerned.

By the time I reached the nightclub I'd burned my way through two more cigarettes. Chain-smoking; another aspect of my former self that had returned faster and with more ease than I would have expected.

Unlike the changing storefronts along the streets, walking through the double doors of the nightclub felt as if I was taking yet another step back in time. Nothing had changed. From the dim hallway to the shabby carpet, it was as it had always been, just maybe more frayed and worn around the edges. No bouncers watched the doors, checking IDs. This wasn't the kind of nightclub that anyone came to unless they were supposed to. And if that particular brand of clientele happened to be under the legal drinking age, there wasn't a Garda in the city who would even consider policing the place.

There may not be any bouncers, but there was always

someone watching. There were security cameras in every corner, covering every possible angle, which was proof of that. And despite the apparent ease of entering the establishment, there was a cover charge – and a hefty one at that. Money loves money.

At the end of the long dark corridor sat a woman in her late fifties, with dark brown hair and a thick blunt fringe hanging too long over her eyes. She was perched on a small, uncomfortable-looking stool behind a desk that had nothing on it except an old silver money box. Yes, nothing here had changed.

'How much have ye hiked the price up in this dive, then?'

The woman looked up, narrowing her eyes despite her already limited view.

'Been a long time since you've darkened these hallways.' Her voice sounded the same, like she needed to clear her throat of the phlegm sitting permanently at the back of it thanks to years of heavy cigarette consumption.

'I missed you, too, Bernice,' I said, crossing my arms.

'Mmm. You might as well go straight in. You never paid before, don't know why you'd start now.'

'Fair point,' I agreed, heading for the black door leading into the club.

'Be careful, Maeve,' Bernice warned, as I placed a hand on the door ready to push it open.

'Always am, Bernice,' I answered, without turning. 'Always am.'

The music was loud and, despite the quiet hallway I'd entered through, the place was full of people dancing, drinking, and talking, or at least attempting to, over the deep rumble of the bass. Some things had changed since my day, I thought, manoeuvring through the people swaying on the dance floor, moving through thick clouds of smoke blown out intermittently from a smoke machine near the DJ box.

By the time I made it to the bar, I was desperate for a drink. But unlike my past visits, I didn't know the bartender racing up and down the bar taking orders, and he didn't know me, so I had to wait to order my drink.

'Jameson. Neat!' I shouted over the music, when he finally got to me.

As the greasy-haired hipster placed the drink on the counter and swiftly pulled the twenty from my hand at the same time, I had to resist the urge to catch up the glass and throw it at his face with the large thick-framed glasses, which I was certain contained clear glass. Neat. I had said neat, and there sitting in my glass were four small ice cubes bobbing around with the sole purpose of destroying a perfectly good drink. Fortunately for him, time was a constant pressure weighing on me, so I simply scooped the ice cubes out and threw them on the ground behind the bar, before walking away without my change and with a partially saved drink.

I made my way back across the dance floor and up the steps to a raised area with tables and some seating. I settled on a spot with a good view of the entire dance floor and the bar. This vantage point wasn't to enable me to see anyone, but so I would be seen. No doubt they already knew I was here, and it was only a matter of time before someone came for me, but I wanted it to be a speedy process.

As far as anyone around me knew, I was a thirtysomething-year-old out for a casual drink, waiting for a friend or a special someone, or perhaps preparing to do a deal with someone, taking in the atmosphere and enjoying a drink. Enjoying a drink slowly, very slowly. Before today, the last time I had enjoyed a drink, other than a small glass of wine, was before Abbie was conceived. The last thing I needed right now was to diminish my senses, but something to steady my nerves was a necessity. Taking another small sip, I savoured the burning sensation as it slid down my throat and into my near-empty stomach. Despite how relaxed I might appear on the outside, I was struggling to remain calm. The time without my baby girl was causing my insides to ache more and more with every passing hour, but I knew what I needed to do. I needed to use that pain, that ache, and turn it into something more useful for this situation, something more fitting.

Very little had stuck with me from my schooldays, but one science lesson finally made sense to me after all these years; energy cannot be created or destroyed, but it can be converted from one form to another. That's what I would do, transform the pain inside me into something more effective, something I could use to get my daughter back safe and sound, so we could return home to Christopher and Abbie.

I took a deep breath to push down the feeling of desperation clawing its way up from my guts.

Less than ten minutes of staring into the space around people, before a man in his thirties, dressed in a black jumper and black slacks, approached and stood next to me, staring straight ahead in the same direction as me. He didn't speak a word, only stood there with his arms crossed and waited. I downed the rest of my drink, and set it on the table beside me, before following him silently.

As we weaved through the crowd, adrenaline surged through my body. A part of me hoped that Sarah was here, that she was waiting for me in the back room where we were headed. It wasn't the most rational part of me – I knew it wouldn't be that easy – but it didn't stop me from hoping.

The whiskey did little to dampen the panic inside me. I wanted my daughter back. I needed her back. Now.

I should be checking on her and her sister, safe in their beds, making sure they were breathing peacefully, and replacing the blankets they had kicked off, before making my way downstairs to join Christopher and return to the latest crime documentary we were binge-watching. This vile nightclub, filled with the scum of the earth who were up to no good, was not where I should be.

How dare they take my child? How dare they put their hands on her? The anger that flowed through me was yet another thing from my old life that came back easily. I was slipping back into so many of my old ways, it surprised me, scared me even. Over the last few years, since marrying Christopher and giving birth to my children, I'd become more and more certain that Maeve King, wife and mother, was the real Maeve, the real me. But the last twelve hours had made me wonder if that was something I'd convinced myself of, just so I could sleep better at night. Maybe I deserved all this. Maybe this was my payment, my penance for the life I had led before. Karma coming to reap what I'd sown.

No, fuck karma. Karma wouldn't take this out on my daughter. Karma could burn in hell, like all the bastards who were standing between me and my child.

'Well, if it isn't *the* Maeve Deane,' said a tall woman with grey strands running through her dark brown hair.

My heart sank. It wasn't Rita, and a quick scan of the back room, including the office located in the corner and visible through the glass panelling on the door, told me she wasn't here.

'The one and only,' I answered, refusing to allow the frustration I felt show in my voice. I was now flanked on either side by two men, both dressed in black clothing.

'You remember me, do ya?'

I remembered her: Lucy Murphy, Rita's cousin. She was reaching the end of her forties and, I was willing to bet, as clueless as ever. If you didn't know better, you'd think she'd worked her way up the ranks, overseeing the running of not just this club, but all the side businesses that were channelled through it. You would assume that she must be a competent, intelligent woman. But no, she'd been pushed up the ranks because of who she was related to, and because she was so absolutely useless it was easier to move her up and let her manage the paperwork than have her actually do anything. That, on top of the fact that she had a tendency to open her legs at the right time for the right men, had landed her where she was today.

Running my eyes over the lank strands of hair devoid of pigment and the wrinkles starting to settle deeper in her face, I wondered if that particular personality trait was still as effective as it had once been. Where would she have ended up if she'd been as unattractive as she was stupid?

'You clean the toilets here, don't you?'

'You'd better watch yourself, you little bitch, you're not part of any crew now.' Lucy took a step towards me.

I matched her immediately, causing the men in black to step forward and grab me by both arms.

'Don't worry, boys, no danger here,' Lucy said, smirking, a couple of inches from my face.

Her 'boys' released me and stepped back again.

I smiled. 'I wouldn't be so sure about that.'

Before the needless back and forth could waste any more time, I lunged for Lucy and in one swift, easy movement was behind her with my arm across her chest and a gun pushed against her temple. Her two lackeys had barely moved, staring at us with their mouths hanging open. Lucy was shaking with temper. Both at me, for getting her into this position, and at her ineffective bodyguards, for letting it happen.

'You let me go this second, Maeve Deane, or I swear to God . . .'

'What?' I asked, pressing the gun harder against her temple. 'What is it you'd like to swear to God?'

'I'll make sure you never see your little brat again.'

It was the wrong thing to say. The second the words left her mouth, I pulled the gun from her temple and shot each of her bodyguards in the shin, for no other reason than I didn't want them to interfere in what I was about to do next.

'No, no, please,' Lucy begged, realising her mistake as I released her and pushed her from me, returning the gun to the back of my waistband beneath my jacket.

Lucy stumbled to the ground, looking up at me as she scooted backwards. 'Don't. Please don't. I'm sorry, I'm sorry. Don't.'

I could barely hear her pleas over the screams of her bodyguards.

She had been part of the same circles as I had moved in, back in the day, so she knew nothing good was about to happen.

I reached down and caught the scrambling woman by her tacky blouse and pulled her towards me as I bent closer.

'Where is she?' I whispered, menace dripping off my tongue.

'I can't, I—'

My fist struck her cheekbone before she could finish.

'Where is she?'

'Please—'

I struck her again. This time the skin broke, her face already starting to swell and bruise.

'Where is she?'

Lucy was crying now, looking around for someone to swoop in and rescue her, but her bodyguards had shuffled themselves over to the far wall, more concerned with stopping the blood seeping from their wounds, so they weren't coming to her aid anytime soon.

I raised my fist again.

'Donegal!' Lucy screamed. 'Donegal.' She repeated it, over and over again, her eyes squeezed shut.

'Where in Donegal?' I asked, shaking her blood from my fist.

'Her house, the bungalow on the coast. The one in the middle of nowhere,' she elaborated through her sobs.

I knew where she was talking about. I'd been there once before.

'You can let her know I'm coming,' I said, as I turned and made for the door. Although, I would put money on her keeping her mouth shut, holding out hope that something debilitating would happen to me before I reached Rita's doorstep.

'Fucking bitch,' Lucy muttered as I placed a hand on the door to push it open.

Turning, I pulled out my gun and gave Lucy a bullet hole to match her 'boys'. I was on the other side of the soundproof door before I could fully appreciate her screams.

Making my way back through the crowded nightclub, I called for another Jameson at the bar and threw it down before making my way out into the night air, whiskey adding fuel to the fire burning in my belly.

14

I was halfway back to the terraced house when I realised I was being followed. No one had come after me from the nightclub, I'd made sure of that, but after putting a few streets between me and that dive I'd become distracted making plans for my journey to Donegal. I should have noticed sooner that someone was trailing behind me. I took the next right turn, the opposite direction to the house. The footsteps behind me continued. I checked my watch: 11:45. It wasn't very late, but the streets were uncharacteristically quiet. That was a good thing. I took another right turn, down an even quieter street with fewer houses and fewer people.

The more secluded the area, the closer and braver the footsteps became. Who could it be? Had Lucy sent someone after me? Had someone else seen me leaving the club? Someone looking to settle an old score? Had Davey contacted his people up here?

Turning down a narrow cul-de-sac, which ran behind a line of derelict houses, I was about to find out.

'A little lost, sweetheart?' a voice called from behind me.

Holding my breath and ready to pull my gun, I turned around. I didn't recognise the man standing there. He was late twenties, maybe early thirties, and dressed in a shirt and jeans. If he hadn't followed me this entire way, I'd have assumed he was a random partygoer heading home after a night out. As far as I could tell, he looked entirely ordinary and not at all threatening. He continued to walk towards me. I took a step back, unsure who and what I was dealing with here.

'Pretty thing like you shouldn't be walking home alone at this hour.' He was Irish, possibly a Dub, but his accent wasn't particularly strong. He spoke with a tone that was very nearly sincere, but his body language as he came towards me indicated he was far from concerned about my welfare.

'Who sent you?' I asked, trying my hardest to stop backing up, but there was something about him that made my skin crawl.

He paused for a moment, eyes narrowing, before a slow smile spread across his face.

'Had a little too much to drink, did we?' He made a point of looking around at our very private surroundings. 'Lost your way? It never fails to amaze me how stupid women can be, especially after alcohol.' He was laughing now, a soft chuckle.

I straightened, making myself taller. This guy really didn't seem to know who I was, and by the way he was talking . . .

'Wait a second.' I held up my hand, palm facing him. 'Are you some sick rapist?'

He stopped, confusion clouding his face thanks to my sudden confidence and the question I'd posed.

'What?' he snapped.

'Are. You. A. Rapist?'

He didn't move. His eyes narrowed, as if he was working out some complicated maths problem. He looked behind him and down the empty street before turning back to me, smiling again.

'I see what you're doing. Trying to throw me off. Is that something you picked up in one of those self-defence classes?' His smile widened, but it looked more like he was baring his teeth. 'Maybe you should have started with lesson one: don't walk home alone.'

He moved quickly, pinning me to the high wall running along the street.

I laughed. I almost felt sorry for him. Almost.

'You stupid man,' I said, looking up at him, barely able to contain my laughter long enough to talk, but the moment he leaned back to look down at my face and made eye contact, all trace of humour left my voice. 'I'm going to make sure I'm the last woman you ever try this on.'

'You that good, are ya? I won't want anyone else after you? Let's see, then,' he sneered, reaching one hand down and flicking open the button on my jeans with practised skill.

How many girls had he stalked and trapped like this

before? He didn't have me pinned securely enough to stop me reaching for the gun in my waistband. I twitched to move for the gun, but changed my mind. A bullet would be wasted on this piece of shit, but I needed more space to get to the knife that was stored in the inside pocket of my jacket – the one I'd cleaned another man's blood from, only an hour earlier.

Pushing forward, I pressed my body against his. 'Oh, I can guarantee you won't want to go near another woman after this.'

He moved back, seeming put off by the prospect of a willing participant. I used the extra space, pushing myself back against the wall, reaching inside my jacket and flicking the switchblade open as I pulled it out.

He jumped back as if I'd burned him. 'What the fuck is wrong with you? What are you doing with that?'

It was a funny thing to ask, since men like him were the exact reason a woman would ever need a weapon like this in her pocket. He wasn't the reason I needed a knife, but I would make damn sure I used mine to the benefit of all womankind.

'You could really hurt someone with that, you stupid woman.'

I stared at him for a moment. He meant what he was saying. I couldn't even laugh at that, the fact that he thought *I* was the dangerous one when he was the one roaming the streets, stalking his prey, with the intention of doing what he pleased to whoever he happened upon.

'You really shouldn't insult someone holding a knife,' I warned him. 'It's just not good sense.'

The smile returned to his face. 'Put it down. Now,' he commanded. 'I don't want to hurt you. I don't like the mess.'

I laughed. 'That's enough,' I said, walking towards him.

Now, it was his turn to back up, but I could tell he was simply waiting for his opening, an opportunity to pounce and get the knife away from me so he could get back to doing what he'd followed me here to do. You had to marvel at the arrogance; knife or not, he wasn't really afraid of me, and had no intention of walking away. I'd make sure he regretted that decision.

I closed the blade of the knife and returned it to my pocket.

'Good girl,' he said, smiling.

Before he could advance on me again, I ran towards him and swung my right fist into his jaw, allowing the momentum to turn me around so my back was facing him, and propelled my elbow deep into his guts. I twisted as he doubled over, and drove my knee into his face, holding the back of his head to ensure the maximum number of bones in his face shattered.

He fell to the ground in a heap. As he turned to look up at me, blinking, I swung a booted leg into the air and brought it down, heel first, onto his already broken face, before reaching inside my jacket for my knife once again.

'You won't be catching any more women off guard,' I told his unconscious body.

I finally turned down the street, towards the small, terraced house. I needed to get some sleep to make sure I'd have enough energy for the journey to Donegal in the morning. Pausing at the small patch of greenery across from the house, I wiped both sides of the knife, still tight in my grip, against the half-dead grass before retracting the blade and returning it to my pocket.

15

Then

Jamie opened his eyes and smiled. Last night had been unexpected. Initially, he'd been terrified at the prospect of introducing Maeve to Martin and Rita, but they had left him with little choice. Maeve was pushing to get further involved in the crew, and that would never happen without approval from the boss man – and from the woman who was always by his side. Although they were both in their early fifties, they'd only been married about fifteen years. And while their relationship was both personal and professional, Jamie felt that the marriage had more to do with their business interests, rather than any feelings of romance.

He didn't know why he was so worried. It was a straightforward introduction, especially since they technically already knew each other. Maeve's mother had worked in Martin's hotel, where Rita had been the manager, but the last time

Maeve had seen either of them was when they came to pay their respects at her mother's funeral.

Jamie was still nervous. This meeting meant Maeve would become inextricably involved in the crew, and while the idea of that excited him, he found himself wondering if that was really what he wanted for Maeve; this unpredictable, and sometimes scary life. It's all he'd ever known, it's what he lived for, and after getting to know Maeve as intimately as he had, he knew it was what she lived for, too. Nothing got her hotter than a near miss, and the smile on her face when she got the upper hand in a dire situation was the closest thing he'd ever seen to true happiness. She needed this lifestyle, and he needed her, so why fight it? Why keep her from it? From him?

Martin was an unfortunate, but inevitable, consequence of this life. He was the boss, and absolutely everything was his decision. If he wouldn't allow Maeve in, it would mean the end of their relationship, Jamie knew that. She wouldn't stick around if she had to step back from him and stay on the outside of the world he lived in. She wanted in; she wanted to be someone, make her mark, and Jamie was equal parts hopeful and terrified that she would succeed.

'Time to go,' Maeve said, throwing his jeans at him as she gathered up her own clothes from the bedroom floor. They'd been dressed, ready to leave and grab a bite to eat before the meeting with Martin that evening, but a kiss had turned into a whole lot more and now they were rushing to make the meeting on empty stomachs, albeit much more relaxed.

Maeve was buzzing. It was the only way to describe it. She was on a high, and as much as he'd like to take credit for it after the moves he'd just pulled in bed, he knew it was the thrill of meeting the biggest and most dangerous criminal boss in the country that was spiking her endorphins.

'All right, all right, don't get your knickers in a twist. We'll be there in plenty of time.'

Jamie pulled on his jeans, grabbed a still-topless Maeve around the waist, and kissed her. He couldn't get enough of this woman – and judging from the hands roaming down his unbuttoned jeans, she felt the same about him.

'No, no, no!' She pushed him back. 'We need to go. Now!' She threw his shirt at him before reaching under the bed for her bra and top.

Walking through the entrance of The Harmada Hotel, Jamie felt Maeve stiffen at his side. It was her first time back here since her mother's death. It hadn't changed much. Martin had pumped a ridiculous amount of money into it back when Maeve's mother still worked there, so it was at least another decade away from a complete revamp. Jamie watched as Maeve took it all in, her eyes roaming around the foyer, before stopping at the reception desk where a woman in her thirties was wearing the same uniform her mother had once worn. Jamie squeezed her hand. She looked at him and smiled, the saddest smile Jamie had ever seen on her beautiful face, and something inside him cracked. He wanted to scoop her up into his arms and take her away from here, away from the ghosts hovering around, ready to swallow her whole. But just as quickly, that haunted, sad look vanished and she grinned at him. The face of a woman who wouldn't be fazed by anyone – living or dead.

The meeting went better than Jamie could have hoped. Normally, these meetings were more of an intense interview; few people ever returned, whether of their own choice or Martin's. Rita was abroad on business, which Jamie was relieved about. One obstacle at a time was about all he could handle. From the moment Rita had taken him in, she had been overprotective of Jamie, especially when it came to the women who kept him company.

'Maeve, good to see you again. Glad this time it's under better circumstances,' Martin said, coming around his desk to shake her hand.

Jamie thought that must be a good sign because he had never seen Martin come forward to greet anyone. Usually, everyone came to him.

Maeve gave him a tight smile. Jamie knew the last thing she'd want to talk about at this meeting was her dead mother.

'Take a seat.' Martin gestured to the seats in front of his desk before patting Jamie's upper arm, picking up two generous measures of whiskey in heavy crystal tumblers, and handing them to Maeve and Jamie.

Martin and Maeve hit it off immediately. Maeve was incredible, as usual.

'Nice,' she said, after taking a drink and holding it up to see its colour in the light. 'I don't care what anyone says, I'd choose an Irish whiskey over a Scottish dram any day of the week.'

'Ah, a woman who knows her whiskey,' Martin said, taking his seat behind his desk. 'I like that.'

Her ability to adapt and converse with anyone, to find common ground and relate to someone, was astounding. She was formidable to watch. Jamie smiled as she won Martin over, turning on her charm. She didn't do that with him; she wasn't someone else or someone different. She was herself. Wasn't she? Something tightened in his chest at that thought. He took a deep drink of the whiskey. *No, he thought, don't be stupid.* Not even Maeve could fake the way she was with him.

After twenty minutes of chatting, mostly about the difference in the ageing process between Irish and Scottish whiskeys, Martin stood up, with Maeve and Jamie quickly following suit. He held out his hand, this time waiting for Jamie and Maeve to come to him.

'Good choice,' he said, with a wink, shaking Jamie's hand first.

Jamie stood back, to allow Maeve to the front of Martin's desk.

Instead of a handshake, Martin took Maeve's hand in both of his. 'Welcome to the family.'

And just like that, Maeve was a member of the crew.

Despite his initial apprehension about it all, now that it was done, Jamie was excited.

Let the fun begin.

Maeve's meeting with Rita took place a few weeks later. Jamie was away on a job and was eager to hear how things had gone when he returned home to the townhouse he and Maeve now shared, but the moment he walked through the door Maeve launched herself at him. Wearing nothing but a towel, she wrapped her legs around his waist, her mouth immediately moving to his. He could taste whiskey and cigarettes on her tongue. All thoughts of Rita evaporated from his mind at the feel of Maeve in his arms. There was no time to even speak as she lowered herself to the ground, her mouth still on his, and pushed him against the door he had just come through, nudging it closed and reaching to undo his jeans. She pulled back from him for a second and the look on her face as she stared into his eyes was all it took. He pulled her up, legs back around his waist, and pressed her against the door as he pushed himself into her.

Sitting on the couch afterwards, with her nestled under his arm, he pulled the blanket from the back of the couch and wrapped it around them.

'Well, do tell. Did Rita scare the shit out of you, and that was your way of saying goodbye? Or did everything go well, and that was some good old celebration sex?'

Maeve laughed, pulling the blanket tighter around her as she snuggled into him.

'The meeting went fine.' She shrugged. 'I'm not sure if she's really the type of person I'd choose to spend much time with.'

Jamie stiffened beside her.

'I mean, I'd be broke trying to keep up with her in the bar,' Maeve added, laughing.

After a second Jamie laughed, too.

'I'm glad you're home,' Maeve said.

Her voice was getting softer as Jamie ran his fingers through her hair, a sure way to relax her, often to the point where she fell asleep.

'Me, too,' he whispered.

Jamie stayed rubbing her hair long after she'd fallen asleep, staring straight ahead as something in his stomach turned, but he wasn't sure why.

16

Now

Stepping off the bus at Dublin airport the next morning, my body thrummed with nervous energy. My baby girl could be back in my arms in the next few hours. No, she *would* be back in my arms today. I would hold her close and breathe her in. I had to believe it, because my chest ached at the prospect of the alternative. She had to be there. She had to be safe. There was no other option, no other potential outcome from this journey to Donegal than me leaving there with my child in my arms.

I went straight to the rental place by the short-term car park, to collect the Mercedes E class I'd phoned ahead to ensure was waiting for me. I looked longingly as I passed a BMW S1000RR on the way to my car. A bike was the quickest way to Donegal, especially when you didn't care about penalty points, but it didn't work for the car seat I'd also hired. The car seat I would *need* for Sarah when I was leaving Donegal. Besides, I hadn't ridden in years. The last time had been well before I'd left Ireland the second time. Jamie had always worried that it made me too vulnerable, and although I didn't listen to him for a long time, I felt I'd no choice but to submit to his concerns when he handed me the key to a brand-new Audi TT.

I broke the speed limit, quite dramatically, the entire way, passing only one speed van that I knew would send the fine to a non-existent Maeve Molroy in Co. Louth. My sense of caution had abated with every passing second I spent without my daughter. All that mattered now was speed.

Despite my heart racing at the thought of seeing Sarah, I didn't go directly to Rita's bungalow. First, I needed to stake out what I was dealing with, so instead I made my way along the narrow winding road that sat 600 metres above sea level and ran parallel to the coast. It would give me a clear view of the bungalow below. I'd only been here once before, with Jamie. Rita hadn't known about that particular visit, which is probably why she'd chosen to bring Sarah here. She must have thought she'd be safe. Davey and Lucy would be in a world of shit for leading me here.

I pulled to a stop next to a steep drop where the road widened, and jumped out of the car. Drawing in the pure, clean sea air, for the briefest of moments, my mind stilled and the adrenaline pumping around my body dropped, allowing my heart rate to settle.

Despite managing to cut the three-hour journey down

by thirty minutes, the morning had still moved on, and it was nearly midday. Not that you could tell the time of day here – the thick grey cloud cover was shielding the sun from reaching the Donegal coast.

I sat on the grassy verge, my legs hanging over the edge. The wind whipped my hair over my face. Pushing it back, I licked my lips and noticed a faint salty residue had already started to form. Taking one last deep breath, I turned my attention to my target.

The bungalow sat on its own, with nothing and no one around for miles. Only one car was parked outside: a navy Ford Focus. No one was keeping a lookout, or patrolling the perimeter, as far as I could see, but there was smoke rising from the chimney and being carried on the sea breeze into the heavens above. My stomach churned. She was there. My baby was inside that house. I could feel it in the depths of my being, in the very marrow of my bones.

After seeing so many terrible things, I'd lost the belief I'd once had in God – and after doing so many terrible things myself, I hoped I was right about that lost belief – but here on this cliff edge I looked to the sky and prayed. Prayed for my daughter to be there and for us to leave safely together. I spoke the words aloud.

'God, please let her be okay. Let me get her back, and allow me another chance to be the mother she deserves, someone who can protect her.'

This was the part where I was supposed to make a promise,

try to bargain and offer God something in return for his divine intervention, in an attempt to entice him to ignore the concept of free will and do some actual, physical good, but I had nothing.

Everything pointed to Rita being alone. Unless Martin had returned from Barcelona without Jamie knowing. Either way, I was going in there. Even if she was alone, Rita was still dangerous – and she already had the upper hand, she had my baby. With nothing for miles, and only one car parked outside, there couldn't be an army waiting inside for me. At least, I hoped not. Though, either way, it didn't matter. I'd already decided on the 'all guns blazing' approach. I just hoped it was the right one.

I pulled my gun from my jacket, released the clip and checked it was full, one last time, before reloading it. I stood, put my gun in the back of my waistband, and returned to the Mercedes.

It was time to confront Rita.

I roared up to the bungalow, fuelled by fury and petrol. Whether Rita knew I was coming or not, the rumble of my engine told her I was here now.

The front door was unlocked, and I walked straight into the narrow hallway leading to a small kitchen-cum-living room. And there she was. Rita Regan. Sitting in a wooden rocking chair.

I could only see her side profile, illuminated by the

blazing fire she sat in front of, in the dimly lit room. One of the most dangerous women in the country and there she was, eyes closed, as she rocked and shushed the sleeping baby in her arms. My baby.

I almost gasped out loud. The relief of seeing Sarah nearly had me crashing to my knees and crying out, right there and then, but I couldn't, not yet. Instead, I walked towards her, pulling the gun from my waistband as I approached. I trained the gun on the side of her head, walking forward until it was almost touching her. She knew I was there, but her eyelids didn't even flutter as she continued rocking and shushing.

My eyes slid to my baby, sleeping peacefully, just as she should be at this time of the day, but not in those arms. Her long lashes resting against her pale cheeks full of baby fat. My child shouldn't be here, not in this world. It was my fault. I had put her here. If anything happened to her . . . I shook my head and pushed the gun against Rita's forehead.

Finally, she turned and looked up at me, the barrel of the gun pressing against the skin between her eyes. She continued rocking and shushing, something so normal in this abnormal situation. Never, in my wildest imaginings, could I have pictured my daughter here, in this house, beneath a red knitted blanket, in the arms of this woman. But she was. And I needed to get her out of here, away from this entire world, as quickly as possible.

'That was fast,' Rita whispered between shushes.

'You can thank Davey and that halfwit cousin of yours,

Lucy Murphy, for that,' I said, my eyes never leaving Sarah's face.

Rita turned her head back to the fire. 'Oh, I'll express my gratitude to them all right, don't you worry.' She sighed as she closed her eyes again. 'And I suppose I've Jamie to thank for you even knowing this place exists.'

I didn't answer. Instead, I asked, 'What is all this about, Rita? Why in the name of God would you take my child?'

'You should be grateful it's me who has her. No harm for you to see how easy it was to take her. And from right under your nose.' Rita snorted. 'You must be losing your touch.'

Despite my baby sleeping in her arms, my index finger tightened its grip on the trigger and twitched in response to her remark. I inched the gun to one side and pressed it against her temple.

Looking directly into her eyes, I asked, 'Why, Rita? Why did you take my child?'

Rita returned my gaze, the flames from the fire dancing in her eyes.

'Just as clueless as ever, aren't you, Maeve Deane?' She said my maiden name like it was an insult. 'Now, lower your gun.'

'No, Rita,' I jabbed her harder with my gun. 'I'm the one giving the orders now.'

'Ah, ah, careful now,' Rita whispered, gently sliding her hand out from under the blanket so I could see the glint of her knife in the dim light. She rested it lightly on Sarah's chest, the tip of it centimetres from her throat.

My entire body tensed. There was such a loud roaring in my ears I almost didn't hear when Rita spoke.

'Not so smart now, are ya?'

My breathing accelerated and I could feel the panic flooding through me as Rita readjusted her grasp on the handle of the knife. As it inched closer to my daughter's throat, something in me snapped. Before she could say another word or move that knife of hers, I slammed the handle of my gun down on the top of her head, and pulled the knife from her grasp with my free hand, before throwing it across the room. Rita was dazed but conscious and still had a hold of Sarah, who had somehow stayed sleeping on her lap. I stepped in front of Rita, my gun pointed right between her eyes.

She didn't speak, didn't move. She focused on me until her vision cleared enough for her to see just how serious I was.

'Take her, for fuck's sake, just take her,' she said, holding out both hands, palms up, so I could see she was now unarmed.

I moved the gun to my left hand but didn't lower it from Rita's face as I scooped Sarah up with my right arm, gently bouncing her until she was settled in close to my chest, fearful that she would wake with the movement.

With Sarah finally back in my arms, I wanted to run, to get out of there and as far away from Rita as I possibly could, but I needed answers.

'Why? Why did you do all this?'

Rita gave a small, humourless laugh.

'He knows, Maeve. Martin knows everything.'

17

Then

Metropolitan Police headquarters, London

'Take a seat, PC Deane.'

As I settled into the chair, I ran my hands down the stiff fabric of my trousers, attempting to subtly wipe the sweat from my palms. I'd officially been a police constable for a grand total of two weeks. What could I possibly have done in that time to warrant being called into a meeting with the Chief Inspector, as well as two other men who were dressed in plain dark suits? Their eyes hadn't left me since I'd walked through the door. Looking around the room now, I resisted the urge to adjust myself in the hard plastic seat. I felt like a wildebeest that had unwittingly strayed straight into the lion's den.

Chief Inspector Warren shut the door and rounded his desk but didn't take his seat. Instead, he raised an arm and pointed at one of the other men in the room.

'PC Deane, this is Detective Sergeant Ryan from the Garda National Surveillance Unit.'

I stood and shook the hand of the dark suit on the left. He had short, neat sandy-coloured hair, dark eyes, and freckles scattered across his face, making him look too young to have made it as a Detective Sergeant.

'Nice to meet you, PC Deane,' he said in a thick Cork accent that immediately reminded me of home.

As his hand left mine, I noticed the grey folder he was clasping in his other hand.

'And this is Europol Liaison Officer Silva,' Chief Inspector Warren continued, resting his gaze on the second dark suit.

I shook hands with Silva. His tanned skin, blond hair and lazy blue eyes made him look more casual and laid-back than his Irish colleague.

Returning to my seat, I waited for the Chief Inspector to finally explain what all this was about. But he didn't. Instead, he nodded to the two men and strode from the room.

In the moment of silence that followed, I envisioned relaying this entire occurrence over drinks with the few friends I'd made since moving to England. Jennifer tipping her beer into her mouth, without her lips ever touching the bottle. Amy sitting across from me, sipping her gin and tonic while discussing her next body piercing. We would sit around the same circular wooden table that was both too high and too low at the same time. I would build tension, dramatically stressing the importance of the two men I'd been left alone with, and then—

'Well, PC Deane,' the Europol officer started as he and the Detective Sergeant made their way to stand behind the desk.

Between his accent, name and appearance, I guessed he was Portuguese.

'First, everything that is discussed here today does not go beyond this room – or the three of us – is that clear?'

I nodded, and sat up straighter in my seat, curious but also disappointed that my contribution to tonight's conversation wouldn't be nearly as interesting now. The girls would have to settle for hearing about the ridiculously ripped guy at the gym who asked me out for a drink on Saturday night.

The Europol officer continued talking as the Detective Sergeant remained silent, watching me.

'We're here to discuss with you a highly sensitive matter. A matter that could change your life dramatically.'

18

Now

I froze. Every thought running through my mind stalled briefly. My heart was pounding in my chest. No, he couldn't. He couldn't. There was no way. How? What had gone wrong? How much did he know?

'What?' The question came out like a breath. 'What does he know?'

'Don't bother trying to play the fool, Maeve. The time for that is long past.'

I looked down at Sarah, her soft face still sleeping soundly, and thought of Abbie, of Christopher. This was my worst-case scenario. Martin wasn't punishing me for leaving, or trying to force me back into the crew; he knew I'd betrayed him. I hadn't even allowed myself to consider the possibility, because I thought I'd be dead by now if he knew. But he did know, and this was all his game – a game that would end with him killing my entire family, every single one of them.

It felt as if the ground under me was shifting, rocking back and forth beneath my feet. I stepped back, and slumped heavily into a timeworn armchair beside the fire, laying my hand and gun, still pointed in Rita's direction, on the faded armrest. With Sarah cradled in my arm, I desperately tried to control my breathing. She still hadn't woken. I'd removed her from Rita's lap and yet she remained asleep for the first time in her short life. It was only a small change – something which could have happened as easily at home, when I moved her from my arms into her cot – but it hadn't happened at home, it had happened here, and it made something inside me ache.

'So all of this,' I nodded at Sarah, 'was him?'

Rita nodded. 'He sent Kev and one of his buddies to take her. Only reason I have her now is because he had business to take care of in Barcelona and wanted Kev to join him. I met Kev off the boat in Dublin and brought her here.'

Rita was talking about Killer Kev, Martin's bodyguard, who had earned his nickname from his absolute willingness to carry out Martin's every order, including the swift execution of whoever he might choose, whenever and wherever he demanded. All the while, wearing a cheap black PVC coat. That's who Abbie had played hide-and-seek with, the man in the shiny black coat.

Jamie had once asked him, after a particularly well-paying job, if he was going to finally buy himself a real leather coat, but Kev simply smiled and said he liked how easy the PVC wiped clean. That man had held my baby's life in his hands for hours as they drove to the coast, and then for an entire ferry journey. I'd already been in Ireland while she was crossing the Irish Sea in the arms of that monster. And all under Martin's orders. My stomach turned over.

'So what was all this for? Taking Sarah?' I was still finding it hard to speak, images of Killer Kev with Sarah in his arms running through my mind.

'Martin thought it would be the most . . .' she paused, as if searching for the right word to explain '. . . entertaining way to get you back in the country.'

'And what is his end goal?' I forced the question out but was terrified of the answer.

'Well, now . . .' Rita laughed, but there was no humour in it. 'I'm afraid I haven't been made privy to that particular piece of information.'

I released a breath I didn't know I was holding. I could see her more clearly from my chair by the bright flames, now that she wasn't holding my baby at knifepoint. She looked older than her fifty-odd years, deep lines settling across her face when she relaxed her expression. She'd lightened her hair, a golden blonde replacing her mousy brown, no doubt an effort to camouflage the greys coming through.

'All I know is he wanted you flailing around the country looking for your little one, before ultimately ending up in front of him.'

I pushed my head back against the seat. This was bad. This was very, very bad.

'But then he was called away,' Rita sighed. 'And now he won't be one bit happy that you got her back before he made it home.' She turned, looking me in the eye. 'Don't suppose you'll hang on 'til he gets back?'

I laughed at that. 'Not a fucking chance.'

Rita lifted herself from the chair, stopping briefly as she moved towards the fire. I raised my gun, keeping it pointed at her head.

'Never pictured you as a mother.' Rita looked down at me, a ghost of a smile on her lips. She pulled the wire fire guard towards her before tossing a wooden log into the flames to be devoured. 'Did you really think he'd never find out?'

When I didn't answer, she returned to her chair and pulled it closer to the fire and away from me. 'There's a bag of things for the little one by the door.'

I'd been dismissed. Even with a gun pointed at her head, Rita still spoke to me as if I was nothing more than a lackey being sent off to do her bidding.

I stood, comforted by the familiar weight of Sarah nestled in my arms, and walked to the back door.

Holding Sarah tight with one arm, I turned and trained my gun on Rita's head once again. I should do it. I should pull the trigger. She was involved in this, as guilty as Martin. I should do it, show Martin I wouldn't be easily messed with. My hand started to shake. I couldn't do it. My daughter would wake to a gunshot and look up at me, and I just couldn't let that happen. I placed the gun on a small table by the back door before grabbing the bag filled with nappies, bottles and baby clothes.

'You know it's only a matter of time now,' Rita said, resting back in her chair so all I could see was the top of her head. 'Before Martin kills you all.'

I swung open the door and left.

19

Then

Metropolitan Police headquarters, London

No one had spoken for almost three minutes. I knew that, because instead of looking at the faces of the two men who were staring at me with unnerving intensity, I was watching the clock tick above their heads. My hands were pressed into my thighs, allowing the sweat to soak straight into the rough fabric of my trousers. 'We know that's a lot of information to take in,' Silva said, eventually. 'DS Ryan can take you through it all again if you would like.'

I shook my head, allowing another brief silence before I spoke.

'No, I think I understand perfectly,' I began. 'You want me to return home to Cork City and get close to someone I barely knew when I was sixteen years old, "by any means necessary"?' I paused, opting to leave out the part about selling drugs for him. 'Oh, and he just so happens to be one of the senior members of the biggest crime gang in Ireland, which you want me to infiltrate in order to feed you information on Martin Mulvihill, who is considered one of the most dangerous men in Europe. Did I leave anything out?'

Silva and Ryan glanced at each other, then Silva shrugged. 'No, I'd say that's everything.'

I looked between Silva and Ryan, shaking my head.

'Don't worry,' Ryan said quickly, 'you'll receive thorough specialist training at our Europol base in the Netherlands.'

'Why me?' I asked. 'Surely you have other, more experienced agents who are already trained and would be much better equipped for this?'

'Well, yes, of course we have more experienced agents, but so far, the Garda National Surveillance Unit has had little or no luck getting anywhere near to Martin Mulvihill, or any of those closest to him, and so we asked our colleagues at Europol' – Ryan gestured towards Silva – 'to find us someone who wasn't an outsider – someone from the area, someone with previous, lifelong connections, who might be willing to help us.'

'And when your name and background details came up on our database as applying to become a police constable, we knew we'd found the perfect candidate,' Silva added.

I simply sat there staring at them as if they'd lost their minds.

'Your mother once worked in one of Martin's hotels in Cork,' Silva continued.

'And?' I asked. 'That's a pretty tenuous connection. She didn't even know him—'

'But we have it on record that he went to your mother's funeral,' Ryan chimed in.

That was true. I remembered seeing him and his wife in the queue to offer me their condolences at the time, but I didn't remember much of the interaction.

I shrugged. 'His wife was the manager of the hotel, so I guess they were just paying their respects.'

'Even so,' Ryan went on, 'they know you so—'

'They don't know me,' I cut in.

'But they know *of* you – and that alone is a huge bonus.'

'And so does Jamie O'Leary,' Silva said, 'which would make him a good target for you to infiltrate their inner sanctum.' He was getting more and more excited as he spoke. 'That's who you would need to concentrate on; that's who you would need to reconnect with.'

I shook my head. 'He'd have no reason to trust me.'

'Actually, we know he does.' Ryan folded his arms across his chest, grey folder dangling from one hand. 'We have Garda records from 2003 noting you, Maeve Deane, as one of Jamie O'Leary's underage drug sellers at the time.' I shifted in my seat and started cracking each of my fingers, in turn, with my thumb.

'You have no need to worry, PC Deane,' Silva said, with a laugh. 'That connection is more likely to have helped you rather than hindered you in becoming a police constable.'

Letting out a breath, I placed my hands back on my thighs. 'Look, gentlemen, I appreciate your confidence in me, but I'm afraid I'm not interested. I have absolutely no intention of returning to Ireland, and I'm certainly not about to get myself on the wrong side of someone like Martin Mulvihill.'

'We're willing to offer you quite a substantial salary for this undertaking, and anything you earn while undercover is also yours to keep,' Ryan said.

'I'm sorry,' I said, shaking my head, 'but my answer is still no.'

Ryan looked at Silva, who nodded his answer to whatever silent question was being asked of him. 'It was terrible what happened to your mother, Maeve,' Ryan said, as he unfolded his arms and opened the grey folder to look at its contents.

My heart rate increased at the mention of my mother. I closed my eyes and I could see her lying by our kitchen table surrounded in a pool of her own blood, her eyes open, staring lifelessly towards me. My first thought had been how dark the blood was, which had collected and congealed in the grouting between the tiles. Then I remember thinking how upset my mother would have been about it staining her floor.

I don't know how long I stood there staring at her, and I have no recollection of kneeling beside her and scooping her up into my arms, but I must have made a lot of noise because someone called the Gardaí. I don't remember much else about that day and, honestly, I've never tried to. I stayed with Marnie that night after they'd taken my mother from my arms. And, once she was put in the ground, I was shipped off to England.

I had begged Marnie to let me stay with her but she thought I'd be better off having a fresh start with my mother's much older sister, Fiona, who had moved to London before I'd even been born.

Fiona had been pleasant enough, but she wasn't interested in me, verging on cold and unaffectionate – the polar opposite of my mother, who had been the result of a fertility surge before my grandmother entered menopause. As a result, there was a fifteen-year age gap that turned Fiona from a doted-upon only child into a forgotten teenager, and no real relationship ever developed between the two sisters. Though I was never close to my aunt, I still grieved for her when she suddenly died, just three years after I moved in with her. Perhaps I was grieving my mother, though – at nineteen I'd been more able to deal with my emotions.

That grief and guilt over my mother's death, which resurfaced after my aunt passed away, somehow morphed itself into a desire to join the police force. Maybe it was a way for me to witness some of the justice that had seemed lacking in the world until then. Or maybe it was some kind of repentance for leaving my mother alone at home, to bleed out on our kitchen tiles, while I sold drugs to college students, concerned only with earning enough cash for the Nike runners I'd wanted – the same ones I later found at the bottom of my mother's wardrobe while looking for an outfit to bury her in. 'Multiple stab wounds.' Ryan's voice snapped me back from my thoughts. He was reading from the file in his hands. 'Defensive marks, evidence suggestive of a break-in.' Ryan looked up. 'She fought back.'

I nodded, not trusting my voice.

'No one was ever caught for it,' he went on.

I nodded again.

'If you do this for us, Maeve, we will give you free reign to search for your mother's killer in whatever way you see fit, with access to every resource available to us and Europol.' Ryan closed the file and used it to tap Silva on the arm, who was nodding his agreement.

That's when I realised just how desperate these two men standing in front of me were to get me on board. I was someone whose identity could remain my own, unchanged; I would simply be returning home. And the *pièce de résistance* was that I had no family; there was nothing and no one I cared about that Martin Mulvihill could ever use against me when I'd ultimately need to give evidence against him. I was the golden goose of undercover agents.

Even though I'd often fantasised about it, I'd never truly intended returning to Ireland to find the person who'd killed my mother. Until now.

20

Now

Kent, England

The journey back to Dublin airport had gone smoothly, except for the cramp in my arm from constantly readjusting my rear-view mirror to make sure there was no one following behind. Sarah had slept for another hour as we made the journey from Donegal. Tears had slid silently down my face as I drove, fuelled by a combination of relief that I had her back and sadness that she obviously hadn't slept much in the time she had been with Rita, to be this tired now.

The moment her eyes had fluttered open, I'd pulled into the nearest lay-by to change and feed her. The relief my breasts felt at finally being able to release the milk they'd been storing was second only to the relief of having my daughter safe in my arms. Hand-expressing some meagre drops into scratchy kitchen paper while standing over the sink at Jamie's had done little to ease the discomfort and pain radiating through them.

I had relished those moments in the back seat of the hired car. Holding Sarah up in front of me, I had pushed every thought of Rita and Martin from my mind and smiled at my beautiful baby. Relief had flooded through me as she smiled back at me.

'Mama,' she'd said, burying her hands in my curls as she rested against me.

She'll be okay, I'd thought. She won't remember any of this.

As eager as I was to get home to Christopher and Abbie, Sarah and I needed some time to reacclimatise back to our real lives, and I needed time to readjust to being Maeve King. It was coming up to six in the evening when I texted Christopher to tell him we were stopping off at the Duhon Court shopping centre because Sarah had thrown up on her last set of clean clothes on the plane. Another lie to add to the ever-increasing list. I said that we would grab some dinner and be home as soon as we could.

Sitting in the small Italian restaurant, we both devoured our bowls of pasta. I'd had nothing on the plane, while Sarah had only had a Liga, four rice cakes and a banana. After a quick dose of retail therapy, to get Sarah out of the cheap, coarse yellow onesie she'd been dressed in, and me into a blouse and jeans more representative of Maeve King,

I shoved our old clothes, along with a packet of half-smoked cigarettes, into the bag I'd taken from Rita's, before pushing it down into a shiny metal bin outside the clothes shop. I was excited to get home, but I knew the second I was there I would need to start thinking about what my next steps would be; what I needed to do to keep my family safe.

I drew up and parked outside our house on Redmond Row, glancing back at my happy baby girl, who was now dressed in a powder-blue top and matching leggings, and was playing with her toes. Tilting the rear-view mirror, I moved it from side to side to take in the entirety of the street behind me. I didn't know many of our neighbours, except for a couple of the other mothers who had young children and also attended the local baby group. I'd never had a reason to doubt any of them, until now. Now, I doubted every single one of them. Did Martin know where I lived? They knew about Sarah's vaccine appointment, when and where I would be. They knew where I was parked, even though I'd never parked there before. How had they followed me without me ever realising? Were they that good, or had I become far too complacent in this perfect little bubble of mine as the years had ticked by, uninterrupted by my former life? I should have known, I should have been alert, seen something, anything, that would have warned me, but I hadn't. Had I lost my touch? I turned the mirror back to Sarah. Well, if I had, I hadn't lost it entirely. I'd walked back into the past and done what I needed to get her back. And I'd done it well.

But there was one question that had continued raging through my mind since leaving Rita's bungalow. How did he know? How could Martin possibly have discovered my secret, after all this time? I couldn't think about it anymore. He knew, and as much as it bothered me, finding out *how* he knew wasn't going to help me right now.

The more miles that clocked up between us and Ireland, and the longer I had Sarah back with me, the more it all seemed like a bad dream. It was becoming easier to convince myself that it was all over. That Martin had put me through that horrific game of hide-and-seek to punish me, but now I'd won and it was finished. That's how games went, wasn't it? You played and you either won or lost, but in the end it was over. Finished. Done. Despite everything I knew about Martin, I allowed my mind to settle on that conclusion for the time being as I hopped out of the car with a great big smile plastered across my face. It was time to be happy, loving Mummy Maeve and no one else. Opening the back passenger door, I smiled at Sarah in her car seat, strapped in safe and sound.

'Mummy. Sarah. Mummy. Sarah,' Abbie's voice sang, as she skipped towards us, red curls bouncing wildly, to greet us at the front door.

I crouched down and took Abbie in my arms, still holding tight to Sarah. My two precious girls, safe in my arms. But for how long?

Christopher walked into the hall from the kitchen, drying

his hands on a tea towel. He flicked it over his shoulder as he bent down to become a part of the family group hug.

'You found her, then?' he said.

I pulled back from the hug and looked at him. 'What?'

'Abbie was telling me Sarah was winning in a game of hide-and-seek.' He laughed as we stood, his arm still around me and Sarah as he leaned forward to kiss each of us. 'An impressive feat for a child who can't walk yet.'

'Oh, did she now?' I smiled down at Abbie and winked. 'Did she also tell you that Sarah is currently reigning champion of our very serious Simon Says games?'

Christopher and Abbie laughed. I couldn't even force a laugh, hating that I was making Abbie out to be lying.

'Good to have you back,' he said, cupping the back of my neck for another, longer kiss.

'Good to be back,' I said, smiling against his lips.

'How's Marnie doing?'

A pang of guilt hit me for not really checking in on her, but that relationship was beyond repair.

'Good, good. She'll be fine. A bit run-down is all. Was good to have a catch-up with her.'

'Of course,' Christopher said, heading back to the kitchen. 'I'm just cleaning up after our dinner for two, then I'll get the girls ready for bed and we can sit down and talk.'

I smiled, watching him go. Good old reliable, predictable Christopher. He was so safe; I could always count on him. I think that was part of what had attracted me to him. No, there were no thrilling, dangerous adventures that ended in heated sex in some random laneway or club toilet, and we didn't have a lot in common, but we were right for each other. I'd known it since the day we met. Well, maybe not that first day, but definitely the next one when I'd been less concussed.

There had been times, over the years, when I'd missed the thrill and excitement of my old life, but now that my perfectly quiet, boring life was about to come crashing down around me, I felt stupid, as if I had brought it on myself. As if those foolish thoughts had dragged all this misery down on top of me. I'd always known I didn't deserve any of this, but I had naively hoped that the universe, God, karma or whatever would be too busy dealing with other matters to give me a second thought. I'd hoped I could just quietly coast along in this wonderful life I shouldn't have been allowed to have. But no, my past had come back to bite me on the ass.

I followed Christopher to the kitchen, with Sarah still in my arms, and stroked Abbie's hair and face while she walked along beside me.

'What did you two have to eat?' I asked, giving Sarah a kiss on her squishy cheek as I placed her down in her playpen. 'Want in?' I asked Abbie, who nodded excitedly as I hauled her up and over the white railing.

'My speciality,' Christopher said, rinsing a sudsy saucepan under the tap, 'pasta Bolognese.'

I laughed. 'We were all very adventurous with our pasta today.'

'If it ain't broke,' Christopher smiled. 'Oh, before I forget, there's an envelope for you on the hall table.'

'Okay,' I said, too interested in watching as Sarah and Abbie played with their shape sorter.

'No stamp or anything, so I presume it's another party invite for the girls from one of the neighbours.'

My head snapped from the girls to the hallway and the envelope waiting for me on the table.

'I'll go have a look,' I said, trying to keep my voice light. 'Both of them are in the playpen so keep an eye out,' I called, heading back down the hallway.

Lying on the hall table in front of our first picture as a family of four was a small brown envelope with my name and address neatly written on it in black pen. It didn't look like one of the typical party invites, which normally came in shiny white envelopes and had colourful writing to match the party theme.

My hand shook as I picked it up and tore it open, my body already aware of something my mind refused to acknowledge. Pulling out the white business card, I let the envelope fall to the ground as my hand shot to my mouth to cover the scream that attempted to escape.

No, no, no, please no, I thought, turning the blank card over, but it wasn't blank on the opposite side. Instead, there was a place, a date and a time printed in clear black font:

'The Harmada Hotel, Friday 1st November, 12:30 p.m'. It was a summons.

After a quick dash to the bathroom, where I flushed my earlier meal of pasta down the toilet, I washed my face and went back to my family. So many questions ran through my mind. Which one of Martin's people was close enough to leave this for me? Where were they now? What was Martin going to do with me on the first of November? It was five days away. I had a lot to do, a lot to straighten out in my head, but right now I needed to focus on spending time with Christopher and the girls.

I insisted that I would take care of bedtime, reassuring Christopher that I wasn't too tired. Despite our late arrival home I took my time with the routine. There was no rushing through teeth-brushing and stories so I could escape down-stairs for some peace and a bite of chocolate without hungry eyes on me. Instead, I relished every mundane aspect, cursing myself again for having ever taken any of it for granted.

Once both girls were sleeping, I took it in turns at each doorway to watch them, breathing in and out, peaceful and unaware of the threat hanging over them. A threat I had drawn on them. A threat I would do everything in my power to eradicate. Standing there, watching them dreaming, I made another promise; a promise that no one like Killer Kev would ever lay a hand on them again, that I would keep them safe, no matter what that meant and no matter what I had to do.

By the time I dragged myself away, Christopher was in

the shower. I made my way to the living room and sat staring at a black phone screen in front of a black television screen. Lighting up my phone, I scrolled through my contacts list, stopping at the number labelled 'Florist's–London'.

There was no florist at the other end of that number. It would connect immediately to Officer Silva.

A number only to be used in the event of an emergency.

21

Then

One evening, when Jamie returned home from a particularly taxing day at work, he was greeted by Maeve holding a small white plastic stick, the word 'pregnant' printed on the front. He felt so ridiculously happy. As she threw herself into his arms, tears filled his eyes and all he could do was hug her tight to his chest so she couldn't see the depth of his emotion. His life was perfect.

A few weeks later, Martin called with a job. The son of a previous big player who Martin had forcibly retired had set up his own business and was selling cocaine on the streets of Cork City. Apparently, he had plans to spread his venture further afield and add a greater selection to his menu. It wouldn't have mattered even if he had planned on staying small; Martin would have wanted him dealt with, regardless. That's why he was so powerful. He had a zero-tolerance policy for competition or disrespect of any form in his country. And it really was his country. Often, his zero-tolerance policy punishments involved something a lot worse than sending Jamie to relay a message. Jamie had suggested to Maeve that she stay put, given her pregnancy, and seeing as she'd returned home exhausted after meeting Rita for a coffee, but that comment had earned him a glare so terrifying that he immediately retracted it.

'Let's go, then,' he said, picking up her leather jacket as she walked past him, heading out the door.

They found the young guy they were looking for easily enough. He was called Liam Daily Jr. Son of Liam Daily, one of Martin's former adversaries. Former because, over a decade ago, Martin had cut him into pieces and had those pieces dropped into the sea at different points around the country. A few parts had washed up over the years and everyone, Gardaí included, knew who was behind the brutal killing, but there was no evidence linking it back to Martin.

Liam Daily had been the only person who'd ever come close to challenging Martin, and he'd ended up supplying sustenance to the country's native sea life. Now, it appeared his son was foolish enough to attempt to reignite his father's former businesses – and, consequently, his feud with Martin.

Liam Daily Jr frequented a bar where most of the clientele considered themselves up-and-coming criminals. They were just scumbags, really. A common enough mix-up. People often assume criminals are scumbags, and sometimes that's true, but not all scumbags are criminals. Not real ones. A criminal, a proper criminal, needs know-how and skills, the ability to think on their feet; and they need to be true business people at heart. They're not satisfied with getting in trouble, hanging out with a crew or roaming the streets wearing hoodies all the time. In fact, some of the most successful criminals Jamie knew were also some of the best dressed. Himself included. While he didn't care too much about donning suits every day of the week, he did always wear nice, hole-free jeans or trousers, with good-quality shirts. There were no tracksuits in his wardrobe – at least not anymore.

'Two Jamesons, Mick,' Jamie called as they approached the bar.

'Two?' Maeve asked, settling herself on the high stool.

'What?' Jamie turned to her.

Maeve gave a pointed look down at her stomach, not yet showing any sign of the baby growing inside.

'Jesus, I forgot you couldn't drink with that.'

'That?' Maeve snapped.

'Ah, you know what I mean. Relax, I'll take care of the drink for you.' He winked as he poured one glass into the other.

Jamie watched Maeve as she turned away, scoping out the bar and its occupants. She'd been a bit off lately. Rita had assured him it was probably the pregnancy hormones messing with her head, but he was beginning to wonder if it wasn't something more than that. Maeve didn't want anyone knowing about the baby yet – Rita included – but he hadn't been able to help himself. The excitement had bubbled up inside him and pushed the words out over a few drinks they'd shared last week. Lately, though, that excitement had been tinged with something else – fear, he suspected. From the moment he fell in love with Maeve he was afraid she'd change her mind about living this life with him, and leave. When he'd found out she was pregnant he'd been overjoyed, but now he worried that maybe this baby wouldn't bind them together; maybe this baby would make Maeve finally see sense and leave him and this life they led.

He shook his head and threw back the rest of the whiskey with one quick, efficient swig and stepped off the stool.

'Go time,' he announced, heading for the back of the bar, where he'd spotted the man they were looking for. Lacking her normal zeal when faced with an opportunity for violence, Maeve stepped down and followed. Jamie turned, stopping Maeve and grabbing her face between his hands.

'You sure you're up to this?'

She smiled up at him. "Course I am.'

She pulled his hands from her face, pushed in front of him and made her way towards the darkened alcove at the back of the bar.

Jamie watched as she walked right up to Liam Daily Jr and, without hesitation, cupped the back of his head and slammed his face into the table. The other three men at the table shot to their feet, one reaching for her. But before he could touch her, she caught his hand, slammed it down onto the table and, with a knife he hadn't seen her reach for, pinned it in place. The man roared in pain.

Jamie stepped forward and placed a hand on Maeve's shoulder. No one else made a move. No matter how lethal Maeve was, or what damage she could inflict, his presence meant they were all only one step away from Martin Mulvihill – and that was enough to stop anyone in their tracks.

Liam was rubbing his face. It didn't look as if his nose was broken; maybe Maeve was losing her touch. Martin wasn't wrong when he'd called him 'a young pup'. Well, his exact phrase was 'a young pup that needs putting down', but he always talked like that. Jamie knew that if Martin wanted this guy dead, he'd have sent Killer Kev, or involved himself somehow. Martin relished the parts of the job that others completed as a duty. That's why he was so terrifying. He was several leagues above your average criminal. And that was exactly why the rest of the bar kept their heads turned away, and why no one would call for help.

If Liam Daily Jr was twenty, it didn't show. He was young and stupid, Jamie thought. Taking on Martin in any area was a foolish move, and only someone young, naive and very, very green would ever even contemplate it. Or else, perhaps, someone with a grudge against the man who had murdered his father. Jamie felt bad for the lad. He felt bad for all of them, if he was being honest, but in this eat-or-be-eaten world, Jamie would make sure he was the one with the fork and knife. Figuratively speaking, of course. Literally speaking, he always had a knife. He pulled the switchblade from his pocket, flicking it out as he turned towards Liam.

'How's ye're night going so far, gentleman?' he asked, as Maeve pulled her knife from the soft tissue of the man who was desperately trying not to scream or cry in front of his boss.

Maeve took a step back, allowing Jamie to take charge. That had been the agreement on the way over. While Maeve was more than efficient at getting her point across, it usually involved a lot of violence and, in her condition, Jamie was more inclined to go the 'scare the shit out of them' approach, using Martin's reputation. Maeve had been reluctant at first, but seemed relieved when he insisted, her hand subconsciously going to rest on her still-flat stomach. He'd made a mental note of that – sometimes he needed to insist. It would make it easier for her to take that step back.

Jamie grabbed a chair from a nearby table and took a seat next to Liam, careful to avoid the drops of blood spattered on the table in front of him.

'Well, Liam, my friend, it seems we're having a spot of bother with a bit of crossover of business.'

Liam didn't say a word, just stared at Jamie as he spoke.

'And I'd have thought you, of all people, would have a clear understanding of the repercussions of any such issue.'

Liam's nostrils flared as the muscle along his jawline twitched, but still he remained silent.

Jamie wasn't fazed. He simply placed a white business card on the table in front of him, again dodging the red spatters. The card was blank, but everyone at the table knew what it meant; it was Martin's calling card. A warning.

On the next card there would be a place, date and time printed across it. No one wanted that card. That was a summons. That could mean a deal was to be made, a deal that would benefit only Martin. Or, if not, an execution would occur. If you didn't turn up, the execution was guaranteed. Martin loved to do it that way. It was one of his games, allowing people to decide their fate, while having absolutely no say in it whatsoever.

Liam, in fairness to him, didn't seem all that bothered by the card. That was his first mistake. His second was pulling the gun from his jacket pocket. His last mistake was aiming it at Maeve.

It all happened in less than five seconds. Jamie saw Maeve, the look on her face when the gun appeared. The fear, not just for her but for the life she was carrying inside her. With a shock, Jamie realised she was frozen. He reacted immediately, shoving her out of the path of the gun while simultaneously elbowing Liam in the face, breaking his previously unbroken nose, before grabbing Liam's hand with the gun and burying it into his own stomach. It was Liam himself who pulled the trigger, his mind not catching up with the fact that he now had the barrel of the gun pointed at himself.

Jamie turned back to Maeve. She was on the ground

looking up at him – she must have stumbled when he'd pushed her – a look of terror on her face. Jamie was confused. This wasn't the first time things had gone wrong when they were on a job together. It wasn't even the first time someone had pointed a gun at her. Maybe it was Liam's age that had shaken her, but that look on her face . . .

Jamie saw it then, darkness spreading across her trousers. He didn't understand. Had she wet herself? Why was she reacting like this?

She ran her hands over the wetness before turning her palms towards him.

Her hands were stained red.

22

Walking through the Cork City Library, meandering up and down the rows of bookcases, I looked just like everyone else wandering through the wide archways that had been carefully designed to work with the high ceilings.

After fifteen minutes of browsing, I made my way to the back of the library and slipped into a room used for small events and workshops. The blinds were drawn and the small glass panel on the door had been covered with a blank sheet of paper. Sitting in two hard, plastic orange seats, looking as if they were dressed in the same dark suits they'd worn six years earlier, were Detective Sergeant Ryan and Europol Liaison Officer Silva.

This was my first face-to-face meeting with Ryan and Silva since my career as an undercover officer began. Working deep undercover meant the only connection I had to them was through the coded letters sent back and forth between me and my aunt's 'friend' Hazel in London. While Hazel did exist, meaning everything would stand up to investigation, any relationship between us was completely fictional.

'I'm out,' I said by way of greeting when the door closed firmly behind me. There would be no time wasted on formalities.

Ryan stood. 'We understand, Maeve,' he said, his Cork accent still thick and instantly recognisable. He gestured for me to sit in the plastic chair across from them, then checked the door was closed fully before returning to his seat. 'But you need to appreciate where we're coming from here.'

Silva leaned forward. 'We're so close, Maeve. We have him. But the only way we can be certain of this is if you remain in place until it's time for you to testify.' While Silva's Portuguese accent made his tone more soothing than Ryan's, the words were still not what I wanted to hear.

I shook my head. 'I'm afraid this is only a courtesy meeting, gentlemen.' I stood, wishing I hadn't even taken the seat. 'I'm out. It's already done. I'm on a flight out of Ireland first thing tomorrow morning.' I nodded at them both before heading to the door.

'This is unacceptable,' Silva snapped.

Both men rose from their seats.

'No!' I shouted, turning back to face them, one hand gripping the smooth, cold door handle. My tether to freedom.

Both men stilled.

'What's unacceptable is that I have given you everything, my entire life, for the last six years. I've given you all you need to put the man you've trawled after for decades behind bars – and *still* you want more from me.' My voice was starting to break, but I continued. 'I've given you the name of every known associate I came into contact with, the details of more than a dozen of his businesses throughout the country, how he moves his drugs, where he launders his money, at least five murders he's been involved in. I have nothing left to give you!'

They stood there, looking at me, apparently blindsided by my decision to leave. Neither one of them producing the words to convince me otherwise.

After a few moments of silence, I spoke again.

'I asked you once before to let me get out.' I looked each of them in the eye. 'You've received no additional intel since then.' I laughed once, shaking my head. 'You didn't need any more to make your move. But what I've lost in that time—'

Emotion suffocated my words and swallowed them down. I started at the realisation that my hand had drifted to my stomach. Dropping it to my side, I turned the door handle.

'Only contact me again when it's time for my testimony.'

23

Now

My finger hovered over the 'Florist's' number as my mind wandered back to my final conversation with Ryan and Silva. I had been in the UK for seven months and they had arranged for us to speak on a secure conference call.

'I don't know how many ways you want me to say it, I will *not* be testifying against Martin.'

'You can't do this to us, Maeve. You are single-handedly destroying this entire investigation. You owe us this testimony!' Silva was practically screaming.

'I owe you fucking nothing!' I'd said, matching Silva's volume. 'You ordered raids on every single one of Martin's businesses that I told you about, the second I left the country. You knew that would put me at risk, and we all know it was done as punishment for me leaving. I'm not putting myself at any more of a risk. Goodbye.'

In the end, all the time I'd spent undercover, all the

effort and resources they had put into me, had all been in vain. Martin was clever, and every illegitimate business I'd thought was his wasn't in his name. He paid people a lot of money to take ownership of those properties on paper and deal with the circumstances if they ever came to the attention of the authorities. There were a lot of people willing to do stupid things for money out there. Even so, Silva and Ryan had remained confident they had enough to get him with my testimony. A testimony I had intended to give. I really had. But by the time they contacted me to tell me they were moving forward with the case they'd built, I was married and fourteen weeks pregnant with Abbie. And I intended to live happily ever after.

I returned my gaze to the phone number on my screen. I should ring, tell them what was going on, ask for their help. But if Martin knew the truth, then that information had come from somewhere. And no one, apart from Silva and Ryan, should have known about me.

Instead, I dropped the phone onto the coffee table. No, I wouldn't involve Europol. I could only really trust myself. Besides, whatever Martin was going to do next, bringing Europol to his doorstep again wouldn't help me. I would do this on my own. They had trained me well; I could only hope it was well enough.

Back upstairs, I glanced in on the girls once more before climbing into bed next to a freshly washed Christopher. He was reading the business section of the morning's newspaper.

Rereading it, no doubt. I smiled at my husband as he looked over at me before folding the paper and placing it on his bedside table. He was handsome, almost too good-looking, but his strong jawline kept him on the rugged side. I reached up and stroked his face, the face of a man who, even though he didn't know it, had saved me from a terrible existence and given me a life, a purpose, and a family. I truly loved him for that. But it was also the face of a man who had no idea who was sharing his bed. He had no idea who I really was. The days when I allowed it to, it ate away at me, knowing how hurt he'd be that I'd lied to him from the day we'd met.

I often played the conversation out in my head. I'd tell him and explain how I'd gone undercover, working for the greater good, sacrificing my twenties to put some bad people behind bars. He'd be shocked, upset that I'd kept it all from him, but he would take me in his arms and tell me he understood. But it wouldn't end there. Spurred on by the brief reprieve from guilt, my confession would allow me to keep going. I'd tell him about all the awful things I did while undercover. About the drugs I sold, the punishments I doled out when things went wrong, the assassinations I witnessed and did nothing to stop. And then I would tell him about Brian Walsh, the homeless drug addict willing to do anything for a fix, who had thought my mother an easy target for some quick cash when he followed her into our house. I would tell Christopher how, despite Silva and Ryan's promises, it had been Jamie and Rita who ultimately helped me track down my mother's killer. How I had laughed inappropriately when I first heard his name. It sounded so ordinary, so harmless. Ryan had said that my mother had fought back, that she'd sustained defensive wounds before Brian Walsh pulled a knife from the butcher's block in our kitchen and buried it in her eighteen times. When I found him, sleeping rough at the back of a closed-down restaurant, he didn't fight back much at all.

And then, I would tell Christopher how I had beaten Brian Walsh so badly that he now spends his days in a hospital bed, blinking at the ceiling, being fed by one tube as his excrement fills another.

That's when everything would change. That's when he would look at me and wonder who it really was he was married to. It would be the beginning of the end for us.

I'd been absorbed into a dark and terrible world, and I became a dark and terrible woman in the process. A woman my family would be frightened of, if they truly knew her. They could never know the truth. How could Christopher love me if he did?

'You want to talk?' he asked.

'Nope,' I answered, as I slid a leg over his lap, straddling him.

'Fine by me.' A smile spread across his face as his hands settled on my hips.

This is what I need, I thought.

I needed to forget everything, to feel his body against

mine, to feel him inside me, to remind me who I was, to anchor myself to the woman I had become, before I had to return once again to the woman I was.

The next day, I reeled off the story I'd spent the night preparing. The sex had been a good distraction, a very good distraction, and it had brought me some reprieve from the thoughts swirling around in my head, but I'd woken in the early hours, reaching for the button on my phone to light the screen and tell me how little sleep I'd managed to get: 1:42. I'd lain in bed staring at the dark emptiness in front of me, knowing there would be no more sleep for me this night.

I told Christopher that my visit to Cork had made me think that maybe it was time to go back and do something I'd been putting off for the last sixteen years – go through my mother's things in our old house, and finally sell it.

The house had been left to me, but I hadn't crossed the threshold since the day of my mother's funeral. And thanks to inheriting my aunt's estate after she passed, I never needed to. I should have cleared the house years ago, sold it and been rid of it, but I hadn't. I'd left it to rot, knowing that the second I returned, everything would come rushing back.

Christopher was surprised but he wrapped his arms around me and told me how brave I was. Guilt ripped through me at that, especially since I had no intention of stepping back inside that house. It could sit there, idle and empty, for another sixteen years, as far as I was concerned, but it was the only logical reason I would return to Cork. I was too afraid to wish any more ill health on Marnie.

'Do you want me to see if Mum and Dad can take the girls for a couple of nights so I can come with you?' Christopher asked.

He always wanted to help, to look after me. Another reason I loved him. But I loved him even more for knowing I rarely wanted anyone's help, and accepting that.

'No, it's okay. I'll be fine.'

'Don't worry, I understand,' he said, kissing my cheek. 'But if you did need my help, you just have to ask, I hope you know that.'

There was something in the way he said it, that for a split second I thought maybe it wouldn't be the craziest thing in the world to tell him everything, that he'd still love me no matter what.

'I'd do anything for you, Mrs King.'

Whatever momentary lapse in judgement I was having stopped immediately. I believed him, he would do anything for me – Maeve King – but not Maeve Deane. He wouldn't want to help her; he'd be disgusted by her.

'I know you would,' I smiled. 'But this is something I need to do on my own.'

'I understand, you need to face your demons solo.'

I almost laughed. If only he knew how accurate that statement really was.

The last time he'd referred to me 'facing my demons' we

were talking about me taking Abbie to the local parent-and-baby group. At the time, it had felt like one of the most difficult life experiences I'd ever endured – which said a lot, considering my mother had been murdered when I was sixteen and I'd worked undercover with some of the most notorious criminals in Ireland. None of that had prepared me for the politics and backhanded compliments that existed in the world of motherhood. The first group meeting I'd attended was mad; it felt as if I'd traded battles over money, guns and drugs for arguments over breastfeeding or bottle-feeding, co-sleeping or crying it out, attachment parenting or free style. Half the time I didn't know what they were even talking about, and I had to frequently resist the urge to tell them all to mind their own business when my answers to their probing questions evoked alternating nods of approval and frowns, followed by the damning phrase, 'Oh, well, that's okay, too.'

In all my years actively working as a criminal, I had never felt as intimidated as I did when, at that group, I admitted to allowing Abbie into our bed at night if she wouldn't settle.

'You're so lucky you can take the easy option,' one of the mothers said, patting me on the hand. 'I would feel so guilty if I didn't teach little Louie here how to self-soothe, just so I could get some sleep. Well done, you.'

She was belittling me in the nicest way possible – and all it did was make me yearn for the days when it was acceptable, encouraged even, to send a fist straight into the jaw of anyone who disrespected me.

That day, I learned that even in this new picture-perfect life of mine, I would still encounter and interact with horrible, rotten people. The only difference was I couldn't knock them out.

'When are you going?' Christopher asked.

'I was thinking I'd head off on Thursday, hopefully get everything done over the weekend, and be back home by the Monday.' I so hoped to make that timeline a reality, even though I doubted it very much.

'Sounds good. Things are a bit quieter at work after that trip to Milan, so I'll speak to the office and take a few days off to look after the girls.'

'That's great.' I smiled as I wrapped my arms around his neck and kissed him.

'Well, it's a lot easier than dealing with two hyper girls in the evening if I ask Mum and Dad to take care of them.'

I laughed, still hanging from his neck. 'Very true,' I said, kissing him again. 'Thank you.'

What would Christopher say if he knew just how much I had to thank him for?

24

Two nights before I was due to leave and return to Ireland, Christopher arranged for us to go out for dinner. Just the two of us. I didn't want to leave the girls and, after all that had happened, there was no way I was going to leave them with a sitter, but Christopher had organised for them to have a sleepover at Bev and Ian's.

'We can have some dinner, a couple of drinks,' Christopher had said, sliding his arm around my waist, 'and then come home to an empty house.'

'Oh yes? Is that right, Mr King?' I had smiled up at him, wrapping my arms around his neck. 'And what do you have in mind for how we should spend that time?'

'Well, Mrs King,' he'd said, bringing his face close to mine, 'I have every faith that you can come up with something to fill that time.'

He'd closed the gap between us, his lips moving against mine in a slow, easy kiss.

Dinner was blissfully uneventful. The conversation

between us flowed easily, as it always did, with any silences filled with smiles, each of us reaching across the table to hold the other's hand. Everything with Christopher was effortless. It always had been.

Sometimes, sitting on the couch together in the evenings, too exhausted to speak, never mind move, after getting the girls down, I remembered my previous life and the man I'd shared it with. There had never been a scenario where Jamie and I could be in such close proximity and not grope hungrily at one another.

There were times I missed that passion, that excitement, but that didn't mean I missed Jamie. Christopher was everything I wanted – all I needed – and, sitting across the table from him now as the candlelight cast shadows that danced across his freshly shaved face, I knew I was exactly where I wanted to be.

I smiled as he told me how, while I was away, Abbie had attempted to force the neighbour's unwilling cat into her toy pram to be her baby. As he spoke I felt the smile freeze on my face and my stomach twist at the realisation that, in a few short days, I'd be sitting across from a very different man, having a very different conversation.

Back home, the three glasses of wine I'd had, in an effort to settle my nerves, caused me to fumble with the house keys before dropping them to the ground. I bent down to pick them up, laughing. Christopher bent down and took the keys from me as he held my hand and guided me back upright. I stopped laughing when I saw the look on his face.

'You okay, Maeve?' he asked.

I didn't answer straight away, just stared into my husband's bright blue eyes. In that moment, beneath the porch light, he looked as if he knew about all the worries and fears storming inside me.

Laughing again, I reached my hands up and into his hair.

'Of course,' I smiled, 'just eager to get into this empty house with my husband is all.'

'Oh, well, then . . .' His face broke into a wide grin, all the concern melting away. 'Allow me.'

Before I knew it, it was Wednesday afternoon and the early Thursday morning flight I'd booked to Cork was looming over me, waiting to take me back to Ireland and away from my family.

I didn't want to go. I didn't want to leave them. I wanted to bundle them all up into the car and head to the airport, take a flight to anywhere, and hide. But it would be pointless. A meeting had been set, and Martin wasn't the type of man you could ignore. He'd find me wherever I went, if I even managed to get there safely. He'd know the second I decided to run, and he'd stop me. After opening that hand-delivered brown envelope in my hallway at the weekend, I was certain about that.

I had soaked up every moment with my family over the

197

last few days. Sarah had refused to leave my arms for two straight days after returning home, but then returned to her normal self after that and practically jumped from my arms into Bev's when they babysat. She'd also fully weaned herself off the breast in that time. The hours she'd spent away from me had accelerated that process and I'd always regret the fact that our last feed had been in the back of a strange car on a random road in Ireland. She didn't physically need me anymore, and while I was relieved to make my absence as stress-free for her as I could, I knew I would always be angry that those precious moments had been snatched from us. Somehow, I kept my composure during those days with my family, despite the constant urge to scoop them all up into my arms and sob, because they were so beautiful and wonderful and I didn't want to leave them.

I did, however, realise something very important in that short time. I had thought I couldn't be the soft-hearted, mothering woman I had morphed into the day Abbie was born. That she would be of no use to anyone now, and I'd need to revert to the woman I'd once been, but I was wrong. Mummy Maeve was exactly who I needed to be. The mother who'd stop at nothing to keep her family safe.

It was my last afternoon at home, and I needed to pack. I had put it off, desperate to prolong the inevitable, but when Christopher announced that he was taking the girls to the park, to give me some time to get ready, without my 'helpers' undoing the folding and emptying out my bag every time I turned my back, I was out of excuses. At first I tensed at the idea, but the playground was only around the corner from the entrance to our village. It was a built-up area that was always busy. Martin wouldn't pull anything in a public place in a nice area frequented by normal, upper-middle-class British families. He knew there were few things that could launch a manhunt faster than bringing the masses their worst nightmare right to their doorstep.

When the door closed behind them, I pulled out my phone and typed in a number I hadn't used in years. It was so engrained in my memory from a time when our mobile phones didn't carry the burden of holding all the information we needed, and our brains once had to play their part. I composed the message I knew I'd have to send the moment I pulled that card from the envelope. Three small words.

—*I need you.*

That was all I wrote, quickly hitting the send button before I could change my mind. I sat cross-legged on the floor of our bedroom, waiting for a reply and hoping that I was doing the right thing.

An answer came quickly. There were no questions.

—*I knew you would.*

I blew out a breath I hadn't realised I was holding. I could have sent that message anytime, but I didn't want Christopher around when I did. I didn't even allow myself to think of Jamie when I was around Christopher. It felt like a betrayal for some reason. And on top of all the other secrets I kept from Christopher, now including the fact that his youngest daughter had been abducted and retrieved from an Irish crime lord, the fact that I had spent time with my ex-fiancé added another, different layer of guilt to my already guilt-ridden conscience.

I wasn't even sure how I felt after seeing Jamie, but I knew I hadn't felt nothing, and that was enough to make me sick to my stomach every time Christopher smiled at me.

I didn't know for sure how much Jamie would know. I had lucked out that Rita hadn't told him the truth about me before I'd come looking for Sarah, but he would have demanded answers from her after my sudden return to rescue my kidnapped daughter. I had to assume she'd told him everything by now, including how I'd been undercover the entire time we were together. Even after all this time, I didn't want him to feel I'd deceived him. I mean, I had, there was no denying that, but our relationship had been real. Everything I'd said, I'd meant – but would he believe that once he knew the truth? I sighed. Another man who didn't really know me. Well, I'd find out soon enough.

I arranged to meet Jamie in the city when I returned. Trusting him was a risk, there was no doubt about that, but it was a risk I'd have to take.

That was one job done. I had a few more things to get sorted before Christopher came home with the girls. I clicked on the app on my phone labelled 'Menstrual Monitor', which opened a tracking app: Christopher was still at the park. I'd felt guilty loading the hidden app onto his phone after I got back from Ireland, but I needed to know where he was, to make sure he was safe, too. Martin had shown me that anyone could be taken from my life at any moment, and it was absolutely terrifying.

I ran my eye over the documents in front of me, which I had read three times already. Everything was correct. I'd signed on all the dotted lines. My will was sorted, my off-shore accounts containing my earnings from both my time as an agent and as a criminal – the latter much more impressive than the former – would all transfer into Christopher's name, along with the two trust funds I had set up for the girls. I gathered everything up and tucked the papers underneath the false bottom of our built-in wardrobe, along with a sealed envelope containing the hardest letter I'd ever had to write.

The letter was for Christopher. In it, I told him everything. Everything about my past, my work with the Gardaí and Europol, how I had gone so deep undercover that I'd nearly forgotten who I was. I told him how I had hated the person I'd become, what I had done when I found the man who'd murdered my mother. But I also told him how he had saved my life that evening when he'd run into me, or more accurately, when I'd cycled into *him*. I explained that, by then, I'd already decided to leave that life, but that I didn't know if there was even a future for me anymore – before he came along.

I told him what had happened to Sarah and begged him

to find some way to forgive all the secrets I'd kept and everything I'd done. I told him I would understand if he hated me and that maybe it would be better that way, that it might make it easier to continue without me. But most importantly, I told him about Martin Mulvihill, and that if he was reading this letter, then he had to go. Go as far away as he could. Tell no one. Not his parents, or his friends or colleagues. There was no way of knowing who he could trust. Because if he was reading this letter, I hadn't made it. I could only hope that somehow I had taken Martin with me, but if I hadn't, he needed to keep our girls safe. I had allowed the tears to roll down my cheeks as I wrote, quickly wiping them away as I signed my name.

While I hoped I would be home to ensure the documents remained hidden, the realist in me knew there was a good chance I wouldn't be. Opening another app on my phone, I drafted a message to Christopher telling him to pull up the base of our wardrobe in the event of anything happening to me. It would automatically send on Sunday night, unless otherwise instructed.

And just like that, I was done. Ready to leave. To go and face whatever the consequences of my former life were about to subject me to. A tightness formed across my chest at the thought of what lay ahead of me in Ireland, but I pushed all those whirling possibilities from my mind. It was useless to speculate. I had been summoned. I was going back there; I had to face Martin. And as terrifying as it was, it was a fraction of the terror I felt at the thought of what would happen to my family if I didn't.

Rita seemed certain that Martin's next step would be to kill me and my family, but I had never fully trusted Rita's predictions of Martin's actions. He didn't always react as she thought he would. I often wondered if that was because she didn't know him like she thought she did, or if she hadn't managed to convince him to do what *she'd* wanted.

If Martin wanted me and my family dead, we'd be dead by now. He knew where we were and had already shown how easily he could get to me and my family. But he had sent me a summons instead. That meant there was still a deal to be made.

Whatever the future held, I was running out of time. My flight was at 5 a.m. and I'd decided to take a taxi to the airport, a somewhat naive attempt to get back to Cork without being immediately noticed. I had no idea how close whoever was watching me was, and whether they might have placed a tracking device in my car. It may only delay the information getting back to Martin by a few hours, but every second mattered.

The next morning, I kissed each of my girls, who were still sleeping soundly in their beds, and whispered into their small ears that I loved them and would keep them safe. Then I shouldered my bag, took a deep breath, and descended the stairs.

It was time to go.

Christopher walked me to the taxi waiting in front of the house.

'All set?' he asked, with a sleepy smile.

For a second, I couldn't speak. I looked up into his face, illuminated by the street lights, and paused.

'It's all going to be okay,' he said, taking me in his arms and hugging me tightly. 'I know you're worried about leaving the girls and going back inside that house after all this time, but you're strong.' He gave a small laugh. 'You're one of the strongest people I know, and you'll get through it. You'll face your past, and it'll all be fine – and before you know it, you'll be back home here, to me and the girls, with a weight lifted off you.' He kissed me on the forehead and I quickly swiped at the tears starting to fall. 'I'm proud of you.'

'Thank you,' I choked out, before kissing him and letting his mouth swallow all my silent pleas.

'I love you,' he said, raising his hand in goodbye as I jumped into the back of the taxi.

'I love you, too.' I gripped the cracked-leather seat beneath me so tightly I could feel it give way in parts, but it was all I could do not to jump out of the taxi, wrap myself around him and tell him that I'd changed my mind, that I didn't want to go back to my mother's house, that I was just going to stay home with him and the girls.

I was on my own, as I always had been. As I'd been when my mother was killed, when my aunt died, and every day since, when I thought about who I really was and how I was masquerading as someone else.

That feeling of loneliness amplified inside me and settled in my bones. I could feel a pressure building and pushing down on me, and only me. I was almost numb under the weight of it. Staying perfectly still, staring at the little blue tree swinging rhythmically beneath the rear-view mirror, I felt completely alone.

25

County Cork, Ireland

As I pulled up outside the Stone Lodge in Dunpool Woods, the sun was starting to rise in the sky, though it was still low enough not to have pushed through the trees. I was about to kill the engine when a news story on the radio caught my attention.

> *Gardaí have confirmed that the man who has been recovering in hospital since he was discovered last week on a Dublin City Street, badly beaten and with the word 'Rapist' carved into his forehead, has been connected to almost a dozen sexual assaults committed in the city and surrounding areas over the last three years. Gardaí are looking for witnesses to . . .*

I turned it off, smiling at the reminder of my previous visit before stepping out of the car. I took a moment to breathe in the familiar smell of the woods. That heady scent of fresh air, only possible when in such close proximity to this mass of trees, filled my lungs and settled me somewhat.

This time, I had phoned ahead and informed the couple from the Gate Lodge of my impending arrival. After accepting a hasty explanation about my previous visit involving a last-minute business meeting, they assured me the lodge would be ready for me and I wouldn't be disturbed. They must have been curious about the woman who paid well for the maintenance of a house she rarely visited, but they never questioned me.

Inside, the lodge was warm. Tapping my hand against the piping-hot radiator, I smiled. They must have set the timer on the heating for my arrival. Opening the fridge and seeing it stocked up with milk, eggs and butter, and finding a fresh loaf of bread in the bread bin, I decided to add a little extra to the Gate Lodge couple's next payment. If I got the chance.

I sat at the small kitchen table, sipping a cup of tea and eating a buttery slice of toast, and found myself wondering how all this was going to end, and who I needed to be in order to end it, once and for all. Did I need to be the woman I was? Or the woman I pretended to be? The agent? The mother? The criminal? The mousy woman at the parent-and-baby group who let the other mothers belittle her and her parenting decisions? The woman who felt like a failure as a mother after every visit to the GP's surgery? Or the woman who made a rapist cry in fear, and didn't back down from a man with a gun pointed at her head? Who? Who did I need to be now?

I wondered if there would ever be a time when I could be myself. Who was I? Would I forever have to slot into a role, a character? I laughed to myself. Hopefully, I'd have the opportunity to deal with this identity crisis in the future.

I'd spent almost my entire adult life playing a role. I could keep it up, if it meant protecting my family, but maybe after all this was over, I could find a happy medium. Maybe being Abbie and Sarah's mother didn't mean losing the woman I'd once been, maybe it just meant changing her. Tweaking her, for the world of motherhood, instead of smothering her.

The last time I'd really been free to be whoever I wanted was back when my mother was alive and I didn't have to worry about the world around me – my mother did all that for me. That familiar pang hit me again, of just how much I missed her, of how much her death had affected me and changed me fundamentally as a person. I hated the man who killed her. He'd destroyed a part of me when he took her life and I'd destroyed the rest when I'd found him. I'd crossed a line I never thought I would, and as much as it had left its mark on me, what I'd done to that man, I'd do it again ten times over. Maybe that was the real issue. I didn't really feel the guilt I knew I should. And not only that but I'd relished it. I still took satisfaction from knowing that, every second of every day, he suffered in a hospital bed for what he did to my mother. A quality that made me question myself as a good, wholesome mother but that made me confident when going toe-to-toe with the likes of Davey O'Leary and Rita Regan.

My mother's death left a gaping hole inside me and when Jamie and I lost our baby, tearing me apart all over again, I thought it would swallow me whole. But then Abbie was born, followed by Sarah, and that hole began to heal. For the first time since I was a teenager, I felt complete. I felt like I belonged somewhere. That was until I started to question every single decision I made as a mother. I so desperately wanted to do every little thing right, but by the time one baby became two, I felt as if everything I did was wrong. I would lie awake in bed every night wondering what I could have done better. Was I doing the right thing breastfeeding? Would Abbie resent the time I spent feeding her sister? Should I be letting them sleep in our bed?

I questioned everything I did, because I wasn't sure who I was. Not really. How could I be trusted to make choices for them, to guide them, when I didn't even know who I was myself? It was yet another time in my life when I desperately yearned for my mother. I couldn't ask her for advice about parenting; I felt as though I'd been left to grope blindly in the dark. The few things I could remember, I could pass down. But how my mother had raised me in the early years was gone, forever.

Returning to Ireland last week, it had frightened me how easily I'd fallen back into some of my old ways, my old mannerisms, even my old thought processes. It had made me question who I was, more than ever before.

I stood and added some hot water from the kettle to my half-empty cup of tea. Sitting back down at the table, I pulled out my phone and sent a quick message to Christopher to let him know I'd arrived safely. Then I scrolled through the messages with no name, only a series of numbers, my thumb hovering over the keyboard. I was meeting Jamie at midday. There was no need to contact him, the arrangements had been made, the details were there in the last message he'd sent. So why was I sitting here thinking of messaging him? What exactly did I want to say? I locked my phone and threw it down on the table. I put my head in my hands. That feeling in the pit of my stomach at the thought of seeing Jamie later was nerves, nothing more. Wasn't it?

I had been so naive about undercover work, assuming I would find it easy to differentiate between right and wrong, good and bad. And, for the most part, it was. But in those small moments when the lines blurred, when I couldn't see my enemies in my friends, or the villainy in those I considered family, that was when everything became dangerous, when it all went wrong.

Falling in love with Jamie had been the first sign that I couldn't keep the lines clear in my head. I'd lied to myself for a long time about how I really felt about him. He was my easiest route in, straight to the centre of Martin's inner circle, and I did everything I needed to make sure he wanted me, that he trusted me, that he wouldn't just let me observe his world but allow me to become a part of it. Exactly how Europol had told me to do it. The way he made me feel had nothing to do with it. It was merely a side effect of the mission. At least, that's what I told myself.

Despite my denial, I fell in love with him. Head over heels in love with him. Maybe I would have tried to get out of the undercover game sooner if it hadn't been for Jamie. But I didn't. I stayed because I wanted to, not just because it was the job I'd signed on for.

No doubt Silva and Ryan had been happy that my hormone-saturated self had become so involved in the world they'd wanted me to infiltrate. I was an investment, as far as they were concerned. One they were eager to make a maximum return on.

When I first realised the lines had blurred beyond all recognition, I'd tested the waters. Mentioned the idea of me stepping away from the undercover work in one of my update letters to them. That's when they had brought up Brian Walsh and the lengths they had gone to in making sure that what happened to him didn't rebound on me. The letter had been dressed up as an 'intel update', but I saw it for the threat it was.

26

Driving through the same multi-storey car park where I'd abandoned my first rental car, I scanned the level where I'd parked previously. The car was gone. Hopefully, it had made its way back to the rental company. Continuing onto the next level to find a space, I hoped I'd have the opportunity to return this car myself.

I pulled my long grey wool coat tighter around me, shivering as I made my way into the heart of the city, despite the warmth the afternoon sun had brought.

There would be no private meeting for me and Jamie. I reasoned that it was a strategic move. He was the same Jamie I'd remembered when we ran into each other last week, but last week I had been his ex-fiancée – the woman who had left him, but he understood why. This week, I was the woman who'd betrayed him, who'd used him to get close to his boss, and lied to him for the entire six years we were together. That was why, this week, the Jamie I was about to meet could be an altogether different man.

But that wasn't the only reason for the public meeting. There was a part of me that hoped that sitting across from Jamie in a noisy, bustling Starbucks would keep me focused. Keep my mind firmly on the task at hand and keep me rooted in the present. I couldn't allow myself to become absorbed in the past, to look at him and remember everything we'd once had together. There could be no distractions.

I pushed open the heavy glass door of the busy coffee shop and made my way inside. I couldn't see him, but I knew he was there somewhere; he'd have selected a good vantage point with as much privacy as the place allowed.

I didn't look for him right away. Instead, I went straight to the counter to order a great big cup of caffeine in whatever form they cared to give me.

Turning around with my coffee in hand, I saw him. He was sitting in the corner at a small table, facing the counter. His eyes were trained on me and, for the briefest second, when our eyes met, I paused. In that one moment, seeing him sitting there in such an innocuous place, flashes of our life together played through my mind, and I remembered how much I'd loved him, how much I'd wanted a life with him, and how devastated I'd been when I realised that would never happen. I blinked, and I was back in the coffee shop with people impatiently pushing around me.

Jamie noticed my hesitation, and from the look on his face I could tell he'd gone to the same place as me. Remembering the life we'd had together and mourning what we'd lost.

'Thank you,' I said, by way of greeting. I set my coffee cup down on the table, across from his matching one, before taking the seat opposite.

He raised his eyebrows in a question.

'For meeting me,' I elaborated, taking a tentative sip of my hot coffee and trying to gather all the thoughts that had scattered the second I'd seen him.

'No problem,' he answered, smiling as he reached for his own cup.

I took a deep breath. Might as well dive right in.

'What do you know?' I asked, watching him carefully. I needed to assess his reaction to everything I said. I needed to gauge how he really felt about me after finding out the truth. He was in a position where he could help me – but he could also hurt me, if that was what he wanted.

'Everything.'

I couldn't help but wince at the sad look that creased his face.

'Rita told me everything when she came back from Donegal.'

My stomach clenched at the mention of Rita's name. Had this all been a huge mistake, thinking I could come to Jamie, thinking that just because he had loved me once, I could trust him now? Was I a complete idiot? No, but I was desperate, and without his help I was completely on my own. That dark, lonely feeling pushed down on me again but I had to ignore it and keep going while I still could.

'Why didn't you tell me last week?' he asked.

'I didn't realise anyone knew. It had been nearly five years without even a whiff of anyone finding out.' I took another sip of my coffee. 'I honestly thought someone – Davey, most likely – had taken Sarah to mess with me and get me back on Martin's radar, just to stir shit. I never imagined this.'

Jamie nodded, but he didn't speak.

'I'm sorry, I, I was just . . .'

'Doing your job?' he finished for me. 'I get it, don't worry. I understand what it's like to have to do things for your job.'

It had never before occurred to me that Jamie had any qualms about what he did. He'd seemed to relish the anarchy of the life he immersed himself in. But, then again, I must have, too. No one had ever suspected that I didn't enjoy what I did, so I guess it worked both ways.

I sat back in my seat, both hands wrapped around the hot mug, and looked at him, really looked at him.

Could he be someone other than the man I always thought he was? I knew, or at least I thought I did, that he was one of those good bad guys. He was kinder, nicer, less inclined to cause anyone serious harm, unless absolutely necessary, but ultimately he was a criminal, by choice. Yes, I may have been swallowed whole by the criminal world, but the only reason I'd entered its mouth in the first place was because I'd been undercover. What was his excuse? And while he may have loved me in the past and been willing to do anything for me, I'd seen him turn on people for a lot

215

less than tricking him into a relationship and masquerading as his lover for six years.

I would need to tap into those feelings he once had for me, if I could. I hated myself for it, but I needed him on my side, and I'd do whatever I could to make sure he was.

Before I could say anything else, he spoke again.

'I must hand it to you, though, you sure had me fooled.' He sat back in his seat.

His eyes hardened, and I realised I was about to be on the receiving end of the Jamie O'Leary that so many people were afraid of.

'I mean, not many people can fuck like that and not mean it.'

'Not many people have a skill set as particular as mine,' I answered with a small smile, looking him straight in the eyes.

'I don't know. Are your acting skills really that good?' His eyes wandered over me.

I resisted the urge to pull my coat across me and instead leaned forward, allowing the low V-neck of my black jumper to inch even lower.

'No. I didn't need my acting abilities for everything.'

Jamie smiled, putting his elbows on the table and leaning towards me. 'What do you need from me?'

I pulled the white card from my pocket, but this time I laid it in front of a different brother, and this time it wasn't blank.

'He knows where I live, Jamie.'

Jamie raised his eyebrow. 'You think he didn't know that all along?'

My eyes widened but I couldn't find the words to respond to that revelation.

'So, you've got a summons,' Jamie nodded. 'How can I help?'

I blinked, trying to gather my thoughts once again.

'Find out what he plans to do with me? I need to know if this summons is to make a deal or if it's an execution. I need to know how to play this.'

He didn't answer. Instead, he continued to stare at me from across the table.

'Please?' I added.

'And what exactly is in it for me?' he asked, with a smile. 'The satisfaction of helping an old friend?'

'What if I promise that if I get the opportunity to kill Martin, I'll take it.'

The smile fell from Jamie's face as he sat forward in his seat. 'You know that's a death sentence.'

'And you know that I might have no other choice,' I answered, edging forward in my seat.

He looked down at the table, considering what I'd said.

'And with Martin gone, I could take his place.' It wasn't a question; Jamie was telling himself.

I reached out and took his hand resting on the table. 'Or you could leave?'

He looked up at me, something like hope in his eyes, and I hated myself for not phrasing it better, that I didn't mean with me.

'You could get out of this life, find someone, have a family,' I rushed to clarify. 'Be free. With Martin gone, no one would stop you.'

Whatever hope had been in his expression melted away. It was only small changes; his eyes narrowed slightly and dimmed, his jaw tightened, and the corner of his lips turned down just a fraction.

'We both know there's no life outside of this one for me, Maeve, and you don't have to make me any deal.' He adjusted himself in his seat. 'I was always going to help you.'

I raised an eyebrow at him. 'Why? After everything I did to you – all the lies.'

Jamie shrugged. 'I also know that none of us ended up behind bars. And I'm not a fool, Maeve, I know what we had was real. That may not have been your plan, but I know you loved me.'

I nodded. 'I did. I truly did.'

Jamie smiled, but there was so much sadness in his eyes that I had to look away, down at my coffee cup.

'And besides, I owe you that much,' he said.

My head snapped up, confused.

'To help you save your family, after everything you lost because of me,' he clarified.

I winced at the crack in his voice as he spoke. 'Jamie, what happened, the baby, none of that was your fault. You have to stop blaming yourself.'

'Maybe one day,' he said quietly, before standing up suddenly. 'Why don't we go get something stronger to drink?'

27

The second I returned to the lodge I threw my keys onto the kitchen table and engaged all the locks on the door, including the deadbolt. I started to strip, shedding clothes as I made my way to the small bathroom to take a very hot shower. I needed to wash off everything that had occurred beneath the fluorescent lights in the coffee shop and the low lighting of the bar that we retreated to afterwards. It didn't feel right. I loved my husband very much, I shouldn't have agreed to a drink with Jamie. Our business had been done, I should have left then, but he'd looked so broken when I'd mentioned the baby.

One whiskey in and the conversation began to flow easily and led to reminiscing about the past.

'Do you remember your first time in The Pirate Rooms, when one of the Keane boys thought you were an easy target to get to me?' Jamie asked, his arm resting on the back of the bench seat behind me.

I reached forward to pick up my Jameson. 'Oh, I remember.' I took a drink from my glass. 'It took weeks for those bruises he left on my neck to fade. The prick,' I added, returning my glass to the table and turning to look at Jamie, who was closer than he'd been before I reached for my drink.

He moved closer still. 'Well,' he said, laughing, 'I'm sure they faded long before any of the bruises you gave him.'

I laughed. 'True.'

Jamie shifted another inch towards me, and for one second I thought he was going to kiss me. When he continued moving forwards, I realised he was only reaching for his drink.

'And the mortification of pissing himself in front of the entire patronage of the club on a Friday night definitely took longer to fade.'

We were both laughing as he leaned forward again to return his glass. This time, he didn't move back in his seat fully, and we were suddenly face to face. So close that I could smell his Dior Sauvage aftershave. The same one he always wore. I was back in our bedroom, watching him in the en-suite as he stood, shaving topless in front of the mirror, me admiring how the muscles of his back rippled with the movement of his arm.

The gap between us started to close. I couldn't tell if he was moving towards me or I towards him. Involuntarily, I licked my lips as I looked at his. I was suddenly very aware that we were pressed together, side by side. But then I was at another bathroom door, watching another man shave; observing my husband as he picked up our daughter to sit her beside the sink. I could hear her laughter as he dabbed her nose with shaving foam.

221

Standing up, I knocked what whiskey was left in both glasses across the table. Mumbling apologies, I walked out of the bar and back to my car. Jamie didn't follow.

By the time I got to the bathroom now, I was naked. I pulled the cord, reached in to hit the power button, and the shower burst to life. Turning the dial all the way up to red, I allowed the small bathroom to fill up with steam before stepping in under the scalding water. I didn't turn down the dial, just stood there for a long time, letting the water wash everything away. All the dirt and grime from travelling, and the lingering taint of shame for what I almost did to Christopher.

Towelling myself off, I heard my phone vibrate in the pocket of the jacket I'd discarded on the kitchen floor. I wrapped the towel around myself and went to get it. A text message from a familiar series of numbers.

—*He's angry but planning on making a deal tomorrow. DO NOT aggravate him, come unarmed.*

Relief flooded through me. Martin *had* summoned me to make a deal. This wasn't an execution. I would do anything to protect my family. And now that I knew he was willing to make a deal, I finally felt as if I had some semblance of control for the first time since seeing that empty car seat.

I was starting to breathe a little easier as I reread the message. 'Come unarmed.' Something tightened back up in my chest.

I could trust Jamie, couldn't I?

28

Then

Jamie arrived back at the townhouse later than usual. He could have been home earlier, but he'd gone for a drink instead. Coming home wasn't as exciting as it had once been. There would be no one running to greet him or jumping into his arms. It had been a month since they had lost the baby, and Maeve had become withdrawn. Throwing herself into work and making sure she was in the thick of the most dangerous situations. She blamed him; he could see it when she looked at him. She insisted she didn't, that she only blamed herself, but that was even worse. Either way, he blamed himself entirely.

He'd tried to console her with the fact that she'd only been nine weeks pregnant and they could try again, but that wasn't the right thing to say. That was when Jamie realised that the moment she'd seen that positive pregnancy test, the very moment the tiny word 'pregnant' appeared in the little window, she'd considered herself a mother. And it had all been taken away from her. *He* had taken it from her.

A spontaneous miscarriage. The doctor had said it could have happened even if she'd been at home on the couch.

But she hadn't been at home on the couch. She'd been on the floor of a bar, where he had pushed her down, with a gun pointed at her. It was difficult not to consider it the cause, not to blame it, to blame the life they led. To blame him. Why wouldn't she blame him? He blamed himself. He shouldn't have taken her there. Shouldn't have allowed her to be anywhere near the bar while he threatened Liam Daily Jr. And he shouldn't have underestimated him either. He should have walked in, dropped the card and all that it meant, and taken off.

He'd been a fool. But now he knew, he'd do better. He'd take care of her. Next time.

But when he came home that night and read the letter she'd left for him on the mantelpiece, he knew there would be no next time.

Jamie,

I love you, you know that. But that doesn't matter anymore. I can't stay here. I've lost myself, and now I've lost so much more. Don't come after me, don't look for me. If you love me, you'll let me be.

Stay safe. Mind yourself.

I'm so sorry.

Maeve

And that was it. Maeve was gone. Just like that, he was alone, and the future he had envisioned for himself had disintegrated. He'd lost everything.

'Fucking bitch!' he screamed, catching the coffee table and sending it flying towards the dresser where Maeve had arranged an array of framed photographs, each showing the two of them in varying states of happiness.

After taking a moment to settle himself, he walked over to the mess he'd created. Only one framed photograph had remained intact and it was lying on the ground. He tilted his head at the two grinning faces looking up at him, allowing himself a small smile before raising his boot and smashing it down on top of them.

29

Now

Walking through Cork City the next morning, I felt almost naked. Despite the dark green, heavy-knit jumper, jeans and boots shielding me from the ever-cooling November air, the lack of a single weapon hidden anywhere on my body made me feel as if I was navigating St Patrick's Street with my breasts out and my ass on display.

I had intended sitting in a coffee shop, passing the morning by contemplating every possible deal Martin might be willing to make, but the nervous energy buzzing through me wouldn't allow me to sit still, and the thought of being confined indoors made me feel anxious. Instead, after a quick call to check in with Christopher, and finding out that the girls were just fine, I walked the city streets hoping I looked like your average window shopper and not someone about to meet the biggest criminal in the country. I kept my check-ins with Christopher brief, yesterday and this morning, feigning being on a roll with sorting my mother's house.

I almost laughed, watching all the other shoppers rushing here and there, as if they had the most important tasks in the world to do, oblivious to what really mattered. They hadn't a clue what was going on around them. I had an overwhelming urge to grab a passing woman, pushing a buggy, who was so absorbed in her phone that she paid no heed to the baby crying for a dummy hanging from a clip over the side of the buggy, out of reach. I wanted to shake her, to scream at her and tell her to wake up. The urge passed, and so did the woman, baby still crying, small arms reaching uselessly over the buggy.

At 10:45 a.m. my phone vibrated, causing me to jump. *Get a grip*, I warned myself, irritated by my lack of composure.

I pulled the phone from my pocket. It was Jamie.

—*All's good. No sudden change of heart. See you on the other side.*

I really hoped I was doing the right thing, trusting Jamie. If I was wrong about him, I could be walking into a trap in a little over an hour. *Too late now*, I thought, once again very aware that there was no comforting, familiar weight hidden anywhere on my body.

Walking through the city and seeing how many shop names had changed, how the restaurants had become fast-food places and the bistros turned into ice-cream vendors, I thought that behind it all they were probably the same.

The same people working behind the same counters, just selling something different. And I knew that behind some, under the cover of respectable establishments and honest businesses, there was still a rotten core, where money was washed and drugs were sold. The quiet cancer that only ever showed up as an occasional lump in some leaked, watered-down news story giving people the briefest glimpse of what happens in their city.

The Harmada Hotel was a fifteen-minute walk away, and I wasn't meeting Martin until twelve, but that's the direction in which I started walking. My feet treading the same path I'd taken, time and time again, because, unless I wanted to take a ridiculously convoluted route on my way to the hotel, I would walk right past my old house. The same house I'd told Christopher I was coming here to clear.

There were times during my six years undercover when I walked past my old house and stood outside the door. I knew I wouldn't go in, but sometimes when I was feeling strong I thought maybe I would next time. Maybe then I'd finally face my demons in that house and visit the part of me that died in there, that day, along with my mother.

Before I had a chance to stop myself, I was on my old street and standing in front of the terraced grey-brick house I grew up in. I ran my hand down the faded green door, feeling the pattern of the wood grain beneath my fingertips. Little pieces of green paint flecked off and fell to the ground. I smiled, remembering how I could taste, as well as smell, the

228

cheap, toxic paint, as my mother and I brushed it on. We'd joked that one of us would probably grow an extra limb by the time we'd finished.

I stood there, staring up at the home that made me who I am, wondering when I would finally find the courage to go inside, when I experienced an unexpected urge to say goodbye to the home I'd shared with a woman who had been an incredible mother – someone I could only dream of replicating. Maybe it was because there was a part of me that knew this might be my last chance to open the door to the past and the memories of the mother I missed each and every single day, no matter how much time passed.

There was a part of me that knew I wasn't, and would never be, even half the mother she had been. My mother had been an inherently good person, while deep down I was, well, 'good' definitely wouldn't be the adjective I'd choose to describe myself. I hoped that devoting every moment I could to raising my girls would go some way to help me atone for the sins of my past, but it didn't seem to matter. Nothing could change what I'd done.

I unhooked the neglected key from my key ring. It was stiff, but with some brute force, the key eventually turned in the lock. I stood there, staring at the door, still closed but now unlocked. Sixteen years. My mother had been gone for sixteen years. I'd been without her as long as I'd had her in my life. Something inside me broke a little more at that realisation. A tear slid down my face and I let it sit there for a moment as I took in the magnitude of what I was about to do. As more tears threatened to follow, I brushed my hand across my face and pushed my way through the door and back into my childhood.

At first, everything was exactly as I remembered it, like stepping into the middle of a memory, but as I adjusted to my surroundings and noticed the thick layer of dust covering every inch of the entranceway, the memory dulled. The vivid colours I remembered from my childhood were now muted; the brightly coloured, mismatched tiles that filled the wide hallway leading to the kitchen at the back were greyer than I remembered. Muscle memory made me place my key in the blue glass bowl on the hall table to my right, allowing me to glimpse my reflection in the dusty mirror – the mirror I'd looked in a thousand times over the years, though it had never seen me like this. I wasn't just older, with faint lines beginning to settle on my forehead. I had gone through more profound changes. It had never seen me as an agent, as a criminal, as a wife, or as a mother.

As I made my way down the hallway, I passed the door to the living room on my left and the stairs on my right, and went straight to the kitchen. I paused at the closed door and looked through the frosted glass at the distorted version of the room beyond. Suddenly, I was sixteen again and on the other side was my mother, lying on the ground by the kitchen table. My hand shook as I wrapped my fingers around the thin, curved golden handle; I could swear that through the warped view, she really was lying there.

'Mammy.' The word escaped my mouth in a whisper.

It was a weak echo of the word I'd screamed, over and over, as I cradled her head on my lap and begged her to wake up. I hadn't called her Mammy for years before that day, having resorted to calling her by her name at times. Something she hated.

'I'm not Gail to you. To you I'm Mammy or Mam,' she'd warn me.

Why had I wasted all those opportunities to call her my mother? Thinking I was a grown-up when, the moment I was without her, I wanted nothing more than for her to hold me and sing to me softly, caressing my hair.

Stepping into the kitchen now, my breath caught in my chest. There was no body, the blood had long since been cleaned away, and the chairs were tucked in neatly under the table.

I went to where she'd been. The last place I'd seen her before she was inside a glossy, hard wooden box. I dropped to my knees and lay down on my side. Just how she'd been, facing the door. Had she lain there staring at it? Hoping I was about to walk through and save her? I closed my eyes, feeling my body become colder and colder as the warmth was leeched from me by the cold tiles.

I started gasping, trying to swallow down air, urging my body to remember what it needed to do to keep breathing.

No, this wasn't a good idea. I shouldn't be here; I didn't need to be here. How could I face my past when my future was so precarious? I opened my eyes.

I stayed where I was, looking around me, desperately searching for something, anything, to keep my mind from seeing my mother as she bled out. As I moved my gaze towards the corner of the room, I noticed something poking out from underneath the fridge. Pulling myself up onto all fours, I crawled over and reached my hand beneath the fridge door, grasping it with my fingertips. It was a piece of folded-up paper. I sat up and rested my back against the fridge as I unfolded it. My mother's neat, sloping handwriting filled the page.

It took a few moments before my vision cleared enough to read the words.

> *Maeve,*
> *I have to go out. If I'm not here when you get home go straight to Marnie's and wait for me there. I'll come and get you. Do not, under any circumstances, stay here on your own. This is very important. Do not stay here. Please.*
> *Love you always,*
> *Mammy x*

That was all it said. My eyes roamed over the words, again and again, trying to make sense of them. The sentence 'Do not stay here' was underlined twice. How old was this letter?

Had she written it the day she died? If she had, what did it mean? So many questions ran through my mind. I didn't even have half-baked answers I could supply. None of this made any sense.

I folded the note and slowly slid it back under the fridge. Maybe she had written it long before she died, at some point when she'd been angry with me and didn't want me lounging about the house unsupervised. Those moments were rare, though, and I certainly couldn't remember a time when she'd asked me to wait at Marnie's until she got home.

I needed to get out of here, away from the awful memories, from that note, which was making me break out in a cold sweat for a reason I couldn't quite put my finger on.

I backed out the door into the hall, afraid that if I looked away, or blinked and looked back again, my mother would be there, pale and cold. I hurried back to the front door, locking it behind me as I stepped out into the city. I pulled my jacket tight around my body and made my way along the quays, hurrying to make a deal with the Devil.

30

I looked across the river at the expanse of glass, reflecting the city back at me. There it was, The Harmada Hotel. The walk from my childhood home hadn't been long enough to settle my nerves. I was also acutely aware that I was following in my mother's footsteps, tracing the path she'd taken so many times en route to her job as a receptionist at the very hotel I was about to enter.

Pausing a moment, I took in the sight of the hotel across the water. I wasn't here to dive back into my past and get lost there. I was here to do everything I needed to make sure my family's future was safe.

At that realisation a strange, almost inappropriate, sense of calm settled on me, like walking out into a cold misty morning and becoming a part of the weather.

Gripping the cold metal of the bridge railing, I leaned over and, for a long moment, stood there staring at the warped reflection of the old stone bridge, speared by grey metal poles along the length of it, all linked together by a smooth, curved handrail. My blurry reflection looked trapped behind those bars.

I stepped back. It was time to go.

'Right this way, ma'am,' the young receptionist said, as she rounded the desk and began walking towards the lift.

I bristled at being called 'ma'am' but, to be fair, I was probably ten years her senior. That didn't make me want to slap her any less, however. I wondered if she knew about the toxic things that happened within the walls of this hotel. Probably not. People didn't like to look too hard if there was a possibility of finding out something they didn't want to know.

I thought the receptionist was about to accompany me into the lift, but instead she stepped inside, swiped a plastic card and typed in a code on the keypad, before stepping back out.

'The lift will open up in the penthouse suite for you now, ma'am.' She smiled, before adding, 'Enjoy.'

I attempted to return her smile, but as the lift doors closed, I could have sworn her smile turned to a smirk. Huh, maybe she knew more than I gave her credit for. That made me feel less guilty for wanting to slap her.

As promised, the lift went straight to the top floor. By the time it stopped, I realised I'd been holding my breath. I only released it when the doors opened into a long empty hallway leading to a large, high-ceilinged room.

There was no noise, no sign that anyone was around, but I knew he was here, somewhere. Waiting for me.

I kept my breathing steady. Martin was a criminal, yes, but he was also a sadist, and his most dangerous quality was that he could read people in a second. He could tell what they wanted, and how far they'd go to get it. A talent that had served him well over the years. There wouldn't be much need to read me, though. That was the price of having a family; your cards were always laid out on the table, in plain view, for everyone to see and use against you. But how Martin would do it, how he'd use the cards against me, remained to be seen. What I did know was that he was imaginative and inventive, and that terrified me.

As I rounded the corner into the open-plan suite, there he was, looking as innocuous as an accountant sitting behind his enormous mahogany desk. His hair had lightened to a mousy brown and I could see that he was greying around the temples. But he was still recognisable as the Martin I once knew – small and lean, not immediately intimidating, but when you looked closer you could see he was wiry. Martin Mulvihill, the most dangerous man in the country, and here I was standing right in front of him, unarmed and completely at his mercy.

There was no one else around, no lackey to pat me down or watch his back, but I knew Killer Kev must be somewhere nearby. He always was. Martin sat there, scrolling through something on the big screen of his iMac. A regular busi-nessman doing regular business.

Only he wasn't. It may as well have been Satan himself sitting there. The moment my eyes absorbed the scene and my brain processed the image of his face, all the other times I'd seen him flashed through my mind in a strange series of stills, pausing on one memory in particular. Him grinning, with a leg raised over the head of a young man, barely into his twenties, who'd 'misplaced' ten grands' worth of cocaine, before he shattered his skull into such tiny pieces that his brain matter was spattered on every available surface, me included. I could see that sick, serene smile on his face when he'd finished as he used his tongue to dislodge the clump of bloodied brain matter stuck to his bottom lip.

'Maeve, thanks so much for coming,' he said now, turning his head towards me before pulling his watery-blue eyes away from the computer screen.

'You sound like I'm here for a job interview.' I stood calmly in front of him, my back straight, despite the intense panic that spread through me when I had his complete and undivided attention focused upon me.

He sat back in his chair; his hands were clasped loosely on his lap.

'You already have a job with me, or did you forget?'

I swallowed as quietly as I could, my mouth dry.

'I—' I began, but he cut me off.

'Although it appears mine wasn't the only payroll you were enjoying.'

As much as I wanted to, I didn't look away. I kept eye

contact with his intense stare. I would not be ashamed, and I wouldn't be apologetic. I had done my job, and I had done it well. Besides, if Martin sensed any hint of shame from me, he would play with it, push it, until it became something he could grasp and squeeze and mould into something he could use against me.

'Oh, you know,' I planted a small smile on my face, 'I like to be kept busy.'

Martin's nostrils flared, but the pleasant smile on his tanned face remained fixed in place.

'And now you're back, stirring up trouble again.'

'It wasn't like I had much of a choice,' I snapped, and immediately regretted it. I held my breath, waiting for the consequences of my outburst.

There was no worse situation I could imagine being in. Without a doubt, if it wasn't for my family I would have been on the first plane I could find, heading to the furthest, most remote destination possible, as soon as I'd heard Martin had found out the truth about me, about who I was. What a luxury it would have been to only have myself to think about. I hadn't appreciated it enough when I was the only person I needed to keep alive and breathing.

'There's always a choice, Maeve,' Martin smiled. 'Although, to be fair, you left me with very few when you ran around my island drawing so much attention to yourself.'

Only Martin could have had my child kidnapped and then acted as if I were the one completely in the wrong.

Implying that I should have gone about finding my daughter in a more appropriate manner, to avoid his summons. We both knew that was bullshit. From the second he found out I'd been working undercover, he was going to have me here in front of him, sooner or later.

We stood like that for a few moments, staring silently at one another. I jumped when he finally spoke again.

'I suppose you're here to beg for the lives of your small ones and that yoke you married?'

There would be no pretences. I knew him, who he was and what he was capable of, so there would be no need for him to be anything other than himself with me.

'I'll do anything.' It was time to be serious now. No more bullshit. I *would* do anything, so I may as well offer it straight away.

'Anything? Now, that's an offer to be considered.' Martin sat back in his chair, the leather squeaking under his weight.

I remained perfectly still, afraid that any movement would trigger him, would cause that nasty psychopathic mind of his to click into place and concoct something even more horrific for me.

'You cost me a lot of money, you know.'

I nodded. There was no justifying what I did. Not to him.

'They nearly even stuck me with jail time.'

I nodded again.

'But it seemed their key witness backed out last minute,' he smiled, folding his arms. 'I presume I've your elder daughter to thank for that sudden change of heart.'

And again, I nodded.

'Fortunately for you, I'm willing to make a deal.'

I didn't nod, I didn't move. I was afraid to even breathe in case he changed his mind. I stood there waiting for him to continue.

'The way I see it, Maeve, you were a good employee. And I imagine you'd be even better without any ties to the Gardaí and Europol.'

I resumed my nodded replies.

'And like you said, you'll do anything?' he asked.

'I will.'

'Then it's very simple. Prove you're no longer working undercover for the Gardaí and then pay off your debt, everything you cost me, by returning to work exclusively for me.'

This was one of the scenarios I'd played out in my head. A deal I thought he might make. We both knew I would never clear that debt. I'd work for Martin until I was no longer of use to him. But this would also mean—

'And obviously you'll cut all ties to your family. Never see them again. If you do, they die.'

And there it was. The real punishment. The quid pro quo he'd been itching to add. But I hadn't walked into this office oblivious to what a deal with Martin would entail. I was always going to suffer, to pay for what I'd done, but at least this way my family wouldn't have to. They'd lose their mother, but that was nothing compared to what else Martin could do. I would have to deal with the devastation that part of the deal would cause me, but right now there was another aspect of the deal that concerned me.

'How exactly do you want me to prove I'm not undercover?'

'How about a hit? What better way to prove you're on my side of the law than to commit murder?'

Murder. Something that would push me firmly over the line – from the side of the righteous to the evildoers – and destroy the last remnants of my soul.

'Who?' I couldn't help but wince at how brittle my voice sounded.

Martin noticed the edge of panic in my question, baring his teeth at me as his smile grew.

'Now, that's the part that I think might interest you the most.'

This wouldn't be good.

'You see, the person I need dead is actually the very one who gave me the information that has you standing here in front of me today.'

Something inside me stilled. My soul? My morals? My conscience? Whatever it was, it stopped bucking and warring inside me, no longer desperate to find another way. Instead, another part of me, a part I didn't even know existed until my mother was killed, stirred and lit a fire in my gut. The possibility that I could buy my family's protection by taking out the very person who had put them in danger in the first place appealed to me more than I cared to admit.

Every foul deed I'd committed for Martin had changed me, stained me in some irreparable way, and while adding murder to that, especially now that I was a mother, seemed wrong, if it was something I had to do, then I would.

'Why?' I asked, hoping I wouldn't anger him. You never knew when you could or couldn't question Martin.

Martin pressed his hands together, as if he was about to pray, placed his elbows on the desk in front of him and leaned forward.

'Well, while I want you back in my employ, I'd rather it didn't get out that I was fooled by you so entirely. As it stands, only you, me, Rita and the O'Leary boys know about you.' He tilted his head, looking at me as if he was trying to see something he had missed all those years ago that would have warned him about who I was. 'Trust me when I say it's in your best interests that it's kept that way. This man sold me the information and, from what I hear, he's currently desperate for cash. I don't want him selling it to anyone else.'

I looked down at the floor for a moment. This was it; this was what I needed to do. To save my family, to make sure they were safe. This was what I had to do. And, for my family, I would do it. Like I said, I'd do anything.

'Who is it?' I asked again.

'Does it matter?' He folded his arms. It was a challenge more than a question.

I shook my head. 'You have yourself a deal.'

Martin's smile turned into an outright grin. 'Don't want some time to think about it?'

'No,' I answered firmly.

'Very good.' He stood holding his hand out towards me. The businessman concluding a business deal.

I stepped towards him and gave him my hand. He didn't shake it, just squeezed it. Firmly. Painfully. Watching my eyes for a reaction. I gave him none.

The deal we had just made was a tentative one. I had worked for the Gardaí – the same police force he had laughed at for their inefficacy – and they had not only managed to infiltrate his organisation but his inner circle. One laugh, one snigger from the wrong person would be all it'd take for him to gut me in public for all to see and learn from. A warning to others: to the Gardaí, to Europol, to any other agents hiding in the ranks of the Irish criminal world. I would need to be a good little worker bee. Do everything I was told, and make sure the information about my indiscretion went no further.

'Let's start with the execution, then, shall we?' he said, letting my hand drop from his grasp.

'Consider it done.' I turned to head back the way I came, desperate for the reprieve of the closed lift door, away from his searching stare. 'Send me the details.'

'Maeve.' He said my name like a command.

I knew better than to disobey. I stopped and turned, cursing myself for not waiting until I was dismissed. This was not the time to make mistakes, this was the time to obey, to be the dutiful lackey.

'I'll contact you when it's done.' A promise. A threat.

'Yes, sir.' There was no sarcasm coating my reply, only genuine compliance as I stood still and waited.

Martin allowed a few moments to pass before he spoke.

'That's a good girl,' he nodded. 'Off you go, then.'

31

Back in the lift, when the doors closed, I took a deep breath. My girls would be safe, Christopher would be safe. I'd never see them again, but they would be safe, they'd live, they'd grow up, and they'd all have one another. Martin's deal was more than I could have hoped for, and despite everything, I was grateful. Devastated, but grateful.

But what would I say to Christopher, to stop him from coming to me? From looking for me? And never seeing my girls again? I couldn't think about any of that right now.

Despite the urge to collapse in a heap on the floor of the lift, I kept perfectly still and stood ramrod straight, unblinking, until the doors opened up on the ground floor. I made my way out of the hotel and into the fresh air. No doubt Martin could see me. No doubt he had been watching my every move on the security feed, from the moment I'd entered his hotel until the moment I left. I refused to display any emotions. I wouldn't give Martin that kind of power. My emotions were mine. They were the only thing I still had any control over.

Once I stepped outside, and started walking through the busy city streets, the need to be alone was overwhelming. There were so many thoughts swimming through my mind, but the relief that Christopher and the girls would not be harmed kept me going. I knew it was almost time to deal with the task I'd been assigned, to ensure my family's safety, but as much as I tried to calm the thoughts, I couldn't. After processing what I now needed to do, there was little space left for anything else, especially rationality. Everything that had been bubbling under the surface was threatening to unravel me completely.

Back at the lodge, I lit the fire, hoping to remove the cold sting from the air, which the central heating was struggling to cut through. I moved an armchair to sit directly in front of the fireplace. Staring at the flames, I soaked up the heat, hoping to ease the cold that had settled in my bones from the frigid evening air.

Watching the flames dance in the grate, the only source of light in the room, I allowed myself to feel everything I'd been ignoring. It was now or never.

I thought suddenly of the paperwork and the letter I'd left for Christopher in the wardrobe, and realised that I'd have to return home, just once. I couldn't let him find them, and I needed to make sure that he never wanted to see me again. Something I'd only achieve face to face. I would have to fine-tune that part of the deal with Martin, but I was sure he'd allow it. Another way of making me suffer.

What would I have to say to Christopher, to make him never want to see me, and never want me around the girls again? The thought of it made me sick. How could I do that, and also let them know that I would always think of them, that they were, truly, the greatest children any mother could ask for. To let them know that I loved them with all my heart, and always would. Thinking of how they'd react to being told their mummy was leaving, and would never come back, was when the tears started. I pulled my knees up to my chest, and, still staring into the flames, cried fat, heavy tears.

Sarah was young, much too young to understand, but she'd miss me. I knew that much. She'd look for me whenever someone came into the room, like she did now. I wondered how long it would be before she stopped doing that, before she realised that Mummy would never be the person coming through the door to pick her up and cuddle her, never be the one to comfort her when she was sad or to tuck her into bed, kiss her forehead and hold her hand until she fell asleep. Would it be days? Weeks? Months? Would she always feel like there was someone missing from her life?

I wiped my face on the sleeve of the oversized jumper I'd pulled on as I walked in the front door, turning the green fabric a darker shade with my tears. And then I thought of Abbie. Abbie was old enough to ask questions, to be hurt and upset and angry at the injustice of it all, the unfairness of not having her mother. She'd ask why, over and over, and beg for me to come back. What would Christopher say to ease her pain? They'd hate me for leaving them. I knew that, because a part of me hated my mother for leaving me – even though she'd had no say in it.

At one point, I'd thought there was nothing in this entire world that could ever keep me from my babies. When they were born, I couldn't imagine ever leaving them. I still couldn't, but I would. And there'd be no going back. My tears turned to sobs, my chest heaving as I struggled to catch my breath. My heart was breaking. I pushed my hands against my chest in an attempt to keep it together, to ease the pain, but there was nothing I could do to stop it, to keep it from hurting.

I sat crying in that armchair for hours, alternating between desperate chest-heaving sobs and silent tears that fell down my cheeks, while I watched the fire burn lower and lower. Long after the embers had burned out, leaving me in complete darkness, I got up from the armchair, my entire body aching. The tears had stopped, but only because my body could no longer produce them.

In bed, I buried myself beneath the duvet for a night of fitful sleep, filled with nightmares in which I was reaching for my children, but someone kept pulling them away, just beyond my grasp.

Early the next morning, I woke up screaming their names.

32

Washing my face in the bathroom that morning, I stopped to take in my reflection in the mirror above the sink. My face was swollen, red and splotchy, but that's not what caught my attention. It was my eyes – and the look that had settled on my face. Something had changed inside me last night. I'd mourned the loss of my family, grieved for the part of me that was a mother and a wife, and accepted that there was no going back. And that change was there, in my eyes, written across my face. Something had died inside me, and I had become hardened because of it.

I would do what I had to do. I could do it. Of course I could, if it meant keeping my family safe from Martin.

I would have to be on my best behaviour, because as much as Martin might say I'd been a 'good' employee, there was no way all this was about utilising my skill set. For Martin, this was all about control. He felt that I had played him for a fool, and so now, to regain the upper hand, he would do exactly the same to me.

I wondered what child's game his twisted mind would equate this to, and decided on Simon Says. Obey every command, every order, but make one false move, put one foot wrong, and be punished. And he'd made it very clear what my punishment would be. He wouldn't hesitate in killing my family, and I had no doubt that he would be waiting for me to mess up. Maybe he even hoped I'd reach out to my undercover contacts – although he must be confident he was burning that bridge by forcing me to murder someone.

In the kitchen, I picked up my phone from the table where I'd heard it chirping and buzzing repeatedly while I was drying my face. There was a message from Christopher, checking in and seeing how I was getting on. I typed a quick reply, saying all was fine, just a lot to go through, and asked how he and the girls were. My thumb quivered over the keypad before I typed the sentence:

—*I'll be home soon. Love you all xx*

As soon as the message was sent, I clicked on the message waiting for me from Jamie.

—*Heard a deal's been done. Congratulations? I'm sending on all the info you need for the hit. Good luck.*

I took a breath before clicking on the next message. A downloadable pdf file containing a photo and an information sheet. I flicked the kettle on, to make a cup of tea, before sitting down to read all the information I'd need to commit murder.

I zoomed in on the photo of the man I needed to kill. He

wasn't immediately recognisable as the man I'd last seen in the Cork City Library over four and a half years earlier. His sandy-coloured hair was longer, and his freckles no longer gave him the appearance of youth – now scattered across a much more tired-looking, creased face – but there he was, looking up at me from my phone, Detective Sergeant Nathan Ryan. I gripped my phone tighter with one hand and covered my eyes with the other, pressing hard against my temples, which were beginning to throb.

Martin, you bastard.

I sat like that for a moment, before taking a breath and looking back at the photo. I wondered what had happened to age him beyond the years that had passed, but then I thought of what Martin had said, how this was the person who had sold him the information about me.

Scanning through the pdf file, I read that he had sold me out to Martin for the underwhelming sum of €35,000. I slammed my phone down on the table. Thirty-five thousand. Thirty-fucking-five thousand euros! That was the value he had put not only on my life, but on the lives of my husband and children. I'd kill Ryan all right, and I wouldn't feel bad about it. He deserved to die for what he had done to me and my family.

I relished the anger building inside me, replacing all the other emotions and giving me something substantial to focus on. This was something I could use. I'd make the bastard pay for doing this to me, for putting me in this situation.

Picking up my phone again, I continued reading. There was the Eircode of a car park he would be in between 4:30 and 6:30 this evening. There was only one CCTV camera, which covered the pedestrian exit from the car park, not the actual car park itself. It was a black spot, the perfect place for a murder, provided there were no witnesses. He would most likely be unarmed. There were no guidelines or stipulations attached to the hit, aside from the cardinal rules: don't get caught, and don't leave a trail to Martin.

I banged my fists down on the table as I stood to make my way to the spare room and get ready for tonight. The table was still quivering as I kicked the spare room door closed behind me.

A combination of adrenaline and anger had me walking in and out of the rooms of the lodge, until that wasn't enough. I began pacing outside, continually lapping the house in an attempt to calm myself. I had decided to carry out the hit at 6:30 p.m., using the cover of darkness to my advantage, but I couldn't sit still and was ready to leave by 3:15. I had dressed plainly in black skinny jeans and a short black jacket, zipped up to the neck. My black wig was fixed in place, skimming the base of my jawline, above my shoulders, the full fringe licking the top of my eyebrows. I had layered up my make-up, so that it was smoky and heavy around my eyes, making me unrecognisable to Ryan, unless he looked very closely, and by the time I got that close to him I'd want him to know it was me. I strategically armed myself, my handgun easily accessible in the back of my waistband, my favourite switchblade resting in one of my jacket pockets, a piece of cable tightly wound up in the other.

The plan was to make it look like a robbery gone wrong, the usual cover for murder. An oldie but a goodie. I needed to be careful and ruthless with the kill, but not so efficient that it looked like a professional hit. That meant it had to look messy and rushed, while being anything but. It would mean a more painful death than a simple bullet to the head, but right now that was fine by me. He hadn't given me or my children a moment's thought when he sold me out, so that was the price the prick would have to pay.

I'd spent so long blaming myself for everything that it was a relief to have something else to focus on, someone else to blame for all that had happened. Better still, to have someone I could hurt, someone I could punish.

I couldn't wait any longer. I was tired of the pacing, the sitting down and standing up, the walking from room to room looking for nothing in particular. It was almost 4:00 p.m. I double-checked the information sheet, even though I already knew everything it said, word for word. He would arrive at the car park at 4:30 and leave at 6:30. I knew what I had to do. I knew how to do it. Now, I just had to go through with it.

The adrenaline pumping through me was causing my entire body to vibrate. Shaking out the tremors in my hands,

I grabbed the car keys and made for the front door. Fuck it, Detective Sergeant Nathan Ryan could die a little earlier than planned.

The car park turned out to be a small overflow car park at the back of Cork General Hospital. Parking there was straight-forward. Most people parked in the main car park to the front of the hospital, or along the streets around it, as this car park was quite a walk from the entrance and had steep concrete stairs to navigate. It was quiet, but fortunately not so quiet that I would stand out. There were ten cars scattered throughout, and a quick scout around confirmed they were all empty.

The information sheet had been right: there was only one CCTV camera, and it was pointed at the first step at the bottom of the concrete stairs. I chose my parking space care-fully, between two parked cars, where I had a clear view of every car that came and went through the barrier and every person who climbed or descended the staircase.

I was confident that all I needed to do was make sure no cars were entering via the barrier and that no one was returning to their car from the hospital grounds at the wrong time. Both were easy enough to monitor. I could carry out the hit right here and leave him in his car, to be discovered after I was long gone. There wouldn't even be a need for me to dump the car, something which, more often than not, drew more attention than it avoided.

My restlessness eased. This was a straightforward, simple hit. There was no booby trap laid out for me from Martin – but then why would there be? *Who* I had to kill was already the extra sprinkle of nastiness that Martin had scattered on top of this particular task.

I had to murder this man and prove my loyalty to Martin. I couldn't even consider everything else that would follow – what would happen after I left this car park – because this wasn't the time for thinking about my future. This was the time to concentrate on ending Ryan's.

33

At twenty past four, the daylight started to fade and the handful of street lights surrounding the car park began to splutter into life, giving off a faint orange glow. The car park was quiet. There had been no movement in the time I had been waiting, except for a stray tomcat who had relieved himself on the bonnet of the car parked across from me. No cars had come or gone, so my ears pricked up at the low rumble of a car engine approaching and then pulling up to the entrance barrier. I leaned forward in my seat, gripping the steering wheel while using it to keep most of my face covered.

There it was. The silver 05 Toyota Corolla I'd been waiting for. I actually laughed at the sight of it. The info sheet had stated the details of his car, but it hadn't mentioned how battered it would be. He obviously hadn't used the thirty-five grand on his car. It looked like it wouldn't survive its next journey exceeding ten kilometres.

Maybe Ryan had an addiction? Drink? Drugs? Maybe he liked to spend his down time from the Gardaí at the bookies?

The anger was building inside me again. Was that what all this was for? Had he put my family at risk for the cash he needed to feed his habit? No, I would not feel any guilt after this.

Even so, I was fully aware that this interaction would soon be joining the medley of nightmares that played out in my head in the early hours of the morning, every morning, for the rest of my life.

There was no one around. No one returning to the handful of parked cars. And no security guard, who no doubt only ventured into this car park if summoned from the pay machine. I double-checked that my prepaid ticket was still sitting in the gap under the radio unit, ready to grab for a quick getaway.

Ryan parked his sorry car in the middle row. I gripped the handle of my door, ready to move the moment he did. If I was walking at a brisk pace, I could catch him before he reached the steps leading into the hospital and became visible on the CCTV. I watched, every muscle in my body tightening and preparing to move. As soon as his head appeared over the roof of his car, I pushed the door open and carefully and quietly locked the car before heading straight for him. As I approached, stepping lightly on the worn concrete to make as little noise as possible, I could see he was opening the back door and reaching in for something.

I checked my pace; it was important to catch him unaware. I couldn't risk a struggle that would draw attention to us. I crouched down next to a car, a few spaces down from his. I checked behind me to make sure there was no one watching me, then scooted to the edge of the car, where I could see Ryan's feet and move the second he did. He closed the door and locked the car, slipping the key fob into the back pocket of his jeans, then began making his way to the concrete steps.

I followed quickly, thanking the wind rustling the trees running along one side of the car park for covering any noise I made. I was only five paces behind him and quickly closing the gap, while he continued to fumble with whatever it was he'd pulled from the back seat of his car. I hadn't seen what it was from my crouched position by the car – a bag of some sorts, I presumed – but I was grateful to it for keeping Ryan's attention.

After another quick look behind me, I felt for the knife in my pocket. A swift jab to the lung would keep him quiet while I steered him back towards his car.

I was almost there, nearly at his back, knife ready and poised in my hand. Just as I was about to close the last few steps and bury the blade in him, he slung the bag he had been so preoccupied with over his shoulder; a *Frozen* backpack. I stopped and watched Anna and Elsa get further and further away.

Ryan continued on up the steps, oblivious to how close he had come to a lung full of blood, and all I could do was stand there and watch. I was paralysed.

The moment that small backpack appeared over his shoulder, I had snapped out of 'assassination mode' and back into 'mum mode'. The change was so abrupt that I couldn't move. It wasn't exactly like Abbie's – Olaf was missing from the picture, and there was a dark pink trim in place of the blue one I knew so well – but its likeness had propelled me back to our home on Redmond Row, to the countless times I had helped Abbie slide her arms through the straps before setting off to nursery.

Why did he have a child's bag with him? There had been nothing in his fact sheet about a family, which normally meant there was nothing of importance to note. That he was someone who wouldn't be missed. But that bag . . . it was, beyond any shadow of a doubt, a child's bag, and he was heading into the hospital, alone.

My muscles eventually loosened, allowing me to turn on my heel and backtrack to Ryan's car, carefully scanning the area as I went. Another car was approaching the barrier. I couldn't dawdle here, but I needed to get a look inside his car. The back windows, which I'd originally thought were blacked out, seemed to have sun visors covering them, so I moved down the side of the car to peer through the front passenger window, all the while keeping one eye on the car that was now struggling with the ticket machine. On the back seat was a car seat – a pink Minnie Mouse car seat. My heart rate picked up. He had a child – a girl. Why wasn't that on the information sheet? I turned back to the concrete steps. And what exactly was he doing here?

A heavy feeling settled on my chest as I looked at the empty car seat. I started towards the steps. I needed to find out what was going on.

34

A quick sprint up the steep steps reminded me that I'd let my fitness levels fall in recent years. Thankfully, Ryan had paused for a cigarette at the hospital entrance, in spite of the voice booming from the speakers above his head, incessantly thanking everyone for not smoking on hospital grounds. It gave me a chance to catch up with him. Pausing at the top of the stairs, I adjusted the cuff of my jeans over my boot as he smoked his last couple of drags.

Once he had stubbed out the cigarette and passed through the glass sliding doors, it was easy to track him. I looked like any other hospital visitor as I followed him past the reception area, where no one so much as glanced in our direction, and beyond the hospital gift shop towards the lifts where an older couple were already waiting for one to arrive. I pulled my phone from my jacket pocket and did my best impression of someone completely and entirely absorbed in the digital world residing inside it. I remained like that, head bowed, as we entered the lift and pressed the buttons for the floors we wanted. My eyes slid sideways as Ryan leaned forward to press the number 4 before I appeared to absent-mindedly hit the number 3.

The couple made their exit on the first floor, leaving Ryan alone with me in the lift. He was as disinterested in me as I was pretending to be in him. No attempt at small talk, not even a look in my direction as he stared at the numbers above the lift door. I was confident he wouldn't recognise me with a passing look, but I was glad not to be put to the test – not in this enclosed space.

Once the number 3 lit up, I exited the lift, head still down, eyes glued to my phone, but as soon as I heard the swoosh of the lift doors close behind me my head snapped up, looking for the sign that would show me where the stair access was. I ran up the empty stairwell. I could see the lifts through the small, lined rectangle of glass in the door leading onto the corridor. I couldn't risk being seen again. He seemed like he was in his own world, but then so did I.

In his pale blue shirt and navy chinos he looked as if he'd come straight from work, but the stubble on his face and the dark circles under his eyes suggested there was a lot more going on in his life than his Garda duties. I watched as he made his way down the corridor in the opposite direction, the *Frozen* backpack still on his shoulder. I slipped out into the corridor as he pushed through the double doors at the end of the hallway. I quickly made my way towards those same doors, eager to slip through before he took a turn I couldn't see, but the sign above them stopped me in my tracks: 'Paediatric Long-Term Care Unit'.

I could ask myself why he was here all I wanted, but I wasn't a fool. The answer was there, but I couldn't face it. There had to be something else, anything else, another reason for all of this. There had to be – because if there wasn't, I couldn't even consider it. I'd find out all the facts before I panicked. Taking a deep breath, I pushed through the heavy doors.

Ryan was about halfway down the next corridor, talking to someone at the nurses' station. There was no one else around, so I moved slowly, hovering in the background, until he had thanked the nurse and started to make his way along the corridor. I followed him, keeping my pace steady, and watched as he entered one of the rooms. I smiled at the nurse behind the desk as I passed, upping my pace to a normal walking speed. She didn't stop me, didn't even ask who I was here to visit. The lack of security almost surprised me, but then what kind of sick and twisted individual would sneak into a paediatric unit for any kind of sinister reason?

As I passed the room Ryan had gone into, I slowed, turning to make sure there was no one around. Looking through the slice of glass that ran the length of the door, I tried to glean as much as I possibly could within a few seconds. It looked like a small single-occupancy room, with what I assumed was the bathroom just inside the door on the right; further in I could see the end of a hospital bed, with a curtain half-pulled around it on the left-hand side.

I had no plan for this. I was working off my instincts; I needed to get all the facts before I could do what needed to be done. The corridor was quiet, almost eerily empty. I continued on and turned right, for no other reason than a fifty–fifty chance of finding something that would help me figure out how to get into that room. The answer was right there as I turned the corner; a room labelled 'Utility'. I walked past it and smoothly did a three-sixty, ready to feign a wrong turn, but as soon as I saw the corridor was all clear, I pushed down on the handle and quickly slipped inside. Looking for a bathroom would be my less than convincing excuse if someone happened upon me. Hitting the light switch by the door, a small room full of sheets, towels and toiletries lit up, along with a utility cart tucked in on one side of the room. On the other side was a low portable hanging rail, lined with freshly washed white tunics. Probably an emergency stash for the nurses to change into, if needed, during their shifts.

Perfect, I thought, looking down at my black jeans. They could pass for work slacks. Shrugging off my jacket, I pulled on one of the tunics, wrapped my jacket in a white towel and added it to the bottom shelf of the cart already loaded with supplies for distributing around the wards. I eased open the door and looked out to check the corridor was still clear, before pushing the cart ahead of me and making my way back to the room that held the answers I needed.

35

I knocked lightly on the door, before opening it a crack and calling out in the friendliest tone I could muster. 'Sorry to disturb you, just replenishing some bits and pieces.'

'That's okay, come on in,' a woman's voice answered.

I backed into the room, pulling the cart behind me.

'I'll start in there,' I said, gesturing towards the bathroom as I glanced at the curtain behind me, which a woman was now peering around. She smiled, a small smile that didn't touch her eyes, and nodded before disappearing back behind the flimsy, pale blue fabric.

I pushed my way into the small bathroom, making sure the door didn't fully close behind me, and immediately began to look around for clues. In a glass by the sink was a small pink toothbrush with a pink pig's head clipped over the bristles, and hanging on the back of the door was a yellow fleecy dressing gown. I rummaged for the label: 2–3 years. I stood by the door, pressed my ear to the gap, and listened. The woman was talking.

'They're going to let us know today if she'll be well enough to travel.'

'Who?' Ryan asked.

'The doctor, Nate! Who else would let us know that, for Christ's sake?'

Well, he was definitely still in here at least. And that woman did not sound happy with him.

'Sorry,' he muttered.

'Jesus, can you pay attention for two minutes, this is your daughter we're talking about, after all!' The woman was trying to keep her voice low, but she was seething.

'She's asleep. Keep your voice down. I'm sorry, okay? I'm listening.'

'If she's able to travel next week, they want her in the hospital first thing Wednesday morning, so we need to book a ridiculously early flight.'

'We should just go the night before if that's the case,' Ryan said.

'No, Nate. Every penny is going on her treatment, there's nothing left for an extra night's accommodation. We just can't—' Her voice broke off, and she started to cry quietly.

Someone moved about.

'I'm sorry, love. I'm so, so sorry.'

They were both crying now.

I'd heard enough. It suddenly felt wrong to be there, spying on this couple's grief. Pulling off the white tunic, I grabbed my black jacket from the towel and abandoned the cart, slipping out of the bathroom and, as quickly and as quietly as I could, out of the room.

In my hurry to escape all those emotions and allow the little girl's parents their privacy, I made a mistake. I didn't check the corridor was clear.

I walked straight into a nurse. *Shit*, I thought, *what do I do now?*

But the nurse smiled at me. 'Here visiting Gracie?'

I nodded. 'I was, but I think it's a bad time.'

The nurse gave a small, sad smile. 'Yeah, there are more bad days than good at the minute but, please God, this new treatment in Sweden will help the poor craythur.'

'Please God,' I repeated, before carrying on along the corridor, the nurse already lost in the paperwork she carried.

I was shaking by the time I flung myself back into my car. What was I going to do? What the fuck was I going to do? I slammed my fists into the steering wheel. That sadistic prick! Martin knew *exactly* what he was doing. He had sent me here to mess with me. He didn't just want me to kill a man with a terminally ill child, he wanted me to *know* I was killing a man with a terminally ill child. Why else would he have given me the hospital car park as the hit location? *That bastard, that evil, evil bastard.*

I dropped my face into my hands. What was I going to do? I had to kill him. For my family. To protect them. If I didn't follow through on this part of the deal, well . . . let's just say I had never seen it end well for anyone who hadn't followed through on a deal made with Martin.

All that Ryan had done to me, to my family, it had been to save his own daughter. What would his family do without him? His wife? His sick little girl? How would she get through the new treatment in a different country without her dad?

But what about *my* girls? What about *my* family?

'Fuck! Fuck! Fuck!' I screamed, slamming my fists into the steering wheel with every expletive.

What was I going to do? No answer came to me as that burning question seared itself into my brain. All I could do was sit in the car, staring at the steps I knew Ryan would eventually descend. I could only hope that instinct would kick in and take over when I saw him, that adrenaline and muscle memory would take the weight of my decisions from me.

An hour later, Ryan came back to his car, and suddenly it was as though I couldn't breathe. I felt for the gun in my waistband, pulling it out and resting it in my hand. *Just do it, Maeve.*

'Just do it,' I repeated to myself out loud. But I couldn't move, couldn't pull the door handle, couldn't get out of the car.

I couldn't take him from his family who so desperately needed him. I couldn't be the one to do that. To end his life and force even more suffering on innocent people who were already in pain. I couldn't. But what was the alternative?

Leave my children's fate to the whims of a sick, twisted bastard like Martin? *Damn him, damn him straight to hell for putting this on me, for making me choose between my family and someone else's.*

Ryan was getting close to his car. If I was going to make a move, I needed to do it soon. It was an impossible decision, but one I needed to make – now. He'd made a decision when he sold me out, when he brought that information to Martin. He'd decided to sacrifice my family for his own. An eye for an eye. I pulled the door handle.

By the time I had made my decision, Ryan was in his car, pulling out of his parking space. I rushed for the driver's window, knocked on it and gestured for him to roll down the window while doing my best impression of a woman in need of assistance.

He stopped the car immediately and rolled his window down. 'You okay, love?'

The moment the window opened far enough, I reached inside and shoved my gun into his stomach, simultaneously reaching in with my other hand and pulling the key from the ignition before dropping it to the ground.

'Who are you?' he asked, scanning my face, trying desperately to figure out if he knew me. His eyes widened. 'Maeve Deane?'

'Good to see you again, Detective Sergeant Ryan.'

A look of understanding settled on his face.

I thought there would be some satisfaction from it, from

showing him that there was a price to pay for what he'd done to my family, but his expression changed. Relief softened his features, loosened the tight skin around his jaw. I could see it; this was a way out for him. If I did it, if I killed him here and now, he wouldn't have to see his baby suffer anymore, he wouldn't have to deal with the possibility of burying his child. I'd be doing him a favour.

He'd procured the money needed for his daughter to have one last chance at life, and the most selfish part of him was happy to bow out from the harsh realities of life now. To leave, and have all the worry and fear evaporate from him with his last breath.

I couldn't blame him. In that moment, if someone came up behind me and pressed a gun to the back of my head, there was a part of me that would want them to pull the trigger, too.

'I'm sorry,' he whispered, closing his eyes and dropping his head.

Taking a deep breath, I pushed the gun harder into his stomach. I was about to do one of the most dangerous things I'd ever done, and I already knew I would live to regret it.

'Get your family out of the country and head to Sweden as soon as you can.'

His head shot up, eyes flicking to mine.

'Martin wants you dead, and the minute he finds out that you're not sitting here in this car park with your intestines hanging out, someone else will come – and your family may suffer for the inconvenience.'

His face turned white and his eyes were wide. All he could do was nod as I retracted my gun, returning it to my waistband, and bent down to retrieve his car keys.

'Maeve, I really am sorry,' he said again, as I turned to leave.

I stopped, but kept my back to him. 'Not as sorry as I'm going to be.'

'I had no choice,' he said, pathetically.

'There's always a choice,' I answered, before returning to my car and speeding off as quickly as if I'd completed the task I came there to do.

36

I'd failed. I'd messed up, and let my conscience play me for a fool. What was I going to do now? Had I just sacrificed my children and my husband? And for what? A man who was the very reason I was in this impossible position in the first place. Martin had made me a deal, and I hadn't followed through. There would be no second chance.

I returned to the lodge because I had no place else to go. There was nothing anyone could do to help me now, not even Jamie. I was out of options.

At the kitchen table, I pulled out my phone. Should I ring Christopher, tell him everything, tell him to leave, to get the girls somewhere far away, some place safe? Was there anywhere safe from Martin's reach? Would Christopher even listen to me once he knew the truth? No doubt there were people watching them this very minute. Watching and waiting to pounce, with one word from Martin. I dropped the phone on the table before running to the bathroom and vomiting into the toilet.

I was still retching when there was a knock at the back door. This was it. Time to pay the price for letting Ryan live. I wiped my mouth, and washed it out with some water from the tap, before heading to the inevitable consequence waiting for me at my back door.

Still armed from the hospital visit, I made my way back to the kitchen, but there was no fight left in me. I grabbed my phone and typed out a quick message to Christopher. There was no time for explanations, I could only pray that he'd believe me and do as I asked.

—*Christopher, I'm so sorry. I am not the woman you think I am. You and the girls are in danger. Real danger. Get out of the country, get as far away as you possibly can. Check the bottom of the wardrobe. Everything you will need is there. Clear our savings, then get yourself off grid. Start a new life with the girls. And please tell them that I love them. I always will. And I love you. I'm so sorry – Maeve.*

My finger hovered over the send button as another knock sounded on the back door. It was louder this time, and some-thing snapped in me. No, I would not give up that easily, I thought, quickly erasing the message before I could change my mind.

Flicking the phone to silent, I shoved it into my jacket pocket and went to find out who was waiting for me.

'It's you!' I couldn't keep the surprise from my voice.

'It is,' Jamie said, stepping over the threshold and walking straight past me into the kitchen.

272

He sat at the table, crossing his long legs at his ankles as he leaned back in the creaking wooden chair. I stayed at the open door, surprise stalling me. I had been so sure it was going to be one of Martin's goons, or Killer Kev himself, standing on the other side of the door.

'Might want to close that. You're letting all the heat out.'

'I don't know if Martin knows yet, but there's something I have to tell you,' I said, pushing the door closed.

'I already know,' he said, taking a cigarette packet from his pocket and pulling one out with his lips. He lit it before continuing. 'That's why I'm here.'

I moved to join him at the kitchen table, then stopped dead. Maybe Martin *had* sent someone for me. Yes, Jamie had promised to help me, but I also knew what Jamie was capable of, and how disobeying a direct order from Martin wasn't an option, whether or not he'd like to.

Jamie saw my hesitation and let out a small laugh. 'Don't worry, I saw you choke, and took care of it.' His eyes lowered to the floor. 'Martin doesn't know you baulked.'

A cold feeling spread through my body. 'What do you mean, you took care of it?'

'I mean, there is currently a shitty Corolla on fire in the overflow car park of Cork General Hospital.' He took a long drag on his cigarette and blew the smoke out in a thick line, towards the ceiling. Calm and relaxed, but I could see a weariness in his eyes.

I didn't know how to feel; relief that my family was safe,

or devastation that another family had been destroyed. My stomach turned over, again. I ran back to the bathroom, fell to my knees in front of the toilet and, despite being emptied only moments earlier, my stomach spewed its remaining contents into the bowl.

'You've gone soft.' Jamie was leaning against the door frame, a smile on his face.

'How can you be smiling right now?' I asked, looking up at him. 'Do you know what you've just done to that family?'

He raised an eyebrow in answer. 'You mean, giving them the head start they desperately need to get out of Dodge? I actually feel pretty good about it, thanks very much. Think I might even get my wings after this.'

Now, I was confused. What game was he playing? I was so sick of games.

'What are you talking about?'

'Don't you worry your soft little heart about it.'

'Jamie!'

'I knew you wouldn't be able to go through with it, if you found out about his child, okay? So I made some backup arrangements.'

'What arrangements?' I demanded, feeling as if I might need to put my face back into the toilet.

'I had another car waiting for that pig you were supposed to kill, as well as a wad of cash to speed up the process of getting him and his family out of the country.'

He took another drag of his cigarette as I pulled myself

up from the floor. He moved as if to help me, but paused, opting to stay where he was in the doorway. So that made us even – because my first instinct, when he'd told me what he'd done, was to throw my arms around him. I wanted to thank him, but when I thought about all the ways I'd once shown him my appreciation, I forced myself to keep my distance.

'I don't get it. What's your plan here?' I asked, patting my mouth dry with the hand towel after rinsing it with water from the tap. Again.

We both knew it wouldn't be long before Martin found out that there wasn't a Detective Sergeant Ryan burning inside that car.

'We need to come up with a plan. Rita said that if anything goes wrong, Martin's going straight for your children.'

We stood there staring at each other. Me absorbing his words, him allowing them to get through.

Suddenly it all became too much. A tiredness washed over me, an all-consuming exhaustion. I gripped the sides of the bathroom sink, facing the mirror, and dropped my head.

'I can't do this anymore.' I was talking to myself more than to Jamie. 'I mess up at every turn, every decision I make is wrong. I'm not capable. I'm done.' Looking up, tears were flowing down my face. Every moment of self-doubt and self-hatred that had ever plagued me clawed their way up from deep down inside me, where I desperately tried to keep them contained. I was drowning in it all. I felt that if I stayed right there, staring at myself in the small bathroom mirror, I would see myself disappear beneath all that emotion. And honestly, in that moment, I wanted to. I wanted it all to end, to be free from it all. Yes, I knew exactly how Ryan had felt with my gun pressed to his abdomen.

It was over. I'd failed. I'd killed my family, and now I wanted it all to end.

Jamie grabbed me from behind and spun me to face him, so quickly I cried out in surprise. I'd almost forgotten he was in the room, witnessing my complete and utter breakdown.

He gripped both my arms tightly, uncomfortably so, and shook me hard. 'Snap the fuck out of it, Maeve.'

I blinked up at him. 'I can't.'

He looked at me, searching for something in my face. This was not the reaction he had expected, not from Maeve Deane, his ex-fiancée and former partner.

'What do you mean, you can't? Where's the woman who never questioned herself? The woman who had almost too much confidence in herself and her decisions? Who under-stood her worth and knew her strength?' He shook me harder with every sentence, his fingers bruising my skin.

I had no answers for him. I remembered that woman, but it was like recalling someone I once knew, a very long time ago. In so many ways I'd become a better person since leaving Jamie and the life I'd become so immersed in here, in Ireland. But the person I'd become was haunted and, somehow, less than the woman I'd once been.

Jamie removed his hands from my arms and gently

pushed my chin up with his finger. 'Maeve, look at me. You need to snap out of it.'

'It's finished. I'm dead. They're dead. It's over. I was never good enough for them. How did I ever think I'd be good enough to protect them?' I pulled my head away from him as I spoke.

Jamie caught my face between his hands and forced me to look up at him. His features softened and his voice was quieter when he spoke.

'You *are* good enough for them, Maeve. Don't think you aren't, because of the life you had with me. You were doing your job. I know you did some things you'd rather forget about, but you were always good. Your girls are lucky to have a mother like you, who loves them so much.' His thumbs stroked my cheeks, wiping away the stream of tears flowing slowly down my face. He brought his face closer to mine. 'And forget about your abilities as a parent. One thing I know, with absolute certainty, is that you're more than capable of doing whatever it is going to take to protect your family.'

He was right.

'I'm so sorry—'

'Don't,' he cut me off. 'You don't have to apologise to me.'

I looked up into his eyes, and for a moment I allowed myself to think about what life would have been like if we hadn't lost our baby. Different to my life now, that was certain, but Jamie would have been a great dad.

'I really did love you,' I whispered.

He moved closer still, and his breath was warm on my lips as I closed my eyes.

I didn't know if it was relief or disappointment that flooded through me as his forehead pressed against mine, but my breath still caught in my chest at the contact.

'I know,' he whispered. 'I know.'

37

We stood like that for a long time, our foreheads pressed together, Jamie's hands warm on my face, his thumbs moving ever so slightly to caress my cheeks. I moved my hands to rest on top of Jamie's. But the second I did, he took a step back, threw his cigarette butt into the toilet and walked out, making his way back to the kitchen. A chill went through me at the absence of his body heat.

I turned back to the bathroom mirror. My eyes were swollen and my cheeks tear-stained, but it felt as if I had let go of something – something I'd been holding on to for a very long time. It was as if the act of finally acknowledging all those doubts I had about myself, bringing them to the forefront of my mind, saying them out loud, had lessened them somehow. They were still there, but something in me had changed, or perhaps changed back, and I had Jamie to thank for that. He had reminded me of who I was. I couldn't accept Jamie's confidence in my abilities as a mother, or his assurances that I was good enough for my girls, but he had reminded me that I *was* good enough to make sure they stayed safe. I *was* good enough to stop Martin, and I sure as hell was good enough to finish this, once and for all.

I washed the tears from my face and stayed staring at my reflection as I placed the towel back on the rack. I may be a lot of things, but I wasn't someone who would give up on my family. Martin had tried to break me, turn me into a good workhorse, just like the ones he doted on in his stables. But maybe he'd inadvertently healed something in me, instead. I knew one thing for certain, I'd make him pay for pushing me this far.

I smiled at my reflection. 'I'm Maeve Deane,' I whispered, before following Jamie back into the kitchen.

By the time I sat down at the kitchen table, Jamie had lit a fresh cigarette, the moment we had just shared forgotten. He was the same Jamie who'd sauntered through my kitchen door earlier that evening.

'Well, Maeve, you know what you need to do now.'

Taking the seat next to him, my heart rate picked up at the thought of what was about to happen next.

'I have to kill Martin.' It wasn't a question, but he answered anyway.

'You do,' he said, sitting forward.

'I will.' I smiled, despite the smell from his cigarette turning my already delicate stomach. 'It's not like I have a choice.'

280

He nodded. 'As long as he's breathing, you and your family aren't safe.'

'No need for the pep talk,' I sighed, sitting back in the kitchen chair. 'I know what I need to do. Trust me.'

He stayed where he was, searching my face for the confirmation that I knew what I was doing, rather than simply taking my word for it. He must have been satisfied with what he saw, because a slow smile spread across his face as he leaned back.

'Well, then, let's make a plan.'

'He'll be ready for me.'

'Ah now,' Jamie said, rising from his chair and heading to the back door. 'We both know he's been ready for you the second you stepped off that plane.' He flicked his cigarette butt out the back door before returning to join me at the table. He pulled his chair closer until he was sitting right in front of me, our knees touching, before taking both my hands in his.

He rubbed his thumbs back and forth across my knuckles, and suddenly I was sitting in a hospital bed, bleeding and empty, and he was apologising through his sobs. I pulled my hands away. A small, sad smile crossed his face and he pushed back his chair.

'And where does Rita stand in all this?' I asked, acutely aware that the man who was helping me was like a son to the wife of the man I was hoping to murder.

'Rita is . . .' Jamie stopped for a moment, trying to select his words. 'Impartial.'

I couldn't help raising one eyebrow.

'Don't look at me like that,' Jamie sighed. 'Rita knows what kind of a man Martin is, but she'll never leave him.'

'Okay, Jamie, I get it, she's set in her ways, loves him deep down, blah, blah, blah. What does it mean for us? Now?'

'She doesn't know anything. Not about letting that Garda live, or what we're planning now. She doesn't know any of it, and she doesn't want to.'

I sat back, nodding as I folded my arms. 'But she's giving you information about Martin's plans and whereabouts, whenever you ask?'

'Don't be like that, Maeve. She trusts me to do what's in her best interests.'

'And if those interests clash with mine?' I asked, entirely aware that if Rita was helping us it must benefit her in one way or another.

'They don't,' Jamie said firmly. '*You* need to trust me, too.'

I sat there for a second, searching his face while searching my gut.

I nodded. 'I do.' He hadn't given me a reason not to.

'Now, it's time to turn off those emotions and get the job done,' he said, sliding yet another cigarette from the packet. 'And let's be honest, controlling your emotions is something you're very good at.'

He was right. It's why I had been so good at being under-cover – in the beginning.

'Right,' I announced, standing up. 'How about a cup of

tea before we get to planning Martin Mulvihill's assassination?'

A smile spread across his face, so like that of the Cheshire
Cat in Abbie's *Alice in Wonderland* book, that I couldn't help
but smile back, until it occurred to me, as I filled the kettle
from the tap, that I never knew if the Cheshire Cat was good
or bad.

38

According to Rita, Martin was currently residing in his manor house in Clonakilty, about forty minutes west of my lodge.

'But he'll have security,' I said.

'Yes,' Jamie grinned. 'But we happen to know the head of Martin's security.'

'Oh Christ,' I fell back in the seat. 'You can't be seriously thinking of asking Davey for help?'

Jamie laughed. 'Of course not.'

I sighed with relief.

'*I'm* not going to ask anyone,' he said.

'What?' I sat up. 'Me?'

Jamie grinned again as I shook my head at him. 'Hear me out,' he said, leaning forward.

The plan was a simple one. Have Davey remove his men from Martin's security detail, then I would charge in and take the bastard out.

Not the most sophisticated of plans, and it was by no means foolproof, but given that we were under some serious time constraints, with an empty car burning in Cork General Hospital's car park, it was the best chance we had.

As we talked through the finer details of the plan, Jamie suddenly fell silent.

'What's wrong?' I asked, swallowing down my annoyance at the disruption in our plan-formulating rhythm.

'I can't go in with you,' he said quietly.

I tilted my head to the side. 'Obviously,' I said. 'All of this only works if it doesn't come back to you or Davey.'

To get Davey on board, to convince him to turn on Martin and help me, of all people, the woman he had recently tried to kill, the woman who had shot his son, the deal would need to be something he couldn't refuse – and how could he refuse the throne of the kingdom, in Martin's wake?

Not all to himself, of course, he would have to scoot over and share that particular seat with his brother – a partnership.

At first, I was taken aback when Jamie had suggested it; him taking over I could understand, but Davey was dangerous, volatile. However, Jamie had pointed out that when it came to a choice between Davey or Martin, Davey was the lesser of two evils.

'And besides,' he'd said, 'I'll be there to keep him in check.'

There was one important detail, crucial to the plan's success: there must never be anything to tie either brother to the assassination of Martin Mulvihill.

If they were to take the reins of Martin's empire, they would need the complete support of everyone who had worked to make it so successful. Murdering the boss would not achieve that. While some would back them for it, others would rebel, and infighting would lead to vultures appearing, ready to feed on the weaknesses within the organisation.

That meant, for the assassination part at least, I was very much on my own.

'We've already gone through all this,' I said. My irritation at this ill-timed tangent was starting to push through.

'I can't go in with you,' he said again. 'And we both know Kev will be with Martin. Even in the best-case scenario you'll be outnumbered two to one.'

'Jamie,' I said softly, leaning towards him and resting my hand on top of his. 'I'm out of options. All that matters now is that my family is safe.'

Walking into Henderson's Bar a couple of hours later, it felt as if we were going through the movements of a dance we once knew. Jamie opening the heavy door and holding it as I went through, him trailing me as we headed to the bar, calling for two Jamesons, neat, before we turned, putting our backs to the bar and surveying the goings-on of the scene around us.

We had performed those same movements many different times, in many different bars, but this was the first time that Davey O'Leary was the man we were looking for.

When we saw him, chatting up a woman in a short red dress, with sleek, flat chocolate-brown hair almost reaching her waist, and false nails that reminded me of a crow's talons,

Jamie reached for my hand without turning to face me, and squeezed it. A quiet reassurance I didn't need.

'I guess there's no point suggesting we run? Go somewhere Martin can't find us?' he said.

I squeezed his hand and smiled. There was no need to answer. Jamie knew there was no such place – and that even if there was, I would never leave my family to the whims of a psychopath like Martin.

'Let's go,' I said, nodding towards Davey.

'Lead the way,' Jamie said, giving my hand one last squeeze before letting go and gesturing for me to go ahead.

When I reached Davey's table, he and his lady-friend were so deep in conversation, him stroking her hair, that they didn't realise I was standing there. Crossing my arms over my chest, I smiled at the bandages wrapped around both of his hands. I must have broken the other hand when getting his gun, I thought, while trying to decide how best to get his attention.

I kicked the leg of the table hard, causing the drinks atop it to shake precariously. They didn't spill, but it was enough to get Davey's attention.

The smile on his face morphed into a sneer, like a taut elastic band returning to its original state.

'We need to talk,' I said, unfolding my arms and tilting my head slightly back, to indicate Jamie standing behind me.

'Get out of here,' Davey said, without so much as a blink. It wasn't until he turned his head that I realised he wasn't talking to us.

'Are you deaf?' he asked, turning back to the woman whose hair he'd been stroking moments earlier. 'Fuck off!'

She was a blur of red moving across the bar before I could raise an eyebrow at Jamie.

'The golden couple back together again?' Davey asked as Jamie stepped forward, pulling out two seats for us to sit in, uninvited.

'Nope,' I said, taking my seat. 'But we do have a joint business proposition for you.'

Davey stood. 'You're a stupider bitch than I thought if you imagine I'd make any deal with a two-faced pig like you.' He downed the end of his drink before standing to walk away.

Unfortunately for him, before he could take more than two steps, I had the back of his shirt collar bunched up in my fist. Pulling him back, I sent him crashing down backwards onto the table he'd just vacated.

I leaned over him, my lips almost touching his ear as I spoke.

'We'll be at the back door of your house in twenty minutes. Meet us there. No one can know.' I grabbed his jaw and turned his head so he had to look me in the eyes. 'You're going to want to hear what we have to offer, Davey.'

We could be seen coming to blows in public, but making a deal with so many eyes around would be dangerous.

Letting go of his face, I made my way out the back door of Henderson's, knowing that Jamie would be following behind.

39

The deal was made. Hands had been shaken. There was no going back now, I thought, as Jamie sped along the dark country roads towards my lodge.

The conversation with Davey at his house had gone surprisingly well. It turned out, offering Davey a seat at the head of the table was all it took to make him a whole lot more amenable.

'So, it looks like we're finally going to run this place, then, brother?' Davey asked Jamie, with a smile, raising his glass of whiskey before bringing it to his lips as he crossed his legs on top of his smudge-free glass coffee table.

I turned to Jamie, and a cold sensation went down my back when I saw his reciprocating grin. I really hoped I was doing the right thing, trusting Jamie and helping these brothers achieve so much power. I knew I was in a dire situation when I was entrusting the life of my husband to my ex-fiancé and his brother, and the lives of my children to the man whose baby my body couldn't carry and the man whose son I'd recently shot.

Before I could think about it too much, we were all on our feet and shaking hands like civilised people.

Jamie and I made our way back to his Jaguar, feeling confident in the arrangements we had made with Davey. Or as confident as I possibly could feel with so much at stake. And it appeared the good luck pendulum was finally beginning to swing my way because, as it happened, Davey was overseeing the logistics of a big delivery of cocaine that night, just off the coast of Skibbereen, which was only twenty minutes from Martin's country house.

In a couple of hours, Davey was going to make an urgent call to Martin to explain he'd need to pull his men out to deal with a shipment that had come in heavier on security and lighter on product than it should have. He would assure him that he wouldn't need them for long. To make it look good, Davey would have to kick up a fuss when the delivery landed. It could be dangerous, but Davey thrived in those situations. Bridges would be burned, but he could work to repair them when he took over.

And while Rita was still desperately clinging to her precious, plausible deniability, it was clear she had finally decided between the two men in her life. It shouldn't be surprising she chose the man who worshipped her, rather than the one who treated her like she was a piece of shit on his shoe. She would let Jamie know exactly who remained at the house before I made my entrance and, most importantly, let me in, straight to Martin.

It should all work; it did on paper. Of course Martin would send his men to deal with a problematic business transaction. He could take care of himself at the best of times. And why would he be worried about me? As far as he currently knew, I had completed the hit, and we were still all simpatico. No reason for him to suspect that I was about to make a stupid, idiotic, suicidal attempt on his life.

Best-case scenario, I get in, take care of Martin and get out. Worst-case, I take Martin out and Killer Kev puts a bullet in me. I was not unaware that the worst-case scenario was also the more likely. I may not walk out of Martin's country home, but I'd do my utmost to make sure he didn't either.

We returned to the Stone Lodge to prepare for the night ahead. By the time we were ready to leave, I had an array of weapons stored in every pocket of my clothing and strapped to every available body part.

Jamie returned to his car while I headed to my rental. From here on out, I was on my own. Aside from a few short sentences about weapon choices, we had barely spoken since arriving back at the cottage. We knew that this was goodbye and, however it played out, it was a permanent farewell. Win or lose, succeed or fail, no matter what happened, there was no room for Jamie in my life anymore. And in the life he would hopefully embark on soon, there certainly wouldn't be any place for me.

'Maeve?' Jamie called across the driveway, both of us pausing at our car doors.

'Yes?'

'Good luck.'

I nodded. 'Thanks,' I replied, without turning around. It was easier to say goodbye without looking him dead in the eye. Only when I heard his car door close and the engine roar to life did I allow myself to turn around and watch as he pulled out of Dunpool Woods.

Yes, I *was* the master of shutting off my emotions.

Once his tail lights had disappeared from view, I turned my gaze to the black sky and the never-ending twinkling yellow lights. Suddenly, I was back in Sarah's room, watching the stars from her night light dance around her as she slept.

I smiled and got into my car.

Driving down Martin's long, pointlessly winding, tree-lined driveway, my heart rate started to pick up.

Jamie had texted as I drove there. The coast was clear. Davey must have caused some serious trouble, because Martin had sent Killer Kev with the others to take care of things. This was the opening scene of the best-case scenario.

As I made my way to the front door and pressed the doorbell all I could hear was the pounding of my heartbeat in my ears. I took a deep, calming breath through my nose, to steady my nerves and supply my tensed limbs with some much-needed oxygen.

I stood there waiting, listening to the *bing-bong* noise echo around the large house. I pulled the gun from my waistband, and the weight of it in my hand calmed me more than any amount of deep breathing could. Whatever was about to happen. This was the end.

A sudden feeling of relief at that realisation filled me, and I smiled as I heard the mechanisms of the locks disengage. In that moment, I was exactly the woman I needed to be. The calm, collected, highly trained and self-assured woman I used to be and had forgotten about. *Here we go*, I thought as the door creaked open.

The door opened fully, and standing there in the doorway was Rita Regan. Everything that had happened since the moment when I first saw Sarah's empty car seat instantly came crashing through my mind.

Rita had been involved in that. She'd been in the thick of all the worst things Martin had ever done, and here she was now, standing in the doorway of the home they shared. Jamie trusted her. He always had. But there was a part of me that wondered if that trust had lasted all these years more out of habit than because she'd continued to earn it.

Rita stood blocking the doorway. She didn't speak. She didn't move. The gun twitched by my side. She continued to stare at me, the slightest curl in her thin lips.

She wasn't going to help me. She was never going to help me. I was about to raise my gun, when she finally moved.

'He's in the kitchen,' she said, stepping to the side and gesturing theatrically with one hand, showing the way.

Oh, thank Christ, I thought, as I stepped over the threshold into the house. I nodded at Rita, took another deep breath, and walked past her into the hallway.

This was it. In a matter of minutes this would all be over. I raised my gun, readying it for the task of finally freeing me from my past.

I was surprised by the genuine gratitude I felt towards Rita as I made my way towards the kitchen.

Until I felt the prick of the needle on the back of my neck.

40

The second I regained consciousness, I knew I had been completely and utterly fucked over. Rita had played me for a fool. She'd never been on my side. She was, as usual, doing Martin's bidding. I was an idiot for ever thinking otherwise. She was as bad as Martin. No, she was worse. At least Martin didn't pretend to be anything other than the sadistic bastard he was. Rita betraying me was one thing, but manipulating Jamie so blatantly, well, he'd never forgive her for that. Although, maybe . . .

Blinking rapidly to clear my mind, I felt an ache spread across my chest at the realisation that it was possible Rita hadn't manipulated Jamie, that I had been the only person manipulated in all of this. No, he wouldn't, I couldn't be that wrong about him. Could I?

My mind had filled with so many questions that it took a few minutes for the stark reality of my immediate situation to sink in. I was sitting on the floor, my back propped up against a wooden plank, my hands pulled tightly behind my back.

It wasn't until I tried to pull them forward that I felt the bite of hard, cold cuffs gripping my wrists. Looking down at my feet, I could see they were bound together with a cable tie.

Shit. Shit. Shit. This was the worst possible position I could be in. For me, and for my family. I had no cards left to play. And even if I did, Martin had the upper hand. I'd come to his home unannounced and heavily armed. There was only one reason for that. A reason there was no coming back from.

I pulled my arms again, hard, straining at the cuffs. 'Argh!' I screamed, as the steel bit even deeper into my skin. It was pointless.

I threw my head back against the wooden post I was attached to. So this was it. This was where it was all going to end for me. This was how Maeve – the orphaned child, the undercover agent, the blurred-lines criminal, the mother – this was how she would meet her end. It was probably what I deserved. I hadn't lived the type of life that ended quietly, in bed, surrounded by children and grandchildren. But I had hoped it wouldn't end like this – as the prisoner of a man who would make my death as painful as he could.

I took a breath. The grassy smell of hay and sweaty leather filled my nostrils. I was in Martin's stables, but despite the smell, it looked as if all the stalls were empty.

He probably didn't want his investments bearing witness to anything that might cause them distress. On the bright side, the five infrared heaters that were mounted on the walls of the stables, used to keep his precious horses warm, were all switched on, so at least Martin didn't want me to freeze to death. Although I did wonder if that would be better than what he had planned for me.

I took in my surroundings but the row of empty horse pens, plus a large gas container – no doubt necessary to heat Martin's obnoxiously sized mansion – was all there was of note.

I had no idea what time it was, or how long I had been unconscious, but there was a pink hue seeping in through the small window at the top of the stables, which suggested morning was about to break. I closed my eyes and sat there in the silence, trying to accept the utter hopelessness of my situation. There was nothing I could do and, while I seethed with anger, fear fought to be the dominant emotion, bubbling through me at the thought of what was to come.

'Good morning, Maeve.'

I'd fallen asleep. Whatever drug they'd pumped my body full of was clearly still lingering in my system. There was no way I would have slept otherwise, with the amount of adrenaline coursing through my body. My head ached, and for a moment I didn't open my eyes, despite the presence of the woman hovering over me.

'Ah, now, don't be like that. What did you think would happen, showing up here like that? Did you really think I would step aside and let you walk right in and unload your gun into him? Even *you* couldn't be that stupid.'

'Piss off,' I said, finally opening my eyes.

Rita looked down at me with an almost maternal smile. She took a step closer and bent down, so she was eye to eye with me. She stayed like that for a moment, staring at me, before she slapped me hard across the face. 'You never did have much of a manner about you.'

I took the slap with no more of a reaction than an involuntary blink. I wouldn't give her the satisfaction of crying out.

'Nope, I guess not.' I smiled back at her.

Rita was close to me now. My arms ached as I strained against the handcuffs, willing them to break and allow me to wrap my hands around her ageing neck and squeeze the life right out of her.

'Your manner I could get over. The fact that you are a traitorous whore, I could never forgive.' She spat in my face and I winced as the warm gobbet dripped down my cheek, powerless to wipe it away.

'Then why all the bullshit? Why let Jamie think you were helping us?'

As soon as the question left my lips, I wished I could take it back.

Rita gave a small laugh. 'Us?' she mocked, turning her head to the side. 'Do you hear that, Kev, she thinks her and Jamie are an "us".'

Realising we weren't alone, I looked past her to the man in the shiny black coat, standing by the door at the other side of the stables. Killer Kev. He was laughing, too.

'Well, you see, I *was* helping Jamie.'

I closed my eyes, my body warring with my emotions, as I tried desperately to keep my expression blank so as not to give Rita any more satisfaction than she was already taking from this little tête-à-tête. I was an idiot. Another level of stupid for trusting Jamie. For thinking that, after everything I'd done to him, he would help me; for trusting that he wanted to help save my family in return for the one I'd lost.

It was all too much and, despite my best efforts, as soon as I opened my eyes again I knew that my face had betrayed me and shown the pain I felt. Rita looked almost giddy with happiness at the effect her words had produced.

'Give us a minute, will ya?' Rita turned to Kev.

He slipped out the stable door without a word.

She turned back to me. 'You know, it surprised everyone when you tracked that baby of yours down so fast.'

I looked up, not knowing where this conversation was going, but it would be nowhere good.

'Especially considering how easy it was to take her away from you.' She laughed. 'Oh, Martin expected that would be much harder, Maeve. That's why he sent Kev. And what was it Kev said again . . .?' She paused, as if trying to remember. 'Oh, that's right,' she continued, leaning so close her nose was almost touching mine. 'A walk in the park,' she grinned. I could smell coffee on her breath. 'How easy it was for that nurse to let him know exactly where you'd parked.'

Nurse? Who was she talking about? Nurse Rose? But

she didn't know where I'd parked. *I* hadn't even known where I was going to park that morning. There was no way. And then I remembered. I'd barely crossed the threshold of her office and I'd told her. I'd told Nurse Rose I'd parked halfway down Elmwood Avenue, it had been a part of my first apology that day – a flyaway comment, the smallest piece of information – and it had set all of this in motion. I could see her, holding what I had thought was an impatient hand up to me, tapping away on her iPhone the second I'd mentioned Elmwood Avenue, without missing a beat. That was why I'd never spotted anyone following me; they had just sat back and waited for Nurse Rose to let them know where I would be. She hadn't even needed to work hard for the information, I had offered it up like an idiot before even sitting at her desk.

That sneaky bitch. In that moment, I would have sold my soul to the Devil himself to get my hands on Nurse Rose.

Rita backed away, laughing as she enjoyed watching me fit all the pieces together, relishing the opportunity to reveal exactly how much I'd been played.

'I guess you're about as good a mother as you were a spy.'

I kicked out my bound legs and pulled my hands until I felt the cuffs break skin.

'Ah, would ya look,' she said loudly, standing to face the man who had just entered the stables. 'Some things don't change, do they? That temper of hers is still as wild.'

Martin walked towards us as Killer Kev returned to his

post by the door. Martin didn't speak as Rita turned back to me and slapped me hard across the face.

This time I cried out.

'I'm going to kill you!' I screamed, as Rita smiled down at me.

'Is that so?' she asked, reaching into the pocket of her long woollen coat and pulling out a gun, before pointing it at my head.

I didn't close my eyes, didn't look away. Didn't even blink. I would look her in the eyes as she pulled the trigger and ended my life as I sat on the dirty ground with the smell of horseshit in my nose. I'd make sure she'd see my eyes staring into hers before she squeezed off that bullet. Not that she'd care, but still, the strangest of things could haunt you after seeing someone die, and I'd go full Patrick Swayze on her, given the opportunity.

'Enough.'

Martin spoke quietly, gently, but that one word was all it took for Rita to drop her hand and hastily return the gun to her coat pocket. Martin walked towards Rita until he was right behind her.

'Sorry, Martin. I was just messing with her. I wasn't going to, you know . . .'

Martin reached into her coat pocket as she fumbled over her words. She'd forgotten herself, got carried away by her monologuing.

'Don't worry, love. I understand.' He leaned forward and

kissed her softly on the cheek as he tucked her gun into the back of his own jeans. The kiss did nothing to ease the tightness on Rita's features. If anything, it seemed to put her more on edge. 'You won't be coming in here armed again.'

The stables fell silent for what felt like an eternity before Martin finally spoke.

'Step aside.'

The bite in his words caused Rita to jump ever so slightly. I enjoyed watching her squirm, but that enjoyment was short-lived when Martin, at last, turned his attention to me. Rita took a step back, visibly sagging with relief when she moved out of Martin's line of sight.

Martin stepped towards me.

I kept the pull on my cuffs. The biting pain from the pressure on the fresh wounds helped me to stay focused under Martin's heavy stare.

'Tut, tut, tut.' He frowned down at me. 'I'm very disappointed, Maeve. First, I find out about your work undercover. That you were working against me all that time, when I'd taken you in, allowed you into my home, into my organisation, my family.' He crouched down on his haunches beside me. 'Then you run around my country causing unnecessary havoc, drawing attention to yourself, and still, after all that, I gave you a chance to redeem yourself. And what do you do? You come here, to my home, late at night and fully armed. To do what exactly? To let me know you'd already broken the first part of our deal?' He was surprisingly gentle as he reached out and brushed my hair behind my ear. 'Or perhaps you came here for a more sinister reason?' His hand moved down to my face, cupping my cheek.

I didn't speak, tried not to move. His touch became stronger, exerting more pressure as his hand slid towards the side of my neck and his grip tightened, painfully. I winced.

'Were you going to kill me, Maeve?' His voice was soft, but there was a fire in his eyes that promised pain for what I'd done – and what I'd failed to do.

I didn't answer him. I didn't need to. There was nothing I could say to convince him I hadn't come to kill him, but still, the thought of admitting it so blatantly to his face felt like the wrong thing to do. Killer Kev was making his way towards us. Nothing good could come from his proximity.

'Never seen you so quiet.' Martin's grip was still tight on my neck. 'I like it,' he said, releasing me roughly, using my neck to push himself back up into a standing position.

I winced, closing my eyes, as the back of my head bounced off the wooden fence. My head had barely stopped spinning when the first kick came crashing into my ribs. I cried out with shock at that first kick but kept as quiet as I could with every other one that followed. The only sounds breaking the silence were Killer Kev's grunts of exertion and the thuds as his heavy work boots made contact with my body.

Black spots appeared at the edges of my vision, the pain flooding my body. The last thing I saw before I passed out was the retreating silhouette of Rita and Martin leaving the stables as Killer Kev raised his boot over my left leg and brought it down so hard on my shin that the crack echoed throughout the stables, bouncing off the wooden beams overhead. The darkness swallowed me in that moment, and I was grateful for it.

41

The pain kept rolling through me and there was nothing I could do to stop it. How would I endure this for hours upon hours?

'Maybe you should consider some pain relief? It's going to be quite a long while, Mrs King.'

'No,' I forced the word out, past gritted teeth. 'No, thank you.'

'Very well, I'll be back in a little bit. Press the buzzer if you need anything.'

I closed my eyes and took a deep breath as the pain ebbed.

'You know, if you need something for the pain, no one's going to think any less of you.' Christopher rose from his chair to take my hand, attempting to reason with me for the few, glorious moments between contractions.

'I know that, but I don't want to do anything that might put the baby at risk.'

Christopher looked at me, patting the back of my hand. 'The pain relief is perfectly safe. They wouldn't offer it, if it wasn't.'

'I know, I know.'

'Then maybe you sh—'

I cut him off with a moan as another contraction took over. Rubbing my back, he waited for the pain to subside before attempting to continue.

'Why don't you go get a coffee for yourself, and maybe I'll think about getting something for the pain?'

'Mmm, sure,' he said, with a smile, knowing I was only humouring him. 'I won't be long.'

'Take your time. I'm not going anywhere,' I smiled back at him.

Once he'd left, I wrapped my arms around my baby bump and whispered, 'Don't worry, sweetheart, we'll get through this.'

Tears slid down my face that had nothing to do with the physical pain of the contractions.

'I know that this pain is something I deserve. It's the price I need to pay for you.'

The midwife came back in. 'Can I get you anything, Mrs King?'

'No, I'm good,' I smiled, hurriedly wiping the tears from my face as another contraction took hold.

'She's here. Congratulations, Mrs King, she's beautiful.'

The midwife placed my baby on my chest and, just like that, she was here and all the pain was gone.

She was perfect. Small and innocent. She was mine, and I

was hers, and I would do anything for her. But mingled with the feeling of undiluted love was the knowledge that I wasn't good enough for her. That, while I was the most blessed person in that moment, this beautiful baby girl deserved someone so much better as her mother.

'I'm sorry,' I whispered, over and over, as tears that everyone assumed were of joy flowed down my face.

42

'I'm sorry,' I mumbled, as I swam back to consciousness, interrupting my dreams. I blinked, confused by my surroundings. This wasn't a hospital room, and I didn't have my baby resting on my chest, her warm pink body against my skin. Tears pricked my eyes. No, I was a long way away from that.

I whimpered, straightening up from the slumped position in which they had left my beaten body. I tried to take the pressure off the cuffs, which were biting deep into my wrists.

A moan escaped me as I struggled to find a position that even marginally relieved the pain radiating throughout my body. My left leg was broken below the knee, the shin bone barely contained within the skin. I couldn't be sure how many ribs were cracked. Fortunately, I could still breathe, so at least none had punctured my lungs.

The door creaked from the other side of the stables, and I stopped moving. Was this it? Was this the clean-up? I wanted to fight back, to be strong, but I was done. My mind and body were finished. There was no more fight left in me. And even if there was, I was out of options.

I tried to shift my shoulder, to find some position that wouldn't make me scream with pain, but it was no use. There was no comfortable position for my aching body. Every muscle and patch of skin burned in response to movement, but I couldn't let my captors see that. They could see the marks they'd put on my body, but I wouldn't give them the satisfaction of seeing how much pain I was in. How much pain *they* had caused me.

How brave of them to set Killer Kev on me when I was tied up.

Bastards.

I blinked quickly to clear my eyes. I wanted to see my attackers, to see what was about to happen. I couldn't fully explain it, but I didn't want to lose consciousness again, I wanted to be present for the end. To be aware of what was happening.

I wanted to maintain a small piece of control in a situation I had absolutely no control over. Maybe I was delirious from the pain after the beating. Maybe it was because a part of me hoped that if I stayed present, experienced every excruciating minute of the death that awaited me, Martin's thirst for retribution would be fully quenched and maybe, just maybe, he would leave my family be. Whatever it was, I knew I wanted to see my death coming, and to look it square in the face.

As the footsteps approached, I looked up to the wooden

rafters overhead, imagining I could see past them to the skies above.

In my head, I was outside Europol headquarters, looking up at the clear blue sky, a week away from returning to Ireland as an undercover officer. I had been excited. Ready to embark on an adventure and, finally, find some peace by tracking down my mother's killer.

I wondered whether, had I known where it would all lead, I would have still felt excited. If I had known it would all end here, with me battered and bloody, tied to a wooden post in Martin Mulvihill's stables, would I have smiled up at that blue sky?

I closed my eyes.

'Christ, they've made shit of you.'

Jamie.

His name escaped my lips in an exhalation, a sense of relief, until I remembered he had betrayed me. What a fool I'd been. Trusting someone who I'd deceived for so long.

I hung my head. I should have done this alone.

I hated myself for feeling even the briefest reaction to his voice. For thinking, even for a moment, that he was here to help me, to save me. That he would risk his career, his life, for the woman who'd lost his child and run away. He'd been working against me all along.

I didn't realise how dry my throat was, or how difficult it had become to take even the shallowest breath, until I tried to speak.

'Here . . .' I stopped, to take another breath, as deep as I dared, and to form saliva in my mouth. 'To have a go, too?'

'Yes,' he said, smiling sadly down at me.

So it was true. The smallest, most pathetic part of me had still hoped, deep down, that Rita had been lying.

I'd truly thought he'd forgiven me. That he knew I'd loved him, despite everything. Although I guess, if he did, then walking away from him and starting a whole new life with another man in another country, and having the family Jamie and I were supposed to have, would have been enough to turn him against me, anyway.

'I should have known not to trust you.'

'Yes, you really should have.' He crouched down and brought his face within inches of mine, the smell of Dior Sauvage from freshly shaved skin reminding me of another lifetime.

'Ah, so you've found her.' Martin's voice cut through the moment. He was dressed smartly in a business suit, no doubt for one of his more legitimate businesses.

'Sure did, boss.' Jamie stood and turned to face Martin as he approached, arm outstretched.

'Good man yourself.' Martin smiled as he shook Jamie's hand briefly. 'You did a good job keeping control of the situation,' he told him, with the barest nod in my direction.

I was clearly the 'situation' they were discussing.

Jamie nodded. 'Anytime, Martin. Glad I was of use.'

'You certainly were,' Martin said. 'Now, I've a meeting to

311

get to, so I'll leave you two alone.' He winked at me before turning and leaving.

I shifted painfully to look at Jamie. 'You haven't forgiven me? All of this was just your way of getting back at me?' I didn't mean to phrase it as a question but, despite everything, it hurt that Jamie had done this to me. That he had contributed to me ending up here.

'Now, now,' he crouched down in front of me again. 'Don't be like that in these last few moments we have together.' He looked to the left and gave the barest inclination of his head.

My eyes followed the direction he'd indicated. Despite what Martin had said, he hadn't left us alone. Killer Kev was standing by the stable door watching us. But why did Jamie care if there was someone to bear witness to my humiliation?

Before I could think about it too much, he grabbed my face roughly, his fingers squeezing my jawbone. Looking into his dark eyes, I hated myself for falling for everything he'd said. He'd used the loss of our baby to convince me he was willing to help, regardless of the risk. I hated that it had felt so easy and so natural with him. That despite the years, despite the loss, the lies, the anger, I had trusted him – and even more than that, I had felt safe with him. He had fooled me, betrayed me, hurt me more than I had ever thought possible, and it occurred to me, sitting there in the stables with him grasping my face, that we were now finally even.

I squeezed my eyes shut. I'd sown these seeds, and no

matter how hard I'd tried to avoid it, it was time to reap the consequences.

I opened my eyes as I felt him close the last few inches of space between us, pausing as he looked into my eyes, and in that one look we were back in that hospital room, sharing our grief and searching for answers to our pain, but that memory disappeared as he crashed his mouth against mine. A far cry from the gentle way his mouth once moved against me, in a different life. I tried to resist but with his hand on my face there was no way I could. I struggled as I felt his kiss deepen, but stopped as I felt his tongue push a hard object into my mouth.

Pulling away from him, I searched his face for answers, and, using my tongue, tucked whatever it was into my cheek. It was small and hard, and the best guess I could make after feeling it with my tongue was that it was a metal paper clip. Something I could open my cuffs with? Was he giving me a chance to escape? Why would he do that? How far was I going to get on a broken leg? Killer Kev was a constant at the stable door, if not on this side of it then the other. But if I timed it right, could I make a splint out of something and get away? Maybe. None of it was likely. I was probably still going to lose, but at least now I was back in the game.

Jamie kept his mouth against mine as he spoke, murmuring like a lover in a romantic embrace, keeping his voice low so Killer Kev wouldn't overhear.

'This is all I can do, Maeve. I'm sorry. I don't know what

went wrong. Rita called me and told me to get here and let Martin think I'd just been keeping you busy all this time. We're both dead if I try to take you out of here. It's all up to you. Your car keys are in your car parked behind the house, and your phone and your gun are both in the glove box. Make it count.'

He spoke quickly and quietly, relaying as much information as possible, but I heard each and every word. He pressed his forehead against mine. A soft, gentle movement compared to the angry, violent pose of a scorned lover gripping my face. 'All or nothing.'

'All or nothing,' I whispered back.

'Y'know I never needed to forgive you. All I ever wanted was for you to be happy, Maeve.' He closed his lips around mine in a short, sweet kiss.

We both heard when Kev's heavy boots started to shuffle closer to us.

'I'm sorry,' he whispered, before pulling back abruptly and slapping me hard across the face.

The slap caught me off guard. I quickly felt around inside my cheek with my tongue for the clip. It was still there, the taste of blood filling my mouth. The clip must've cut into me with the slap.

Jamie stood right next to me and patted me on the head. 'That's a good girl.' He turned to Killer Kev. 'Always liked it rough, this one,' he said loudly, with a laugh.

Killer Kev grinned.

I spat a mouthful of blood at his feet. It was an effort to get it to even leave my mouth. The bloody wad of spit landed closer to me than him. He stepped away, turning to give me a wink and a sad smile, before leaving without another word. A single tear escaped down my face as I watched him go, but I quickly blinked back the rest.

Resting my head back against the wooden fence, I closed my eyes. He hadn't turned against me, after all. It was a comfort, even in this situation, that I hadn't been wrong about Jamie. That meant something to me. It meant I hadn't made yet another mistake. And since he had just risked his life by trying to help me, it had been a good decision turning to him. If I got out of here, and if Martin ever got wind that Jamie had helped me, then he was in for a world of pain. He had said to make it count. He didn't mean for me to merely escape, he meant for me to complete the task I'd come here to do.

Killer Kev followed Jamie out. Once I heard the stable door slam shut, I began to shuffle and twitch, under the guise of trying desperately to get my aching body into a comfortable position, in case he returned. Something I didn't need to use much acting skill for. As I shifted myself around, I brought my hands down on the thick mixture of blood and saliva I'd spat at Jamie's feet. I groaned out loud and grimaced before twisting back and returning my hands safely behind me.

I stopped moving, closed my eyes, and took a deep breath as I tried to manage the pain. I wasn't any more comfortable than before. I was actually in even more pain, but as my fingertips carefully felt the small metal clip covered in spit, I allowed myself a small smile. It was foolish. The odds were still completely against me, in every way, and there was no longer a scenario I could envision that had a happy ending, but holding that small piece of metal in my hand tipped the scales ever so slightly.

43

My determination didn't last long. My numb fingers struggled to manoeuvre the unravelled paper clip into the cuffs, which had hours earlier suppressed the flow of blood to my hands. After around the thirtieth time of trying, the clip slipped from my fingers and I slumped against the wooden wall. I was done. Finished. The game was over, I'd lost, Martin had won. I closed my eyes and forced my mind to think of nothing and no one.

I don't know how long I sat there with my eyes closed, staring at the darkness behind my eyelids, but the bang from the stable door opening caused me to snap them open and blink in the light again. Rita strode towards me, looking as if she had a very particular purpose. She was alone, Killer Kev wasn't keeping watch at the door.

'You poor stupid bitch ya,' Rita said, stopping in front of my feet. 'How else did you think all this was going to end? The minute you stepped in front of Martin as an undercover agent, all those years back, you sealed your own fate.'

I didn't look up at her.

'I gave you one chance, for Jamie's sake, and you managed to fuck it up.'

'Because *you* drugged me when I got here,' I spat out, looking up at her.

Rita pursed her lips. 'I had no other choice. Whatever that bollox Davey said to Martin on the phone, it worked too well. He'd sent Kev off with the others to take care of things.'

'I don't get it,' I said quietly.

'Well, you three were so busy making sure the boys couldn't be linked to anything, you forgot about me. How do you think it would have looked if I was the only one here and I just stood by when he was killed? People would wonder, question if I'd been involved, and even if it was just whispers behind my back, I couldn't risk it. You were meant to get your shot with Martin and Kev. That was as much as I could allow.'

I stared at her without speaking. There was nothing to say. She was right – but what good was agreeing with her now?

'And then you go talking about me helping, and you and Jamie as an "us" in front of Kev. Jesus Christ!'

I hung my head.

'And to think all of this started just so you could find your mother's killer.'

I squeezed my eyes shut, unable to face the pain at the mention of my mother.

'And was it worth it? Ending up here now after putting the wrong man in a hospital bed?'

I opened my eyes and looked up at Rita.

'I felt sorry for you, ya know.' Her voice softened, taking on a tone I rarely heard her use – and if she did, it was only ever with Jamie. 'I pitied you for believing you had finally punished your mother's killer when, actually, all you had done was become a workhorse for the very man who stuck a knife in her.'

No, no. She was lying. Nothing had ever linked Martin to my mother's death. Not even a whiff. Ryan and Silva had assured me that there was nothing pointing to Martin. Everything, absolutely everything, had pointed at Brian Walsh. All the intel—

Something in the recesses of my mind cut off my thought process. Rita. Rita had played a significant role in gathering the information that ultimately sent me down that backstreet to find Brian Walsh. Had that all been under Martin's orders?

Rita shook her head slowly. 'You were just so desperate to find someone. Anyone.'

Rita was no longer in front of me. I was staring at my mother's body on the ground in our kitchen. All I could see was the knife – the knife that should have been sitting with its siblings in the wooden block on the counter, but which was now swimming in a pool of blood. The knife that had been ripped from its holder and used to end my mother's life. I thought of the note lying beneath the fridge, my mother warning me not to stay in the house alone. It all made sense now. She knew something was going to happen. She'd been afraid of someone. Had it been Martin? As my mother faded from my mind, Martin appeared. I was reliving flashes of conversations, meals we had shared, drinks that had led to orders and punishments. Each moment raced through my mind like an accelerated movie montage. Then I was watching Brian Walsh's face cave in beneath my bloodied fists. But if Rita was telling the truth, that meant what I had done, the injuries I had caused, had been to an innocent man.

I shook my head, the pain from the movement bringing me back to the present. Rita was still standing over me, her head tilted to the side as she looked down at me.

'No. No. No,' I repeated with every movement of my head from side to side, using the pain to keep me grounded. 'What I did. To that man.'

'I wouldn't worry about that, pet,' Rita said, softly. 'When Martin wanted to make sure you never connected anything back to him, he told me to give you a name, and I did.'

There was a moment of silence before she continued. 'The reason that Brian Walsh fella was sleeping rough was because he'd been thrown out of his house by his mother after it came to light that he'd been inappropriate with his niece.' Rita smiled. 'We did the world a favour with that one.'

'But why?' I asked, my voice rasping from my bloodied, dry mouth. 'Why would Martin kill my mother?'

'Well, now, the answer to that I think you'll find interesting.' Rita sat down on the dirty ground next to me, resting her back against a wooden support beam running the full height of the stables, and stretched her legs out in front of her. Almost identical to my position – except she was free and I was bound.

'You see, as it happens, your perfect mother who you always spoke so highly of, as if the sun shone out her ass,' Rita gave a little laugh, 'was actually working for Liam Daily Snr.'

'What? No! My mother would never—'

'Yeah, yeah, she was too honest? Too sweet? Well, she wasn't,' Rita snapped. 'She was feeding Liam Daily information on Martin the entire time she worked in his hotel.'

'I don't . . . I don't understand.' My mother was a good, moral woman. She would never have involved herself in the feud between Martin and Liam Daily. Never.

'You'd be surprised what the best of people would do for money,' Rita said. 'Martin dealt with her personally when he found out. She'd been seen with Liam outside the delivery entrance of the hotel, accepting an envelope of cash. Silly bitch got sloppy.'

My eyes snapped to Rita's, smarting at the insult to my mother, despite everything. She was staring unfocused into the distance, as if seeing everything play out as she spoke. None of this made any sense.

'Why would she do that? It doesn't make any sense. She wouldn't get involved with someone like Liam Daily.' I was shouting now, but I couldn't help it. As desperate and surreal as this whole situation was, the things Rita was saying were crazy, fantastical.

They couldn't be true. They couldn't, because if they were, that meant I'd been working for the very man I'd been searching for. The only reason I'd done any of this, the only reason I had gone undercover, the only reason I had said yes to Ryan and Silva, had been to find the person who had killed my mother, and instead I'd been running his errands, jumping at his commands and ruining what was left of my life for the bastard who'd destroyed it in the first place.

'Well, she did. And Martin punished her.' Rita closed her eyes and rested her head against the pillar behind her. 'Quickly followed by him finally eliminating Liam Daily Snr.'

I remembered that. The week of my mother's death, the TV news and newspapers were filled with stories of the disappearance of Liam Daily Snr. The week I lost my mother, Liam Daily Jnr lost his father, and the day I met Liam Daily Jnr, I lost my unborn baby. It almost seemed as if there was some kind of karmic curse between our two families.

I couldn't speak. There was nothing to say. Rita stayed silent for a few moments, allowing everything she'd said to sink in, before she spoke again.

'And even after all that, Martin still trusted *you*. Gave you work, allowed you into his inner circle. Even gave you a second chance after finding out you were undercover.'

Shaking her head, she stood and dusted the loose dirt from the back of her trousers. 'So you can imagine the punishment that's coming to you. And your family. All this,' she gestured around her at the stables, 'it's all just another game of Martin's. He'll see how much pain you can take, as you watch what he'll do to those two little girls of yours, until you finally break.'

Rita left then, and as her final sentence soaked into my shock-saturated brain, I flexed my fingers and picked the paper clip back out of the dirt.

44

Hours passed. I closed my eyes, my injured body exhausted. I didn't think I'd fallen asleep but when I opened them again Rita and Martin were towering above me, Killer Kev lingering behind, looking as if he couldn't wait for the festivities to unfold.

I flinched at the sight of them. I flexed my hands, which were still pulled behind me, but were now free from the cuffs. It hadn't taken long to free them after my renewed attempt, but it had taken a lot of massaging before I regained enough feeling and dexterity to deem my hands useable.

All I could do now was wait for an opportunity to present itself, and hope I'd be quick enough, precise enough, good enough, to do this – to finish this the way it needed to finish, with Martin dead. This was now a suicide mission, but I trusted Jamie entirely to make sure my family was safe.

I wasn't afraid, not for me. I was ready to do whatever I needed to. No more looking for another way out. I had one option: kill Martin and die in the process. There was nothing else to consider.

'Did you have a nice catch-up with your ex-fiancé?' Martin asked, the interest in his tone at odds with the sneer on his face.

'Go fuck yourself,' I answered, my hoarse voice letting me down and displaying my weakness.

'None of that carry-on now.' A serpentine smile spread across his face. 'You don't want to make poor old Rita mad and get her into trouble again, do you?' He gave Rita a pointed look, clearly still angry at her earlier outburst.

He turned back to me, crouching down to look me in the eye. 'The last thing I want is for anything to happen that would cause you to bow out of this little game of ours early.' A small smile played on his lips. 'Not when I'm about to add some new players.'

I stopped breathing.

'And if I'm not mistaken,' he continued, stretching out his arm to reveal the gold Rolex, bright against his tanned skin. 'The older one should be finishing up in nursery any minute now.'

Forgetting myself, I moved towards Martin, only remembering at the last second to keep my hands behind my back as if still cuffed.

'Ah now, you should be thanking me for sending someone to help out while Mammy's away.'

'You touch one hair on my child's head and I swear to

God I'll kill you.' I was practically growling. The anger spread through me, anger at him threatening my children, at what he'd done to my mother, at what I'd done because of him. It replaced the pain from the broken bones and damaged muscles the length of my body.

He bared his too-white teeth at me. 'And I thought you'd be happy to see her.' He stood and began to walk away, before adding, 'One last time.'

That was it. There was nothing that could restrain me after that. There was nothing more to wait for. Bringing my hands from behind me, I pulled my knees to my chest quickly, ignoring the sharp pain and the strange way the bones in my left leg moved. With a silent prayer that I wouldn't pass out from the pain, I pushed myself up from the ground, into a standing position, and lunged forward at Martin's retreating back. There was no plan. I had no weapon and there would be no way I could overpower him, but I needed to get my hands on him, to hurt him, even if it was only for a second. I almost had him. Almost.

Rita saw what I was doing and, with irritating speed, jumped between us while simultaneously pushing Martin out of my reach. I wasn't falling back to the ground empty-handed. I grabbed Rita around the neck with one arm and wrapped my other across her chest, pulling her down as we crashed to the ground.

Martin turned, a look of disdain on his face, as if we were only a minor irritation to him exiting the stables. I tightened my arm around Rita's neck, partially cutting off her oxygen supply. Killer Kev hadn't moved an inch; he was unconcerned, as Martin himself wasn't in danger.

'Call your men off my children.' I tightened my arm around Rita's neck, enough to make her thrash her legs in a wild panic. 'Now!'

Martin looked down at us, one side of his top lip pulled up into a sneer.

'Kill her,' he shrugged. 'What do I care?'

My heart sank. He meant it. He'd let me squeeze the life out of Rita right here in front of him, and it wouldn't bother him in the slightest. He was going to make that call. He was going to take my children. Adrenaline was pumping through my body, each limb and muscle ready to spring into action. Even the broken bones were ready to move, pure desperation masking the pain. I needed to think of something, anything. And I had to keep him talking until I did.

'You bastard. Have you ever cared about anyone but yourself in your entire life?'

'I cared about you, Maeve,' he answered, his voice taking on a serious tone. 'You may not have realised it, but I have always looked out for you.'

I loosened the arm across Rita's throat and could feel her body tense against mine as Martin spoke.

'And how did you repay me? You left us. Took off with some man you barely knew.' His voice was rising uncharacteristically. 'But I let you go. I let you go off with your new man, to your new life, with no repercussions. People thought it was a sign I was softening in my old age. They tested me, and what happened to them is on you.' Spittle was flying from his lips.

It was terrifying to see this man who'd always been the pinnacle of control become undone.

'And then,' he was roaring now, 'then I find out you were undercover the entire time, and still I give you another chance. Another opportunity to save yourself, and what do you do? You come here, to my home, and try to kill me!'

His face was flushed, the red heat of his anger coming through despite his deep tan. 'What do you think everyone expects me to do now?'

My arm loosened around Rita; she could have pulled herself away if she tried, but we both stayed still, staring at Martin. He would do everything in his power to hurt me as much as he could, because that's what I had done to him – I'd hurt him.

I had been caught off guard by Martin's roaring and ranting, so much so that I didn't realise Rita was trying to say something to me, whispering and barely moving her lips. She had her head turned towards me as much as she could without catching Martin's attention and distracting him from his rage-fuelled monologue.

'Gun. Pocket. Gun,' she whispered.

Even after the berating she'd received earlier, she'd still come back into the stables armed. After everything she'd done, here she was offering me the one thing I needed to kill this bastard where he stood and save my family. Rita was giving me one more chance.

Silence suddenly filled the stables, more startling than any noise. Martin had stopped talking, looking almost embarrassed by his emotional outburst. He cleared his throat and straightened up, composing himself.

'Anyway,' his voice was soft and controlled again. 'Do with her what you will.' He turned, heading for the door.

I reached a hand into Rita's coat pocket and felt the handgun. I pulled it out and pointed it at the back of Martin's head.

45

'Stop.' The word came out hoarse and small, but Martin heard. He turned slowly, as if sensing the sudden shift in power. If it surprised him to see me holding a gun, he did an excellent job of hiding it. He couldn't even give me the satisfaction of catching him off guard. Instead, he smiled. A smile that made my skin crawl. My hand, already struggling under the weight of my gun, started to shake.

'And what are you going to do with that, Maeve?'

'What do you think?'

'What I think is that you're desperate, and I understand that.' He turned his head, drawing my attention to Killer Kev and the gun he already had trained on me. 'And while shooting me may seem like an option for you, now that you've managed to get your hands on a gun.' He paused and gave Rita a look that promised pain. 'You should consider the fact that Kev here will make sure you don't get another shot off, right before making the call to move on your darling daughters.'

My hand shook. I didn't know what to do. My mind was racing. How close were his men to my children? If I shot him, would Jamie and Davey be able to take control before Kev contacted Martin's crew? I couldn't take the risk, but there was one other option.

'And don't you worry,' Martin said, with a sneer and a wink. 'I sent one of my men who has – how will I put it? – a special affinity for young girls.'

My hand stopped shaking. My breathing steadied and my taut muscles relaxed. There was only one choice I could make. A smile spread across my face, immediately removing the sneer from Martin's.

'You're out of choices here, Maeve. You're going to die either way, so don't make it worse for your children,' he warned, panic beginning to creep into his voice.

Under my arm, Rita held her breath. I had made my girls a promise before I'd left them; that these people would never put a hand on them again. A promise I had every intention of keeping.

'There's always a choice, Martin,' I said, repeating his words back to him and moving my gun a couple of inches to the right.

Smiling, I paused just long enough for Martin to look in the direction it was pointing and then back to me. The look on his face was more satisfying than anything I could have hoped for.

'Don't you da—'

I squeezed the trigger and sent a bullet straight into the path of the large gas tank. I thought it would be instant, but I saw the look of terror on Martin's face and instead of seeing the flames, or feeling the heat of the explosion, I heard it roar, like a raging, vengeful banshee. I remember thinking it was strange that I felt as if I was being pulled backwards instead of being pushed, before everything went dark.

46

Death wasn't what I'd thought it would be. I had expected nothingness. I had thought that nothingness would be peaceful and serene, that I would simply cease to exist. But that wasn't the case at all. There were no fluffy clouds or imposing golden gates looming over me. Instead, I could see my daughters. Not as they were, but as memories. I could see them as I had held them when they were born, kissing their soft, delicate heads. I could see Abbie taking her first steps, remembering how, in that moment, I realised she wouldn't be a baby forever. She wasn't mine; she was on loan, and every moment was painfully precious. I could see Sarah reach for her big sister and hold her hand before she could even sit up. Their bond so strong, formed so quickly. It helped to know they would have each other.

I wanted the numbness I had expected death to bring. Even now, the pain of never holding my girls again cut through me. Was this my eternal punishment? The price I was to pay for the life I'd lived before. But I'd come through in the end, hadn't I? I'd made sure they'd be safe from Martin. No one would come for them now, and they had an amazing father to care for them. I'd miss Christopher so much. I'd miss his face. How, a couple of hours after shaving, he would have a six o'clock shadow to rival most men's best beard attempts. I'd miss the way he always laughed at my jokes, even though we both knew they were awful. I'd miss the way he'd say my name in his awful attempt at an Irish accent, and make it sound as if it contained two syllables instead of one.

'Mae-uve.'

'Mae-uve. Mae-uve.'

'Maeve. Maeve.'

I could almost hear him. But he was shouting. Why was he shouting? I couldn't remember a time he'd ever shouted at me.

'Maeve. MAEVE!'

I opened my eyes – if such a thing were possible in the afterlife – and smiled at Christopher's face above me. I saw a dark cloudless sky, dancing with lights, above him. Maybe I was wrong, maybe heaven did exist. Maybe I had somehow brought it into existence and filled it with everyone I wanted to spend eternity with. I turned my head to see if my girls were here as well. Pain exploded behind my eyes. What the fuck? Heaven shouldn't hurt, should it?

'Don't move. There's an ambulance on the way. Stay as still as you can. You're going to be just fine.'

I blinked up at Christopher. I didn't know what was confusing me more, that I had survived the explosion – the pain I felt through my entire body assured me that it had definitely happened – or that Christopher was here. How? What possible scenario could have led to him being here outside Martin Mulvihill's flame-filled stables?

I tried to ask how, but I couldn't understand the words coming from my mouth, and I wasn't sure if it was my vocal cords letting me down, or my ears. Christopher's face began to spin and blur in front of me before everything went dark again.

This time, there was nothing else, only darkness.

47

A TV commercial dramatically discussing how you get your whites whiter started to seep into my subconscious before someone turned the TV off, and the voices of doctors and nurses – discussing the unusually high level of flu admissions the last couple of weeks – filtered in from the hallway, filling the silence.

I opened my eyes. This time, I knew I wasn't dead. The pain pulsating through every inch of my body was evidence of that. I didn't know what hurt the most: the damaged muscles, broken bones or burnt skin. But judging by the level of pain I felt, it was probably a culmination of all three. I tried to move, but it was impossible, and I groaned instead.

Christopher appeared from somewhere beside me and closed the door of the room, silencing the anxious discussions about flu.

'Hey, hey, it's okay. You're okay. Don't worry.'

Christopher's voice calmed me immediately.

'Chris?' It felt as if razor blades were slicing up and down my throat as I spoke, but at least words were coming out.

'It's me. I'm right here.' He was smiling.

That was a good sign, wasn't it?

'The girls?' I asked.

'They're fine. Perfectly safe, and running rings around Mum and Dad. Don't worry.'

I started to cry as relief washed over me. I tried to move again, but no part of my body would cooperate. Panic rose in my chest. Christopher wouldn't look so happy if I was paralysed, right? Oh God, he would. He'd just be happy I was alive.

'Can't move.'

'You're fine, don't worry.' The look I gave made him laugh as he added, 'Okay, well, obviously you're not fine, but you will be. I promise. You've got a broken shin bone, several broken ribs, and you've sustained some second-degree burns – but nothing that won't heal with time.' He grinned down at me. 'So, to correct my previous statement, you *will* be fine.'

'How?'

Christopher knew exactly what I was asking.

'You didn't think you were the only one who could sneak a tracking app onto a phone, did you?'

'What? How? *What?*' I couldn't understand what was going on. How was he here? None of it made any sense, and trying to figure it out was making the pounding in my head even worse.

'You know what? There are quite a lot of explanations to be given and revelations to be shared. It would probably be better to wait until you've had more time to rest.'

'How?' I repeated, with as much force as my raw throat allowed.

Christopher chuckled. 'Good to see your stubborn streak hasn't been knocked out of you.'

I narrowed my eyes in warning, and Christopher continued. 'Well, as luck would have it, I happened to be holidaying in Ireland and was walking by when—'

'Chris!' I snapped, and immediately began coughing from the exertion.

'All right, all right. I'm sorry.' His face finally turned serious. 'Just relax and I'll explain everything.'

Lying there in the hospital bed, listening to Christopher explain everything, I couldn't help but think that if it was coming from anyone else, I wouldn't have believed a word of it.

'I've known everything about you since the first moment we met,' Christopher began.

That sentence alone made me feel as if I was going to be sick. My attempt at heaving sent a roaring pain racing through me as a nurse rushed in and helped Christopher to gently roll me onto my side. I didn't let on how agonising the movement was, because the nurse was already suggesting it might be time to let me rest, and while Christopher looked more than happy to escape the conversation for another few hours, there wasn't a hope in hell I was going to let him stop there.

'Go on,' I said, after the nurse had left.

'Well, as it happens, I also worked undercover with Europol and was tasked with assessing you, to determine if you'd been compromised or not. They wanted assurances that your intel could be trusted.'

This was insane, I couldn't believe what he was saying, that my husband was telling me this, that he was using words like 'Europol', 'compromised' and 'intel'.

'So you were *trying* to knock me off my bike that day in the woods?' I asked.

Christopher gave a little laugh. 'God, no. That was highly embarrassing. I was supposed to be doing some reconnaissance, but I'd lost track of you. The last thing that should have happened that day was us running into each other. Literally!' He shrugged. 'But we did, and I fell head over heels in love.'

I couldn't help but smile at that. 'I think you'll find I was the one who *actually* fell head over heels.'

We both laughed.

'I can't imagine Silva was too pleased when I left the country with you then?'

'Ah, no,' Christopher said. 'Not in the slightest. That resulted in a demotion and a permanent desk job for me. But,' he shrugged, 'the joke was on him, because I was more than happy to take a position that meant I didn't have to keep so many secrets and go away from you all the time.'

I nodded, still struggling to get my head around Christopher even knowing Silva existed. For a moment we both fell silent, neither of us knowing what to say next.

'Why didn't you ever tell me?' I asked, finally. 'The truth about you, and that you knew the truth about me.'

'I didn't want to compromise you any further, you already knew enough to make Europol uncomfortable and,' Christopher looked at his feet and gave a small shrug before he continued, 'we were just so happy, I didn't want to change the way we were with each other – and honestly, I didn't want you to know about me and my past. The things I did before finding you.'

He looked up then, into my eyes, and for the first time I could see that there were shadows from his past haunting him as well. If anyone could understand that, it was me.

I nodded, closing my eyes as I allowed everything he'd told me to sink in. Christopher knew. He knew everything about me. All the things that ate away at me every time he paid me a compliment or told me he loved me, he knew. I'd always thought if he really knew me, truly knew me, he'd hate me. Hate me for the person I had been. But he'd known, and he'd loved me, regardless. He'd started a life with me, had a family with me.

Lying in that hospital bed, with pain pulsating through my entire body, it felt as if an enormous weight had been lifted from my chest. I was free from all the lies, and all the secrets. Finally.

'Let's both leave the past where it belongs,' I said, desperate to take the sadness from his face.

It worked. He grinned back, no more ghosts dancing behind his eyes.

'So, you came to Ireland when you couldn't get in touch with me?' I wasn't sure of the timeline; I'd spent a lot of time unconscious.

'Kind of,' he answered. 'Europol had actually called me into an emergency meeting in the London office.'

'Why?'

'Well, it turns out DS Ryan finally developed a conscience and told Europol everything, hoping to save your life.'

Tears rolled down my face. An eye for an eye. I hoped Europol and the Gardaí would be lenient with him – for his daughter's sake.

'What will they do to him?' I asked, not really sure I wanted to hear the answer.

Christopher shrugged. 'I really don't know.'

I looked away, staring at the blank TV screen.

'But he did.'

I blinked, looking back at him.

'Save your life,' he clarified. 'A Garda and myself were the first to arrive at the scene. We got into the stables at the back, behind where you were tied up, and I saw you grab Rita and point a gun at Martin. I knew what you were about to do, the second your arm moved, so I started running for you.'

I closed my eyes. We could have both died there in Martin

Mulvihill's stables, leaving the girls parentless. But we didn't. We were here. Alive.

I looked at Christopher then, really studied him. Light bruises were scattered across his face. I turned my head, ignoring the burst of pain that exploded in my brain, and saw that his hands were wrapped in white cotton bandages like the ones covering most of my arms. I looked back up at his face.

'Thank you.' It was all I could manage. More tears spilled down my face.

'Anytime, sweetheart. Anytime.'

'Is he dead?' I asked, quietly.

'Two dead bodies – both male.'

My chest felt even lighter. Martin and Killer Kev. Both gone.

The man who'd murdered my mother had finally paid for what he'd done.

'And Rita?'

'She survived. Mind you, she isn't in great shape. She will be a while healing, but she'll recover in time. Her body shielded you from most of the blast, so she suffered a lot of burns.'

Even after everything she'd done, she had come through in the end. 'Did you get her out, too?'

'No . . .' Christopher paused. 'That was Jamie O'Leary. He had jimmied open a sealed-up back door into the stables by the time we got there. I think he was trying to get you out.'

I winced at the name of my ex-fiancé coming from my husband's mouth.

'Don't worry, I know all about your past with him, too.' He took my bandaged hand in his own. 'None of it matters to me, as long as it doesn't matter to you?'

I could see the question in his eyes: did Jamie still matter to me the way he once had?

Yes, I'd loved Jamie, but I loved Christopher now. Christopher and my girls. There was no more love left for shadows from the past.

'No,' I smiled. 'It doesn't matter to me.'

I closed my eyes. The pull of exhaustion was tugging at me.

'One more thing, before I let you sleep.'

'Hmm?' I asked, not opening my eyes.

'Did you know?'

'Know what?' I asked. The pull of sleep was too strong to even think about what he was asking.

'About the baby?'

My eyes snapped open, and my entire body jerked as my hands flew to my stomach.

'I'm . . . am I? . . . I . . . ?' My words were stumbling over each other and getting caught in my throat.

'I take it you didn't, then.' Christopher was beaming now. 'It's not often the man gets to spring it on the woman.'

Every roll of nausea, every time I had vomited over the last week, ran through my mind. It hadn't even occurred to me at the time. Then every fight, every fall, every kick, every punch I'd received pushed into my memories, along with every drink and cigarette, and panic rose in me again.

'Is? Is everything . . . ?'

He laid his hands gently on mine, resting on my stomach.

'Breathe. Relax. Everything's fine. They said the hormone levels look great. It seems as if you're around five, maybe six weeks along. They'll do an ultrasound soon.'

I started to sob. There were no more secrets, no more threats hanging over me or my family. This little baby would come into a world with no dangers from my past hanging over its head.

'A fighter,' Christopher said, leaning down to kiss my stomach gently. 'Just like you.'

I was smiling as I fell asleep with bandaged hands cupping my stomach. We were finally safe, and I was finally free.

48

Jamie paused at Maeve's room and leaned his shoulder against the door frame, out of sight. He didn't want to interrupt. Maeve was getting some serious bombshells dropped on her. He just wanted to make sure she was okay. That blast had been a stroke of genius on her part. Suicidal, but still genius. Maeve always found a way. Jamie didn't think he'd ever been so happy to see law enforcement in his life – and he certainly hadn't ever expected to be so grateful to meet his former fiancée's husband.

If it hadn't been for Christopher arriving, Jamie would have had to make a choice when the place went up – between dragging Maeve from the stables, or saving the woman he regarded as a mother.

The blast had been bad. Maeve and Rita only survived thanks to their quick removal and the almost instantaneous medical care provided by the Gardaí. Martin and Killer Kev hadn't been as lucky.

He smiled, seeing Maeve hold her stomach. *Good*, he

thought, *those bastards deserved to burn for everything they'd put her through*. And he had little doubt that's how they'd spend eternity. True, he'd probably join them himself one day, but that day wasn't today. Maybe he'd even get the chance to have something like that for himself, he thought, watching Christopher kiss Maeve's stomach. Maybe there would be a route out of this life he led, some day.

But that day isn't today, he thought, as he shook his head and pushed himself off the wall, before making his way down the corridor to Rita's room.

Rita was lying there, her one unbandaged eye closed as she slept. She'd been lucky to get off so lightly, he thought, as he sat in the blue faux-leather seat next to her bed, adjusting the small blue cushion behind him as he did. The left side of her face was almost entirely covered in bandages, along with her hands, which she'd used to shield her face. The doctor had told him she wouldn't regain the sight in her left eye, but all in all, she had been very fortunate. She was alive.

Rita stirred.

'It's just me, Rita. Sleep away a while. I'll still be here when you wake up.'

She turned her face and her good eye towards him, and tried to smile, but she winced at the pain it caused.

'I'll get the doctor to up your meds, don't worry.'

'No, don't do that. I need to be back on my feet soon to get everything in order.' Her voice sounded strained.

Some of Rita's words were slurred thanks to the consistent

supply of morphine pumping into her from the drip attached to her hand. But she sounded strong enough. Jamie had little doubt that she would be up and about as soon as her body allowed, probably sooner.

'You don't have to worry about a thing. Take all the time you need to get back on your feet. Davey and I will take care of everything.' Jamie smiled.

He expected Rita to return his smile, to be relieved that she didn't have to carry the burden of everything Martin had left behind, to be proud that he was manning up and stepping forward to take on a role in which he would be challenged and pushed to his limits by an array of assholes testing him for weaknesses. He and his brother were finally putting their differences aside and working together. It wouldn't be easy, but they could do it.

But no smile formed across Rita's lips. Instead, a sneer he had seen many times before, but rarely directed at him, settled on her face.

'No, ye fucking won't.'

Jamie reached forward and took her bandaged hand gently in his. 'You don't have to look out for me, Rita. Don't worry, I can do this.'

Rita gripped his hand, tighter than he would have thought possible, burns or not.

'I'm not looking out for you. I haven't gone through all of this to have you and that fool of a brother of yours step in and take everything out from under me.'

'I-I-I . . . don't—'

'You don't what?' Rita slurred. 'Know how to form a sentence?'

Jamie had nothing to say. He sat staring at Rita, his mouth slightly open as he waited for her to say something, anything, to help him make sense of all this.

'You don't really think I put all that effort into winding up that two-faced bitch, only to allow someone else to take over *my* fucking empire.'

'Okay, you know what, Rita? Maybe I should leave and let you get some rest. I'll come back later.'

When your morphine dose has been lowered, Jamie thought, as he made to leave, but Rita's tight grip on his hand remained.

'Sit the fuck down. We need to get some things straight before you head out there blowing smoke up the holes of my employees.'

Jamie sat back in his seat again.

'Now, you listen to me. You and Davey will slip back into the same roles you've always had, and answer to me and only me.'

'That's what you want?' Jamie asked, completely taken aback. It had never occurred to him that Rita would take over from Martin. The way Martin had treated her, despite all her bravado and big personality, she'd had as little say in the business as any of them. It had been Martin, and only Martin, who had been in charge. Hadn't it?

'That's not only what I want, that's what's going to happen.

I have no intention of spending another thirty years with my hand shoved up another puppet's arse, all because I don't have a cock and balls.'

'I . . . I don't understand,' Jamie said quietly, thinking maybe he should call the doctor to reduce her pain medication, as she was slurring more and more.

'Martin was a sadistic bastard, but his mind for business wasn't that good, not until I came along. Although the arrogant prick never even realised I was feeding him his ideas and manipulating him into making the most profitable decisions.'

'Okay, Rita,' Jamie began, giving her hand a squeeze. 'I might go get the doc to have a check on your pain relief.'

Rita smiled then, an ugly smile, and suddenly Jamie wasn't so sure it was only the drugs talking. He was about to open the door into the corridor when Rita spoke again.

'That's fine, you don't believe me.' Rita laughed softly. 'It's thanks to men's lack of belief in me – in women, in general – that I managed to get the bastard killed. And by his own daughter, no less.'

Jamie stopped with his hand on the door handle, but he couldn't bring himself to turn around. He had a sudden and strong urge to leave Rita, to leave the hospital room and what she had just said behind him. That one innocuous word that could turn his entire world upside down in the context that Rita had just used it. 'Daughter?'

'I knew, the minute he didn't order her execution when we

349

found out she'd been working undercover. He was willing to give her another chance. Have you ever heard of Martin giving anyone a second chance?' Rita gave a humourless laugh. 'He always did have a soft spot for that Gail. I'd just thought he wanted into her knickers, not that he'd been there already.'

Jamie barely registered leaving the door and sitting back down in the blue chair. *This can't be real*, he thought.

'So *you* got Martin killed?' Jamie asked, his heart pounding in his chest. Rita was talking as if she was high, the pain medication loosening her tongue, but she seemed certain about the things she was saying.

'I asked him one night, after he'd snorted enough coke to drop an elephant, and he admitted everything. That's when I knew I had to do something, when I discovered she was the mother of his child, I knew then that he'd kill me for what I did.'

Jamie had so many questions, but he couldn't speak, shock had paralysed his vocal cords.

Rita continued with her confessional, as if she'd forgotten there was anyone listening. 'But then I realised I was looking at it all wrong, and it was as if all my Christmases had come at once. Finally, I had a way to get rid of the bastard and make him look weak and pathetic all at once.'

She laid her head back on the pillow and stared at the wall in front of her as she continued. 'I needed to wind up Maeve enough that she'd risk it all. Easy to do, to a mother. All I had to do was take her daughter, show her just how easy it was to lay hands on that family of hers.' Her body shook, as if she was laughing, but there was no sound. 'I had one of my men wear a jacket just like that cheap black plastic monstrosity Kev always wears. Martin had nothing at all to do with any of it.'

Jamie could hear her laughter now, bubbling up despite the pain of her injuries.

'Martin didn't even know why she had come back to Ireland, roaming around causing trouble. He had no idea that I'd taken that brat of hers, left her that damn business card of his. It worked perfectly, though. Forced him to finally act, to send her a summons card. To punish her for her betrayal. Or at least appear to.' She snorted. 'Then all I had to do was feed information to you that Martin was going to go for her family, when she didn't complete that hit.' She sighed.

Her words were slowing. The effort of disclosing all she'd done was starting to tire her.

'Would you believe that he was going to give her another chance after that?' Rita asked, turning to look at Jamie, the lid on her one visible eye getting heavy. 'If she hadn't come here to kill him, and he hadn't seen it for himself, he'd still be making stupid deals with her. Looking for excuses to leave her and her family alive. He never even sent anyone for those children.' She grinned as much as her burns allowed. 'I'd suggested it would be a good way to fuck with her, to punish her for coming here to kill him. He was never going to hurt his grandchildren. Soppy bastard.'

Jamie hadn't moved.

351

'That's why you had a gun on you when you went into the stables?'

'Ah, now you're starting to get it. I needed to give her something, anything, to finish him.'

Jamie couldn't believe what he was hearing, but what she was saying was starting to make sense.

'And you'd have Killer Kev as a witness.'

'You've got it now. After Davey fucked up and got Martin to send Kev to that drug deal, I made sure he'd be around the next time. He'd think I'd disobeyed Martin, bringing the gun back in, but he knows better than most that I'm always armed. He'd never suspect I planned for Maeve to get hold of it.'

'You gave Maeve no other choice, she had to kill Martin.'

'Yep, there was no alternative for her.' Rita looked down at her heavily bandaged hand. 'Have to admit, I didn't expect this, though. Thought the desperate bitch would just kill him and chance her arm getting another shot off at Kev. Or just be relieved that she'd be gone before anything happened to her children. But no, she had to go and blow us all fucking up.'

Jamie couldn't believe it. This had been Rita's plan all along. Everything that had happened to Maeve and her family, it was all because of this sick, twisted game Rita had set into motion, to take over from Martin.

But Maeve was free now, finally able to live her life and enjoy her family. Wasn't she? Would Rita be satisfied that Maeve had played her part in all this, and leave her be? He couldn't be sure. He didn't feel sure about anything anymore, except for one thing, he had to make sure Maeve never discovered any of this. Because if she did, he knew for certain that Maeve would never let Rita get away with playing her for a fool.

'What did you do to Gail?' he asked, finally able to find the words.

'Oh, Jamie,' Rita sighed, as the effort of relaying all her devious deeds had caught up with her. 'That's a story for another day. And my Jamie,' she turned to him, opening her eye again, 'you'll be a good lad and keep this to yourself.' It wasn't a question. 'Or you'll end up in the ground with Martin.'

'Whatever you say, Rita.' Jamie stood to leave.

More morphine pumped into her vein from the drip. Her pupil dilated and her speech slurred even more. 'That's my boy.'

Jamie started moving towards the door when he heard Rita continue talking in a whisper.

'Best thing I ever did was get rid of the bastard child that snake had inside her.'

Jamie froze, realisation hitting him. Slowly, he turned back to Rita. Her eyes were closed, and she was smiling as she drifted back to sleep, seemingly unaware of Jamie's presence.

'One small pill in her coffee and he was free,' she murmured.

The reality of Rita's words washed over him.

No, he thought, *there will never be a way out of this life for me. Not now.*

EPILOGUE

Cork City, 2003

Gail was pacing up and down her tiled hallway. She still couldn't believe what she'd seen. What was she going to do? It wasn't until she'd returned home that she realised she'd already made a mistake by leaving work early. If Rita knew, if she thought for even one second that Gail had seen her, she'd be in danger.

Everyone was afraid of Martin, and they should be – to this day, she couldn't believe that she'd actually slept with such a man. But aside from his sadistic, psychopathic tendencies, he'd been good to her. By giving her a job and staying completely out of her life, as well as her daughter's. She appreciated that. But it was Rita Regan who really scared her; Gail had never seen anyone who'd crossed Rita come out the better for it.

She shook her head. All because she'd snuck out of the hotel's delivery entrance for a cigarette, she could now find herself on Rita's bad side.

After a few more minutes of pacing, Gail decided on what she had to do. She would go to Martin and tell him what she'd seen. It was the only way to ensure her safety and Maeve's. He was the only person who could keep them safe from Rita.

Gail went to the kitchen; she'd need a cup of tea to settle her nerves before she had that particular conversation. She scribbled a quick note to Maeve to tell her to head straight to Marnie's if she got home before her. She'd tried her mobile five times, but Maeve hadn't answered.

Gail was about to flick the switch on the kettle when the doorbell went. Her hand stilled mid-air and she turned towards the door, but there was no way of seeing who was on the other side.

She stood there like that until the bell went again. Gail took a deep breath and went to the door.

'Who is it?' she called, hearing the tremble in her voice.

'Just selling raffle tickets,' came a young male voice.

Gail released a breath as she swung open the door, just as a young boy, about twelve or thirteen, took off running down the street.

Strange, Gail thought, about to shut the door again, when Rita appeared, pushing her way inside and quickly closing the door behind her.

'Gail, you're looking well. I thought I'd better come and check on you after you left work early.' From the smile on Rita's face, it was clear that she knew everything.

Gail took a step back.

355

'I was having a look through some of our CCTV footage today, and guess who I saw sneaking out the delivery entrance with a cigarette in hand? Ah now, Gail. I thought you'd quit.'

Gail took another step back.

'But you didn't even smoke it, did you, Gail? I saw you drop it and run back in.' Rita tilted her head to the side. 'Did you see something out there that spooked you?'

Gail took another step back.

Rita knew exactly what she'd seen. It was the reason she was here. Because Gail had seen Rita behind a parked van with a man. They were kissing and his hands were roaming all over her. That man wasn't her fiancé, Martin Mulvihill. It was Liam Daily. And the second Gail recognised him was the same second she recognised she would be in danger if Rita knew she'd seen her.

Gail took another step back.

This time, Rita matched it. Gail was almost halfway to the kitchen.

'No need to look at me like that, Gail. We can't all be as saintly as you are. Besides, it makes sense for a woman to keep her options open. There's no telling which one of them will end up on top by the time their feud is over. Last thing I want is to be on the losing side.'

Rita smiled, before lunging forward.

Gail ran to the kitchen, desperately trying to recall if she'd left the back door unlocked.

She hadn't.

ACKNOWLEDGEMENTS

First, let me start by saying thank you to Cork for having so many wonderful woodlands, hospitals and hotels that I was able to pick pieces and fit them together to create the fictional places I needed for this story.

Now, the first thank-you to a person must go to Jane Gregory for being the first person to ever validate my hours spent writing into an abyss. For that I will be forever grateful.

To my wonderful agent, Stephanie Glencross, at David Higham Associates, who not only helped me shape this book into what it is today and did all she could to make sure it was published but was also ever so patient with my 'just checking in' emails while on submission. Thank you and I'm sorry.

Huge thanks to Bea Grabowska at Headline Publishing Group for seeing what I wanted to do with this story and appreciating Maeve for exactly who she is. And to everyone at Headline who made this a reality; you quite literally made my dream come true.

AMY MURPHY – I feel you should get all caps here to

make sure your name stands out because if it wasn't for your encouragement and willingness to attend every writing and publishing event with me, just to make sure I'd go, I'm not entirely confident that this book would have been written – thank you! Thanks also to Noelle Kelly-Trindles for always keeping me informed of those writing events. I still can't wait to read your work in progress – best premise ever.

Thank you, too, to Vanessa Fox O'Loughlin for facilitating so many of those events in Cork and Dublin. Thanks to you I knew exactly what to do when my book was finally written, which leads me to my next thank-you – Catherine Ryan Howard. Thank you for teaching that free summer school in creative writing at the Cork City Library in 2018 which I was fortunate enough to attend and, on top of teaching me how to pace a novel, thank you for helping me to realise that I shouldn't concentrate so much on trying to get published until I had a book written, and rewritten, and rewritten. . .

And, to round out my thanks to this trifecta of amazing authors, thank you to Andrea Mara who gave me exactly the pep talk I needed at a time when I felt like this would never happen – it was so very much appreciated.

Thank you to Gail O'Brien who, quite a few years ago now, when I mentioned I'd like to write a book, said I absolutely should. Things may have worked out differently without that immediate encouragement.

Thank you to everyone in the Cytology and Histology Labs in Cork University Hospital who asked for weekly updates on how my writing was going; you really kept me accountable. A special mention must go to Sandra Murphy and Martina Deasy – my good-luck charms.

To all my amazing friends and family, especially: Louise and Patrick Griffin, Jennifer Scully, Debbie Cooney, Sinead Teahan, Lynne and Ciaran Condon, Ann Shine, and Linda and Conor Cahill, for always being so interested, encouraging and excited for me through all of this, thank you.

To my mam, Tina, the strongest woman I know, and my dad, Michael, the most selfless man on this entire planet, I probably don't say it as often as I should, but thank you for everything. Thank you for your endless, unwavering belief in me that I can do anything I try – I may not always believe it but I really appreciate it.

To my grandmother, Gobnait O'Regan, thank you for lighting all those blazing fires I sat beside while reading and writing over the years.

To my father-in-law, Eugene, who I consider myself inexplicably fortunate for having known; you are so missed.

To my wonderful, amazing and hilarious girls, Christina and Johanna, you have made my life so much better simply by being in it, and thank you for helping me realise that if I could raise two small humans, anything was possible, including writing a book.

This is an important one. To my husband, John, who has done absolutely everything he possibly could over the years to make sure I got to this point. Thank you for giving me the space, time, means and opportunity to write; I can't even express how much it means to me. I thank my lucky stars every day for that bus trip to Dingle.

And last, but most certainly not least, thank you to you. Thank you for taking the time to pick up this book, to read it through and for getting to the end of this longer-than-anticipated acknowledgements page. Time is precious and thank you for spending a little bit of yours with Maeve.